The Curious Death of PETER ARTEDI

The Curious Death of PETER ARTEDI

A Mystery in the History of Science

THEODORE W. PIETSCH

SCOTT & NIX, Inc.

Published by
SCOTT & NIX, Inc.
150 West 28th Street, Suite 1103
New York, NY 10011
www.scottandnix.com

10 9 8 7 6 5 4 3 2 1

ISBN 978-0-9825102-8-5

Printed in the United States of America

The engraving used as ornament on the title page represents the Twin-flower, *Linnaea borealis*, named for and by CARL LINNAEUS, and described by him, obviously tongue-in-cheek, as "a plant of Lapland, lowly, insignificant, disregarded, flowering but for a brief space—from LINNAEUS who resembles it."

Contents

In humulum ARTEDI

Here lies poor ARTEDI, in foreign land pyx'd
Not a man nor a fish, but something betwixt,
Not a man, for his life amongst fishes he past,
Not a fish, for he perished by water at last.

—Translated by GEORGE SHAW (1751–1813)
from the original Latin of ANDERS CELSIUS
(1701–1744), taken from the back flyleaf
of LINNAEUS's copy of the *Ichthyologia*

Preface

THIS IS A STORY based on fact—nearly all of it true and well documented, taken largely from CARL LINNAEUS's autobiographies of which he left no less than five. The small part that is fictionalized twists and augments the known facts to give another side to a history that might have been. There really was a brilliant young naturalist named PETER ARTEDI who drowned in an Amsterdam canal on the very early morning of 28 September 1735, under mysterious circumstances. And of course there really was a CARL LINNAEUS. It is true also that ARTEDI and LINNAEUS, during the very brief time that was available to them—only six and a half years, from March 1729 through September 1735—took a fervent liking for each other. But, more than just a strong affection, they formed an intense intellectual bond, sharing among other things their revolutionary ideas about order and hierarchy in nature. While ARTEDI has been long forgotten, his friend and fellow naturalist is to this day a historical figure of huge proportion, credited with revolutionizing systematic botany and establishing the Binomial System of Biological Nomenclature. Characterized in nearly all writings as god-like, a person of great kindness and benevolence, LINNAEUS had another side that is little talked about. He had from an early age a most favorable opinion of himself. He was selfish and conceited, unable to tolerate disloyalty or criticism of any kind and always uncomfortable when attention was not directed toward him. "All my youthful powers, both of mind and body, conspired to make me an excellent natural historian—besides my remarkable retentiveness of memory, I had an extraordinary energy and ability of concentration, coupled with a brilliant intelligence and an astonishing quickness of sight." These superlatives and the many others that appear throughout this book in reference to LINNAEUS—as he himself narrates the story of ARTEDI from the vantage of old age—are not my exaggerations intended to turn the reader toward an unfavorable opinion, but rather LINNAEUS's *own* words. His writings are replete with statements of preposterous self-assurance:

"The Lord Himself hath led me with His own Almighty hand. He hath caused me to spring from a trunk without root, and planted me again in a distant and more delightful spot, and caused me to rise up to a considerable tree. He hath permitted me to see more of the creation than any mortal before me. He hath given me greater knowledge of natural history than any one had hitherto acquired. No person has ever proved himself a greater botanist or zoologist. No person has ever written more works in a more precise and methodical manner, and from his own observation. No person has ever so completely reformed a whole science, and created therein a new era."

Delusions of self-worth on a scale of this magnitude may well have elevated LINNAEUS so far above the rest of humanity in his own mind that he might easily rationalize any inhuman act that he might commit, leaving him feeling blameless no matter how evil and self-serving. After all, he and science had much to gain by ARTEDI's early demise.

The Death of PETER ARTEDI

Death threatens from behind, stealing everything away.

—LINNAEUS, *Nemesis Divina* (Divine Vengeance)

WORD OF THE tragic event reached me the next day. I was at Hartekamp at the time, having just recently been employed there to tend to the plants in GEORGE CLIFFORD's gardens—a work which you might recall was culminated in 1737 with publication of *Hortus Cliffortianus* (CLIFFORD's Garden)—when my friend and traveling companion CLAES SOHLBERG, who had just that very hour returned from Amsterdam, called upon me in late afternoon. For reasons that might be surmised, his approach was not an unexpected reappearance—he had been with me at the CLIFFORD country estate only on Tuesday last— but it immediately filled me nevertheless with a cold apprehension.

Accompanied by CARL TERSMEEDEN—and while neither of these good gentlemen was witness to the fact, or so it was said—they together described in some detail what others had seen. The body was found at daybreak by passers-by, floating face up in the Singel at the Nieuwe Haarlemmersluis, about one-third distance between the house of our mutual colleague ALBERTUS SEBA and ARTEDI's own quarters in a lodging house in the Warmoesstraat, near the Nieuwebrugsteeg, in the dock area on the waterfront of Amsterdam. ARTEDI had been that evening before enjoying the pleasure of food and drink with friends at the house of SEBA on the Haarlemmerdijk, as, of course, I well knew beforehand. I myself had been invited to join this gathering, but had excused myself for need of botanical work at Hartekamp, having removed myself to that place some days before—in fact, as I recall, my departure from Amsterdam was on 24 September 1735.

As SOHLBERG and TERSMEEDEN told it to me, and others confirmed some time later, the guests stayed late, absorbed in congenial conversation, and did not end their revelry until well past midnight. ARTEDI was said to have left the house at one o'clock, on foot, the distance being small and he unwilling to pay the cost of a carriage, the latter, in any case, near impossible to come by at that late hour. A clear sky, but no moon that night to help guide the way amid the poorly lighted and unfenced waterways of the town, ARTEDI, full of drink, lost his way or so they say. While progressing along the Haarlemmerdijk just past the fish market at the Nieuwe Haarlemmersluis, expecting to find a bridge, he apparently tripped and fell into the cold black waters, most likely drowning quickly—thanks be to God—never quite knowing what had happened to him.

It was called an accident from the start, no evidence of foul play detected. He was fully clothed, in shirt and breeches, with simple dress-coat, hat and wig, it being yet mild for late September. Walking stick floating nearby, his sword and sheath were still at his side, one shoe on, the other missing, his pockets not turned out, a golden double guinea in the one, nine pennies and four farthings in the other. The constable having been summoned, the body and its belongings were retrieved and taken to the City Hospital. There, a superficial examination confirmed the ample consumption of food and wine. A large swelling on the left side of his head was attributed to the fall, against the heavy stone embankment of the canal.

Expressing my most profound grief, I thanked SOHLBERG and TERSMEEDEN for delivering this sad news and immediately prepared to depart for Amsterdam. CLIFFORD's horses were available to me, as they always were; and there was the stagecoach, but I chose to go by towboat, thinking it faster, for the roads were coarse and muddy from autumn rains.

Arriving there the next day by mid-morning—it was in fact 30 September, a Friday—I went directly to view what remained of God's gift to natural history so early denied his place in posterity. When I beheld his lifeless body, stiff and stark, and saw his livid lips, pale and filmy with the frost of death; when I thought of the unhappy fate and loss of so old and excellent a friend and recalled to mind the innumerable sleepless nights, the laborious days, the wearisome and perilous journeys, the countless midnight hours of exhausting study that the man now lying dead before me had been fain to undergo, and which had preceded his attainment of that standard of learning in which he had no rival to fear—then I burst into tears. And when I foresaw that all the scholarship he had acquired—which, in the fullness of time, should have earned undying immortality for him, reflected unfading glory for his country, and rendered the scientific world untold services—would perish with his death, then the love and devotion that I felt for my friend commanded that the pledge we had once so solemnly made to each other must be honored. I would carry out this promise to be sure, but it was then at that moment that my guilt began to weigh heavily upon my soul.

CHAPTER I

Early Years

"Man is created for this purpose, that there might be someone
to regard God's work, and the things brought forth by Him,
and that while he admires the creation, even learns to know the
Creator." It is these words of the eminently learned JOHN RAY,
which especially encouraged me to observations, so that I now
with all my heart desire to investigate nature.

—LINNAEUS, *Den Osynliga Världen* (The Invisible World)

I FONDLY REMEMBER those early cherished years of our acquaintance,
our many long and intimate conversations, most especially during those
dark autumn and winter evenings of 1729 and 30 in front of the fire in
my rooms at Uppsala. Many hours, often extending late and into the
early morning, were occupied with intense talk of the three Kingdoms
of Nature—minerals (those things that grow), vegetables (things that
grow and live), and animals (things that grow, live, and have feelings); of
order and hierarchy in nature; of names and of naming; of method to be
applied in describing and classifying natural objects; and a myriad other
related things, into which I will delve further as this account continues.
But, much talk too was of a highly personal nature. I learned then that
my dearest friend had sprung from the most modest of beginnings;
although surely I might have guessed it, without having been told, considering his meager financial state in the time that I knew him. And,
while on this subject, I must say, I too was not much better off—for all
my early years I was woefully ill-clothed and ill-fed, unable to procure
badly needed books and the like. I was forced more than once, when
my shoes needed mending, to patch them with folded paper, instead of
taking myself to the cobbler. I dare say the acute lack of proper nutrition
during the whole of my younger days quite badly affected my general
health in later years.

But as for ARTEDI, he came from a family that was settled in the
County of Västerbotten in North Sweden. The first of that lineage

known even to him was born about 1635. This ancestor was the son of a poor peasant farmer who resided in the village of Hiske, in the rural parish of Umeå, which itself lay on the coast of the Gulf of Bothnia at the mouth of the River Ume. This grandfather of our future naturalist called himself PETRUS MARTINI ARCTAEDIUS, employing an antiquated variant of the family name. Desiring to better his potential, and not wanting to repeat the dreary life of his father—and most likely his father before him—he enrolled at the University at Åbo in southwest Finland. The next I know, if memory serves, he returned to his homeland to take up teaching duties as a newly appointed master of the Piteå Grammar School at Härnösand. Not content with that, however, he proceeded in September of that same year (it was 1663) to take priest's orders and was presented to the perpetual curacy in his native parish in 1666; there he remained till 1690, when he was promoted to the care of the living of Nordmaling on the shores of the Gulf of Bothnia. And so this ARC-TAEDIUS, by these means, forged for himself a rather respectable if not well-remunerated life as a clergyman, a path followed almost exactly by his two sons, OLAUS and MARTEN, whose mother was a certain ANNA GRUBB, married to ARCTAEDIUS in about 1668. Additionally, there were three daughters, but if details were told, I do not recall them.

     * * *

While I sat listening—and, I must say, I was told this story more than once—I could not but reminisce upon my own humble background. My father NILS INGEMARSSON, who later took the name LINNAEUS, in homage to the lime tree, which in Swedish is *Lind*, an ancient symbol of the family, was born in 1674 in the parish of Wittaryd in Småland. He was also of poor independent peasant stock but, given a good taste for learning while very young by the kindly SVEN TILIANDER, Pastor of Pietteryd, particularly in the art of horticulture, he managed in some way to find the resources to attend the University of Lund. Applying himself very diligently to his studies, he was eventually admitted into holy orders of the Lutheran Church by Bishop CAVALLIUS and by 1706 he had received the appointment of Perpetual Curate of Stenbrohult, which position gave him ample free time to tend to plants in his beloved garden at Råshult, the dwelling of the Curate. Having soon thereafter married the pastor's seventeen-year-old daughter CHRISTINA BROD-ERSONIA, his firstborn, whom they named CARL after the King, was brought into the world between the hours of twelve and one in the night, dividing the 22nd and 23rd of May 1707—a delightful and most beautiful season of the year, when the cuckoo calls to the summer, in the Calendar of Flora, being between the months of frondescence and florescence. My mother, I am quite certain, wished for a child of the gentler sex; however, my father's joy quickly abated my mother's sorrow.

But I have now diverged widely from the primary purpose of this narration, and, biding patience, these facts and circumstances will come out later as I continue.

* * *

So, there was then this OLAUS ARCTAEDIUS, son of PETRUS MARTINI, whose date of birth was probably 1670. For all likes and purposes he did much the same as his father—studied at Åbo University, was four years later ordained at Härnösand, and in 1701 obtained the perpetual curacy of Anundsjö, this town a lovely place even then, situated inland about fifty miles almost due west from coastal Nordmaling. Shortly thereafter he married HELENA SIDENIA, said to be beautiful in the extreme, the daughter of PETRUS SIDENIUS of Stockholm, a Master of Philosophy and a well-respected Court Chaplain in that city. There were five children of this marriage, of whom PETRUS ARCTAEDIUS the younger, our naturalist to be, was the oldest but one. The date of his birth, according to the Parish Register of Anundsjö, was, by the Gregorian Calendar, 10 March 1705.

The ARCTAEDIUS family continued to reside at Anundsjö for upwards of ten years, but in 1716 a document, addressed to the Swedish Crown by the Consistory at Härnösand, quite suddenly and unexpectedly altered their lives, especially that of the young ARCTAEDIUS:

> Whereas the incumbent of the living of Nordmaling, PETRUS MARTINI ARCTAEDIUS to wit, was of advanced age, had been blind for over two years, and was in great bodily distress, they, the Consistory, sought leave to approve an application made by the said incumbent, praying that his son OLAUS might be

empowered to succeed him in the discharge of his duties, which application had, moreover, received the unanimous support of the congregation of the parish.

In reply thereto, an authorization conferring the father's living on the son was signed by KING CHARLES XII in Lund on 26 September 1716. O happy day, for this change of dwelling brought with it a distinct bearing upon the future of ARCTAEDIUS, son of OLAUS. The natural characteristics and climatic conditions of the new environs, quite different from the old, offered to this young and eager boy, already burning with interest in the forest and field, far more incentives and variable opportunities to pursue an inborn proclivity for the study of nature. Now it was that ARCTAEDIUS at a very tender age openly voiced his strong desire to devote himself to the study of living things—plants and animals in general, but especially fishes for which he had acquired a special fondness. Thus, it may be well imagined that removal from the pine, spruce-fir, and birch-covered mountains—I might better say hills—of Anundsjö to the rocky rich shores of the Bothnian Gulf must have been a new and special joy for him. Here, at the meeting of land and sea, all things were readily at hand from which to procure an unending quantity and variety of living curiosities for his collection and examination. Least not to be diminished in importance also was the kindly climate of Nordmaling, offering considerably greater opportunities to study nature in her various aspects, and of observing the ways and lives of all manner of creatures in their several natural surroundings.

*   *   *

In like manner, I too, at very early emergence from infancy, declared my liking for nature. My parents, blessed be to them, received me, their first born, with joy, and devoted their greatest attention to impressing upon my young mind the love of virtue, both in precept and example. I was nursed in beauty, fragrance, and pure delights. From the very first time that I left my cradle, I almost lived in my father's garden, which he set to work to lay out immediately after attaining his position at Stenbrohult, and which soon became the most beautiful garden in all the province, planted with choice trees and some of the less common shrubs and the rarest of flowers. The flowers in fact became my first playthings. When I made a fuss, as children do, I could be quite easily pacified at once if a flower was laid in my hand. Thus were kindled, before I was out of my mother's arms, those sparks that showed so vividly all through my lifetime and which eventually burst into such a vibrant flame. My early proclivity for nature was many times displayed during those first years, but perhaps best made evident to those around me on the following occasion. I was scarcely four years old when I went with my father to a picnic feast on a lovely peninsula that jutted out into the great lake of Möckeln, one of the most beautiful places in all of Sweden—away to the south were lovely beech woods, and to the southeast charming meadows and other leafy trees; the high mountain ridge of Taxas lay to the north and pine woods to the northeast. When one sits there in the summer and listens to the cuckoo and the song of all the other birds, the chirping and humming of the insects; when one looks at the shining, gaily colored flowers; one is completely stunned by the credible resourcefulness of the Creator.

On that day, and in the evening, it being a very pleasant season of the year, the guests seated themselves on some flowery turf, listening to the Pastor, who, wanting to amuse his guests, made various remarks on the names and special properties of the plants, showing them the stems and roots of *Succisa, Tormentilla, Orchides*, and various others. I paid the most uninterrupted attention to all that I saw and heard, and from that hour I never ceased to harass my father with questions about the name, qualities, and nature of every plant I met; indeed, I often asked more than my father was able to answer. But, like other children, I would forget immediately what I had learned, especially the names of the plants. Hence my father was sometimes put out of humor, and refused to answer me, unless I promised to remember what was told to me. Nor had this harshness any bad or long-lasting effect, for I always retained with ease whatever I heard from that time on. So it was that all my youthful powers, both of mind and body, conspired to make me an excellent natural historian—besides my remarkable retentiveness of memory, I had an extraordinary energy and ability of concentration, coupled with a brilliant intelligence and an astonishing quickness of sight. But let us now return to my dear friend.

* * *

It was in the autumn of 1716 that ARCTAEDIUS was sent to school at Härnösand. Here, he soon made himself stand out as rather different from the rest. The ordinary boyish amusements were not much to his liking, his out-of-school hours devoted instead to the collecting of plants, of shells and beetles and the like, and to the dissecting of fishes. In his coursework, he did as well as most, without showing anything out of the ordinary; that is, with respect to any special kind of brilliance. He early acquired—as, of course, did I as well—the rudiments of Latin, which knowledge gave him ready access to the archives of scholarship and of science in particular. In addition to many other things, he greedily devoured the writings of the medieval alchemists, a perhaps unusual preoccupation for a young boy that would have meaning later on. And so it was that ARCTAEDIUS, after passing successfully through the Lower School, was promoted to the Gymnasium, or Upper School, at Härnösand, and in due course proceeded thence to the University, furnished there with the highest possible certificate awarded.

Now it would seem most natural that ARCTAEDIUS would follow his father, and his father's father before him, to the University of Åbo. But it came to pass that that good institution, for reasons that do not concern us here, had been obliged to close its portals, and though by this time reopened and reconstituted, it had not attained to anything like its former status. Consequently, it was to Uppsala University to the south that he turned his direction, his name

Petrus Arctædius Angermannus

inscribed in the official register of the school on 30 October 1724. And here it may be helpful if I explain that the appendix "Angermannus" intends to connote "from the district of Ångermanland," province of northeastern Sweden. As for our subject's redirection to Uppsala, what good fortune that destination proved to be, for had he not decided so, our paths might never have intersected.

It was also the assumption and fondest wish of his parents that ARCTAEDIUS should follow in the steps of his father and grandfather to study theology and philosophy, with the further hope in mind that he might even soon succeed to the care of the living of Nordmaling. But in decided rebuff to this course of action, despite it being his father's natural desires on his behalf, ARCTAEDIUS took a turn of direction toward the study of nature. To his credit, and thanks be to the grace of God—for otherwise the world might not have been blessed by the contributions of this naturalist to be—he found the strength to follow his convictions, to succumb fully to the pull toward natural history that he felt so strongly even as quite a young boy. So too he allowed himself to fall for the taste he had acquired for inquiries kindred to those of the alchemists of the Ages. Thus, in the end, his father's oft-repeated and well-intentioned injunctions and warnings to shun the pursuit of worldly and pernicious objects of study were to be of no avail.

* * *

At this point, I cannot but help to draw another parallel with my own history. In like manner to my friend of whom I speak, I too was most persistently directed toward the clergy. Early in my schooling I took to shunning the usual exercises intended to educate young men toward church service and to giving myself up instead to that science to which my mind was principally turned, namely, the knowledge of plants. I therefore often wandered about the outskirts of the town, and made myself accurately acquainted with all the plants I could find. I developed a sore dislike of those studies that were considered as preparatory to admission into holy orders, and the same predilection for others in which I had experienced so much pleasure. In rhetoric, metaphysics, ethics, the Greek and Hebrew languages, and theology, my contemporaries, I must admit, left me far behind; but in mathematics and particularly physics, I was as much superior to them. Also quite easily surpassing my classmates, and not without some surprise to my masters, I became a most excellent Latin scholar. I later used that language with great fluency, much to my good and long-lasting benefit—I can say now, looking back, that most of my immense foreign correspondence and my numerous academic treatises and lectures were thus penned. And, while I speak of writing, I might add here that I made a special effort at an early age to perfect my hand, thus to make something pretty of it, knowing that much attention can be gained by a neat and tidy look of things. For this reason, I labored long to sharpen my style, becoming quite pleased with it before long, especially the design of my signature:

Carolus Linnæus Smolandus.

Botany, however, a science at that time almost entirely neglected, was what fully engrossed my attention. When still quite young, and wholly on my own accord, I displayed an unusual precociousness in bringing together a small library of books in this branch, including ARFWIDH MÅNSSON's *Een mykit nyttigh Örta-Bok* of 1642 (An Extremely Useful Book of Herbs); ELIAS TILLIANDER's *Catalogus Plantarum* (Catalog of Plants), 1683; JOHANNES PALMBERG's *Serta Florea Suecana* (Swedish Flowering Plants), 1684; OLOF BROMELLIUS's *Chloris Gothica* (The Gothic Chloris), 1694; and OLOF RUDBECK's (the elder) *Hortus Upsaliensis Academiae* (Garden of Uppsala University), 1657. I recall quite distinctly an inability to comprehend clearly the details of the last two of these works, but that notwithstanding I continued to read them and the others, day and night, until I had committed them fully to memory. Hence, within my group of schoolmates and masters, I early acquired the name of "the Little Botanist."

At age seven, I was put under the private tutorship of one JOHAN TELANDER, a yeoman's son from Diö in Stenbrohult Parish—a morose and ill-tempered man by all measures, who was quite better equipped to extinguish talents in a young lad, rather than to develop them. I did poorly with his guidance and escaped to the garden whenever I could, much to the annoyance of my poor mother. In fact, it was largely through her design some three years later (it was now 1717)—if for nothing else but to wean me from plants—that I was sent off with this tutor (who was hardly suited to bring up a child) to the Lower Grammar School at the cathedral town of Växjö, distanced some 30 miles to the northeast of Stenbrohult. Here, the brutal masters, according to the custom of those times, pursued equally brutal methods, much preferring harsh punishments to kindly admonitions and encouragements. Two years later still, I was placed under the thumb of another private tutor, GABRIEL HÖÖK, who, being of a somewhat milder disposition, had better talents also for teaching. But, still, no matter—try as I might, I could not eradicate the bad taste, might I say hatred, that by now I thoroughly felt towards the ordinary studies of a school.

Still at Växjö in 1724, I was graduated just barely by my masters and passed on to the Gymnasium, where I continued my unhappy studies in those subjects then considered as preparatory to admission into church service. I well recall my dear father when he came to that school in the autumn of 1726 (it was 1 September of that year to be exact) to receive an accounting firsthand of my progress. That kind Pastor—who, by all who knew him, was regarded as most honest and trustworthy, ignorant of the world's deceits, despising its fashions and vanities, always friendly, merry, happy, and humorous—had hoped for, and was quite prepared to hear from the preceptors, a flattering account of his beloved son's progress in his scholarly studies. But, alas, he was told quite the opposite. While everyone was willing to allow how pleasing were my manners and how admirable my moral conduct, it was thought right, on the other hand, to advise my father to apprentice me to the learning of some handicraft, to some tailor or shoemaker, or to some other manual employment. Any one of these would be in preference to incurring any further expense towards giving me a learned education in theology, for which I was decidedly inept and evidently woefully unfit. The old clergyman at first instant grieved mightily at having thus lost his labors, and at having supported his son at school for twelve years, at considerable expense, to no purpose. But somewhat later, he was much heartened by conversation with Dr. ROTHMANN, eminent provincial physician and senior master at Växjö, at which school he lectured quite admirably on logic and physics. Calling on this good doctor with hope to be given relief from a nagging malady to which he had been subject for some weeks, my father was quite joyful to be given a cure, but also to hear a favorable suggestion. Remarking however correct might be the opinion of his colleagues, with respect to my ineptitude for those theological studies that my father and mother had planned for me, so much stronger ground was there for hoping that I would distinguish myself in the profession of medicine. These comments afforded so much the more comfort to the old clergyman. They were advanced confidently and decidedly by ROTHMANN, who at the same time handsomely offered— in case my father's circumstances or inclination did not admit of my being maintained in that course of studies—to take me into his house, and to give me board and instruction during the year that it would be necessary for me to remain longer at Växjö. A short time afterwards, that worthy doctor gave me a private course of instruction in physiology based on the Boerhaavian principles, with so much success, that I, when later examined, was quite able to report in the most accurate way possible everything I had been taught. This good doctor also put me into the right method of studying botany, by stressing the need to search for the practical utility of what I had acquired. But of more significance still, he stressed the absolute necessity of studying that science in the systematic manner of the late TOURNEFORT—that celebrated French botanist and long-time Professor of Botany at the Jardin du Roi in Paris who, you will remember, founded his system on the premise that a plant's correct nomenclatural description and classification is best determined by putting the greatest weight on differences in the structure of the flowers. ROTHMANN required also that I make drawings of the plant classes contained in VALENTINI'S *Historia Plantarum* (Natural History of Plants), which publication, as everyone knows, is by all measures only a shortened version of TOURNEFORT'S great *Institutiones rei Herbariae* (Organization of Plants) of 1700, which book was, upon my first glance, ablaze with light for me. After that time, and upon this excellent instruction, I devoted the whole of my mind to placing every plant I could find in its own class after TOURNEFORT'S method, using ROTHMANN'S personal copy of the former's work, which he so kindly made available to me, and which was altogether quite costly and well out of my reach otherwise.

While still under the continued and most excellent sponsorship of Dr. ROTHMANN, it now being 1727, my father, and my mother too— that dear sweet woman who lived with her husband in love, harmony, and with good sense for twenty-seven years and three months, bringing up their five strong children in a praiseworthy manner—while somewhat more appreciative of my wants, were still of a mind contrary to the desperate desire I had to place my future within the arms of natural history. But, thanks to Almighty God, an event unfolded that removed the last impediment to my escape. On the occasion of a small afternoon gathering of friends in my father's garden, at which I was there as well, my father, in deep discussion, said, "Yes, it always happens, what a man enjoys doing he succeeds in." Later that day, I challenged this good man, asking him if he in all honesty held to that contention. He, for a second time, admitting to this belief, I responded: "Then you must never ask me to be a priest, which I have absolutely no desire to be." Eyes filling with tears, my father replied with sadness, "God give you success, I shall not force you to do that for which you have no desire." And so it was in this way, thanks to the kind and gentle understanding of my father and the generous support of my most worthy benefactor Dr. ROTHMANN—but not least also to my own unwavering determination and most excellent God-given attributes—that I was freed most happily to distinguish myself in the profession of medicine and to accomplish wonderful and great things in the pursuit of natural history.

*   *   *

So too ARCTAEDIUS, while thus causing considerable worry and disappointment at home, broke with family traditions to lead a life in natural science, a branch of knowledge to which he was resolved to apply all his energies. But, at the academy at Uppsala just newly enrolled he learned soon enough, much to his consternation—and to mine as well, for I suffered the same disconnection some few years later when I arrived there from Lund in late August 1728—a course of study in natural science was at that time almost non-existent. Thus, it was, for example, that ARCTAEDIUS was the only student of his day to declare a desire to study chemistry, this interest extending back to his early intrigue with the science of alchemy. Of course, it should not be forgotten that he was obliged to join himself to the medical faculty, for it was only there that any instruction in natural history was then offered. But even here in those days the opportunities were meager. Only two professors of any worth belonging to that faculty had made any kind of good name for themselves in the area of natural history. These two, however, might have served well enough if it were not for the fact that by this time, in the autumn of 1724, both were well advanced in years and had all but retired from taking any meaningful share in the work of teaching, and what small teaching they did do was no longer effective. There was some sense also that these two, once renowned leaders of the medical faculty, from whom ARCTAEDIUS had hoped to gain so much, were now, to describe it in a blunt way, seriously neglecting their work. One of them was LARS ROBERG, 60 years of age when ARCTAEDIUS matriculated, and the other, OLOF RUDBECK, somewhat older in his 64th year.

These learned men enjoyed a favorable reputation when young, both holding their posts on the medical faculty as Professor of Medicine at Uppsala University by Royal Appointment. They had from an early time divided the subject matter under their joint purview: ROBERG, as lecturer and demonstrator of practical and theoretical medicine, thus taking surgery, physiology, and chemistry; and RUDBECK taking anatomy, botany, zoology, and pharmacology. By all that was said about him, the first of these two men was a fair naturalist and a skilled anatomist, yet the teaching he did while ARCTAEDIUS attended at Uppsala was very small in quantity. In fact, there is no record of ROBERG having offered any public course of lectures at all. Professor RUDBECK, who was known as RUDBECK the Younger, to distinguish him from his father of the same name—who was by all measures considerably more famous than his son—was widely considered to be a very gifted and learned man, to whom ARCTAEDIUS was especially attracted by reputation. He had traveled widely in his younger days, journeying through Denmark, Germany, Holland, and England, where he made large and valuable botanical and zoological collections. There is little question also, as is well borne out by his early instruction, that RUDBECK possessed a solid knowledge of the first principles of botany, knowledge said to have been acquired from his eminent father, who was hard at work on a great botanical work, the *Campus Elysii* (Elysian Fields), when almost completed it was destroyed in 1702 by the great fire of Uppsala. Within a very few hours, this conflagration destroyed the greater part of the town, the castle, churches, the University, and the botanical garden, as well as the immense manuscript and the many thousands of copper plates already engraved that would have served to illustrate this great work. The elder RUDBECK, shattered by this tragic turn of events, died a few months later. The son, who had been assisting his father in this botanical effort, almost equally depressed and forlorn, abandoned his academic duties of researching and teaching in natural history—most unfortunately for students like ARCTAEDIUS who were so eager for this learning—to follow his intense interest in the study of languages. Thus, for the first three years of ARCTAEDIUS's time at Uppsala, Professor RUDBECK the Younger was, as a matter of fact, entirely inactive in his prescribed department on account of his being engaged in scientific inquiries in the domain of philology. It was lamented by many that he abandoned botany in 1702 to work on his *Thesaurus Linguarum Asiae et Europae Harmonicus* (Lexicon and Relationships of the Asiatic and European Languages), an immense compilation in which he tried to prove that all languages derive from Hebrew, but, in the end, all his time and efforts came to naught for it was never published. When, in 1727, RUDBECK returned his attentions to his professorial duties, at the age of 67, he delivered, over a two-year period, a course of lectures on the *Birds of Sweden*, which was occasioned by the presence of our young ARCTAEDIUS, who eagerly got out of it all he could.

I was made aware of this deplorable situation at Uppsala not only from the heartfelt complaints told to me later by my friend, but also more directly from personal experience as well. While still at the University of Lund, where I had gone in the summer of 1727, my old benefactor Dr. ROTHMANN advised me to leave that city and remove myself to Uppsala, where the good doctor assured me I would meet with considerably greater advantages for the completion of my medical studies. There I would find the celebrated Professors ROBERG and RUDBECK, a very rich library, and a most extensive botanical garden to help gratify my unquenchable thirst for botany. Eagerly adopting my kind patron's advice, I betook myself to Uppsala, where, for all the reasons lamented by ARTEDI, I soon repented my decision. Yes, it is true that RUDBECK gave a course of study about his *Birds of Sweden*, which animals, by the way, were very cleverly drawn and colored. And just before the first Easter of my arrival, ROBERG gave four public lectures on *De Historia Animalium* (Natural History of Animals) of ARISTO-TLE, in light of the principles of DESCARTES, and lectured privately as well on *Praxis Medica* (Medical Practice)—I attended all of them, but like the others I was disappointed; in the circumstance it was better to buy the books. But during those days at Uppsala no one heard or saw any anatomy, nor anyone any chemistry. I myself never had the opportunity of attending a single lecture on botany, either private or public. Nor, might I add, was there anything to speak of in the way of collections or other materials pertaining to instruction in natural history, those curiosities that might have once filled the cabinets of ROBERG and RUDBECK long since gone to the deprivations of time. It is thus not a question to be debated: the student of natural science in our day, at Uppsala and elsewhere in our country, was almost wholly dependent upon his own ability to teach himself the knowledge he sought to acquire. Those men who called themselves teachers were not in any position to afford him more than the most meager of assistance. However, despite these unexpected and disappointing, might I say deplorable, circumstances, ARCTAEDIUS applied himself with great assiduity—much as I did myself—to his chosen branch of science, and, thanks to his good parts, he was soon accounted one of the most promising of the students attached to the medical faculty, a development moreover proven by the events that were to follow.

CHAPTER 2

My Most Intimate Friend

It seems to have been a case of instantaneous mutual attraction….

—NORAH GOURLIE, *The Prince of Botanists,* 1953

I ARRIVED at Uppsala in early September of 1728, where, unbeknownst to me, for I had not met nor had I heard mention of him, ARTEDI had taken up residency four years prior—it was during his years here at the university that he took the direction to change his family name from ARCTAEDIUS to ARTEDI, that designation by which I knew him and the name with which he made his mark. Here, in this town, determined as I was to study natural science, I immediately sought to make the acquaintance of others of like mind. But when I asked for the names of students engaged in similar studies, I was told, and very much surprised to hear, that there were none with this inclination in all of Uppsala save PETER ARTEDI. In fact, this ARTEDI, as I soon learned, was foremost in everyone's mind in this connection, for it was evident that he was the only medical student who at the time had distinguished himself by his diligence and erudition. Notwithstanding these wide praises for his expertise related to things of the natural world, I was told also, and soon learned for myself, that he was quite capable in other departments as well. He was exceedingly well versed in literature and modern languages, was a profound philosopher, and possessed a sound knowledge of medicine. He had the power, moreover, of giving the most admirable addresses on many different subjects, wherein he displayed keen judgment and a thorough acquaintance with his topic, so that none of his listeners, on leaving the lecture room, could fail to accord him the distinction of being a very great and learned man.

Intrigued to discover also that this ARTEDI had, very much the same as I, given up theology for the wonders and joys of nature, I asked further for his whereabouts. Imagine my disappointment upon discovering that he had taken himself some weeks before back to his home village of Nordmaling, whither he had been summoned by the news of an illness of his father, which eventually ended in the poor man's death.

As I was later told by ARTEDI himself, and could witness first hand by examination of the result, the interval spent by my friend in Nordmaling—a trying time to be sure, to witness the slow lapse of life of him to whom you owe your being—was not entirely spent at the bedside. He took this opportunity to complete a work that he had begun many years before as a young boy: "A Short List of the Trees, Bushes, and Plants that are Indigenous to the Glebe-Lands in Nordmaling and Villages Lying Within Its Immediate Vicinity." Seeing this manuscript, although small and of little importance to the larger aspects of our science—giving little more than a record of the flora of Nordmaling at that time—I was surprised to see the scholarship. He, through this effort, quite plainly demonstrated a profound knowledge and following of the system introduced by the great TOURNEFORT, as so well laid out in the latter's *Institutiones rei Herbariae*, yet ARTEDI entered a number of new things for which I had had no previous thoughts. It is certainly the case, in the productions of both authors, that the orders that hold the trees and bushes are placed separately by themselves, and well separated from the orders that contain the herbaceous phanerogams (plants of a seed-producing kind, in which male and female genitalia are easily seen), which embrace as well the cryptogams (plants in which seeds cannot be found and genitalia are well hidden, including algae, fungi, mosses, and ferns). But, while TOURNEFORT ends his classification with the trees and bushes, ARTEDI, quite surprisingly, starts off with them from the very beginning. This innovation, in addition to a large number of other independent modifications in the overall presentation, constitutes, I must say, rather remarkable improvements. Of other quite favorable enhancements, let me just mention but a few. Coniferous trees and that group that holds the birch-alder assemblage were combined as one by TOURNEFORT, whereas ARTEDI divides them into two well-differentiated parts. The bird-cherry is accepted by ARTEDI to contain the stone-fruit, and in his presentation, it is well separated from bilberries, red whortleberries, and their ilk; whereas, the renowned French botanist weds not only all of these species as one, but combines them together with the elder-tree, the honeysuckle, and other more-or-less related forms, in one and the same grouping.

Horsetail and nettles, if one will believe ARTEDI, have little or nothing to do with one another, situated in the latter's classification in quite distant sections, whereas TOURNEFORT combines them all, together with hemp, the hop, spinach, *Mercurialis*, etc. In like manner, *Pyrola* and the water-lilies, according to ARTEDI, must rightly be contained within two quite different classes, but TOURNEFORT, seemingly ignorant of the large distinctions between these two, puts them together along with *Hypericum*, that beneficial vegetable better known to most as St. JOHN's wart. And so it goes on, much the same in this way, these few examples being only small indications of the independent points of view—of which I took full notice and committed all to memory for my own future employment—well expressed by my good friend. All in all, I must admit that I was somewhat more than astonished that this newcomer to natural history, albeit only two years my senior, could have accomplished such a feat in the way that I saw it in its final form. But, no matter—the work, dated by its author 24 February 1729, as we shall see, was never published, and what is not published, does not exist.

Discharging the last duties to his dear departed father, the obligations of which detained ARTEDI at Nordmaling throughout the winter, he did not return to Uppsala until late March 1729, at which time I sought him out immediately, as I was quite anxious to meet this fellow student. I can still remember in vivid detail our first encounter: I saw him before me, lofty of stature and spare of figure; his hair was long and his face reminded me of that of JOHN RAY's. He struck me as humble-minded, not hasty in forming an opinion, but yet prompt, firm and withal mature, a man of old-world honor and faith. It rejoiced me to remark that our talk turned at once upon stones, plants, and animals, and I was much moved at having so many of his scientific observations confided to me without the least hesitation or reserve, upon that very first occasion on which we met. I sought his friendship, and so far was he from withholding it, that he promised me his services too, if such I needed, a promise he afterwards most loyally kept. This sacred friendship, thus spontaneously sealed, we fostered uninterruptedly for almost six years in Uppsala, at all times with the same fidelity, but with ever-increasing warmth and attachment. He was my closest and most intimate friend, and I was his.

* * *

I must admit, and I have no qualms in saying this outright, men from an early age were the center of my emotional world. Women as such always held a distant second place—I abhorred them in general and was disgusted by their bodily functions; yet, at the same time too, and again this is an admission that I do not feel ashamed to utter, I occasionally felt sexually attracted to them. I especially had no fondness whatsoever for scholarly women. Thus, I strictly forbade my daughters, of which I was later to have a total of four, to attend school of any kind. To my way of thinking, it was the duty of a wife to bring their daughters up as good housekeepers and mothers. Very often having one or more of my poor and hungry students to my house for dinner, I always made invitations of this kind dependent on a solemn promise that they not bring with them books from which French or such things could be learnt. Although I did my best to refrain from it, I did not seldom find myself lecturing severely of feminine customs, and here I give but one example: Women clothe themselves in our terrible winter as if they were out in an Italian summer; could a spider web hold them, it would please them better. Outside Europe one never sees the whole of a woman's face exposed, but here with us the face is not big enough, but they need show themselves down to their breasts, and thus add half the body to the face, which is both a wicked and injurious treachery with which to beguile men. Such misses complain over the least draught in the house, but in church or when out elsewhere, where they will show their rank, they can sit with a bared breast and that with goodly patience; and the better to attract men's eyes, they hang gold chains, pearl necklaces, and diamond crosses round the neck and on the breast. All my life I felt a strong need to wage a war against these and other senseless conventions.

I regarded women and marriage as economic necessities, which men need and could undertake because women, being fools, marry for love. When I was a bachelor, without stable means, and unable therefore to make my way in the world, I knew quite well that I had no other alternative but to pay my addresses to some young lady of fortune, who first could make me happy and then I her. I then proceeded to do just that, securing the knot of matrimony in June 1739 to one SARA ELISABET

MORAEA, daughter of JOHAN MORAEAUS, the physician at the Falun copper mines in the province of Dalecarlia, where I spent the Christmas holiday of 1734, with my long-time companion and fellow student CLAES SOHLBERG, at his house in that town. People would not have hesitated to call this Dr. MORAEAUS wealthy, for certainly in this poor region of west central Sweden, he was truly the richest of all. Yet I was to be disappointed later on to finally realize that my father-in-law was quite fond of his money and did not want to give up any part of it to his son-in-law.

As for the true direction of my emotional outlets, I sincerely loved my students. In fact, they were the only real objects of my love, apart from my young daughters—ELISABET CHRISTINA, born 1743; LOVISA, 1749; SARA CHRISTINA, 1751; and SOPHIA, 1757—and my many animals. Loving all things imbued with life, I kept over the years numerous dogs, cats, parrots, and monkeys. I most fondly adored a gentle raccoon to which I gave the name SJUBB and which, I might add, was the subject of one of my most delightful papers: "The Description of an American Animal given by his Royal Highness for Research," published by me in the *Proceedings of the Swedish Royal Academy of Sciences* in 1747. To my great sorrow this most pleasing creature came to a tragic end, attacked and killed by a large and mangy dog. After searching hard for several days we eventually found his body, upon which I immediately performed a detailed dissection, being especially interested in the curious structure of the raccoon's sexual organs.

As for my students, I always made a point to give them praise openly and extravagantly, even on occasion when it was not warranted or much deserved. I gave them all pet names and called them my "mates" and my "apostles." I struggled and fought for them as best I could. I secured scholarships for them when it was possible; and when it was not, I augmented their means liberally from my own purse. When sufficiently aroused, that being more my normal attitude than anything else, I warmed them with my enthusiasm and spurred them on. To the obvious recoil of some outsiders looking in, I often took to hugging them and kissing them in public view. Firm in the belief that the shape of the head holds significance as to intellectual attributes, I often examined, in public as well, the outer form of the skull of my most beloved disciples to judge each one's memory, intelligence, and inclinations.

Many of my students were quite good-looking. FALCK was, I well remember, quite tall, upright, muscular, and handsome—the face was oval, manly, and pleasing. PEHR LÖFLING, not unlike FALCK in his fine appearance, was often my captive slave as I dictated my *Philosophia Botanica* (Philosophy of Botany, one of my greatest works, which you will remember I published at Stockholm in 1751) and other products of my labors to him from my bed, a secretarial duty that he sincerely told me he did not want ever to end. It may sound silly now, but I distinctly recall missing one of my favorites so badly that I wrote to a friend begging that he "take burning firebrands and throw them at Professor KALM so that he might come without delay to Uppsala, for I long for him as a bride for the hour of one o'clock at night."

We were a fine lot indeed, the good Professor and his mates. They truly loved me and I them. The extent to which together this band of eager boys promoted and advanced the study of natural history cannot be easily measured, but leave it to say that in no kingdom in Europe, might I say, in all the world, could botany be said to be in a more flourishing state. I well recall with deep fondness our glorious summer forays made every Wednesday and Saturday, marching over hill and valley, with my flock of 200 or more pupils, collecting plants and insects, and any other living thing save those larger curiosities that were either too strongly tied down or could more easily escape our grab. We made observations of every kind, shot birds, stuck pins in grasshoppers, dissected worms, and kept close minutes of every action and discovery. After botanizing from seven o'clock in the morning till nine at evening time, we returned triumphant, with flowers in our hats, dancing and singing, the Father surrounded by his children, with drums and trumpets blaring, through the city to the garden of Uppsala. Foreigners and people of distinction from Stockholm and other places often attended these gay excursions; indeed, at this time, and under my profound guidance and persistent force, the science of nature had attained the highest degree of popularity. I was very much esteemed and well loved by all.

Despite the almost inescapable emotional attachment that I had for my students, I was always careful to keep my distance in the sense that they were never my friends, the reason for this having to do with how I saw the results of their work in relationship to mine. As it should be, I always believed quite fervently that I alone should be given the sole credit for the work that they did. While I certainly mourned, for example, the premature death of LÖFLING in 1756, I was disturbed more at the thought that I was just about to further science through his assiduous work and that this opportunity by his permanent and early departure had been lost. I always believed myself to have a kind of right to see and describe first those plants that my apostles found, and greatly appreciated that politeness on their part. When a few times I found that courtesy lacking, I could not control my profound disapproval.

From an early time, I resolutely encouraged, and in later years made it almost a requirement—might I say more like a duty that could not be circumvented—that my students travel to distant lands for the purpose of exploration of unknown places, and for the discovery and acquisition of natural objects of divers kinds. Now it was that these journeys were arduous to the extreme, some more so than others, demanding more than normal human strength, and often leading to dire results. More than once, as instigator and sponsor, I sent members of my beloved flock to martyrdom in the name of science. By pestilence or accident, all for the promotion of discovery, lives were given, and given gladly in that supreme and precious quest to add to universal knowledge, through which the Professor and our nation might shine more brightly among all learned peoples. The first to go in this way was my dear TÄRNSTRÖM, a beautiful boy and intimate companion on many of my botanical forays around Uppsala, with whom I charged, among other things, the task of procuring a growing tea bush in a pot, or at least seed of this valuable plant. I requested also that he bring me a living goldfish that I might present it to Her Majesty Queen LOVISA ULRIKA for her collection—which, I might here interject, was quite excellent, more so in the departments of shells and insects than any other, many procured from the Indies, and rivaling the finest in the world—in exchange for still more royal gratitude and favor. TÄRNSTRÖM was the best of the lot, having progressed so far in botany that no one in the Kingdom could compare with him; but, alas, in 1746, well before he had a chance to do anything for me of importance, he died in Cochin China of a tropical fever, an event that struck me like a hammer and made me unendingly miserable.

Next it was HASSELQUIST, always delicate and badly off, if not sickly, never fit for strenuous work, but whom, despite his frailty, I sent to Egypt in 1749. At Smyrna, three years later, at the tender age of 30, he succumbed to fever, dying like a lamp whose oil is consumed, in consequence of his excursions and fatigues in the Holy Land. Unhappily, he left a debt of a rather large sum—14,000 copper dalers, to be exact—which I was forced to pay, although some relief was had by petition to the Royal Scientific Society. The personal loss to me was considerable, and was made up for only in part by recovery of his manuscripts, which, when I began to read them I could not stop before I read them all. I must say I never held anything before that was so greatly filled with new and real observations as these—they penetrated me as God's word penetrates a deacon. Works such as this had never come out before and, once edited by me, I longed for their appearance in published form like a lover for the wedding day. No trouble was spared over my reworking of the text and, although my many other obligations put the final result off until the year 1757, the book was printed in Stockholm under my authorship with title *Iter Palestinum* (Journey to Palestine).

And so it was much the same with the others: LÖFLING, my most beloved pupil, who, among all my disciples, none had gone as far as he, was laid up in a tertian ague, after which be became dropsical and died miserably at the Mission at Merercuri, in Guiana, in 1756, forfeiting his life for FLORA and her lovers who bitterly mourned his loss. I grieved for him mightily, but luckily his manuscripts and travel journal survived, the best part of which I published in 1758—a lively read that I chose to call *Iter Hispanicum* (Journey to New Spain), in which the descriptions of new American plants take up a full 185 pages.

Sweet FORSSKÅL in Arabia, while I most desperately grieved his loss, sent me, very fortunately, just before he died of malaria in 1763, a stalk and flower of an unknown tree, a plant then wholly new to science, later named by me *Amyris gileadensis* from which is extracted the

Balm of Gilead. By favor of this gift I was deeply gratified, for this very species was the object for which I specially charged this faithful apostle.

Then there was JOHAN FALCK—not to be confounded with his younger brother ANDERS FALCK, the astronomer—whom I sent to Russia, the Caucasus, West Siberia, and Kazan. It was at the latter place, for reasons known only to him, but afflicted certainly with hypochondria and sufferings of every other kind, not to mention opium addiction—some say also he had by that time completely lost his sanity—that he slit his own throat and thereby took his life in the month of March of 1774. And finally, I might include in this list of tragedies, ANDERS BERLIN, who, while collecting for me in Senegal in 1773, and before there was any chance to send to his teacher the objects of his labors, was attacked and hacked to death at a tender age of 27 by the local inhabitants of that strange and wild country.

In all of this, amidst the melancholy fate of these my sacrificial lambs, each cut off in the flower of their days, there were, of course, the more fortunate, but in no way less daring of my apostles, who struck out for distant foreign lands. By safe reappearance in their welcoming homeland, they were thus able to enjoy the untold rewards of their success during their own lifetimes. The best of these was PETER KALM, an excellent naturalist, born to the rigors of natural history, who in 1748, journeyed to North America, visiting the British colonies of Pennsylvania—where in Philadelphia he called upon that able scientist BENJAMIN FRANKLIN—Delaware, New Jersey, and New York, and venturing as far as southern Canada. Returning to Sweden in 1751, he delivered to me an extraordinary collection of dried plants and seeds, which specimens happily found their places in the pages of many of my publications, most especially my *Species Plantarum* (Species of Plants) of 1753, which, you will remember, included more than 700 species in total, of which about 90 were due to the diligence of this brave servant of botany. In no small thanks for this effort, I immortalized KALM with the naming of *Kalmia* for the mountain laurel.

Then there was ROLANDER who upon my instruction went to Surinam and St. Eustache in 1755. He managed to return to me in 1756, but by this time his mental faculties were completely deranged, claiming most emphatically that he had discovered a bush in Surinam that produced real pearls, and how these pearls were the elixir of life. He brought back with him little more than several dozen long-desired cochineal insects alive in a jar, all of which died before I could see them, disappointing me greatly. The fault for this considerable loss lay with the gardener, who, upon receiving the jar, opened it, took out the plant, cleansed it from the dirt—and as well from the insects—and replaced it back in the jar, so that the insects, though they arrived alive, were then destroyed in the garden, before I could even get sight of them. Thus, this unfortunate error removed all my hopes of rearing them to advantage in the conservatory. As it were, the procurement of living cochineals, being the chief reason for sending ROLANDER to Surinam, had been for many years primary on my list of desires to add to my entomological studies. Thus to lose them now when so close was grievous to me beyond description—for many weeks thereafter I suffered the most dreadful fits of migraine, made only worse by this ungrateful pupil who gave what remained of his collections to my competitors and thus proceeded to slander me everywhere he went.

Let me mention also in this tribute PEHR OSBECK, who I sent to Canton and Java in 1750 as a ship's chaplain for the Swedish East India Company. I well recall my nervous impatience when fully a year after his departure I had received no word from him. Fearing that some dreadful event had removed him from this life, and that all my good efforts on his behalf had been wasted, you can imagine my great relief, to learn by letter dated 27 November 1751 of his success in obtaining *Melastoma*—a genus within which are classified certain shrubs and trees, the curious berries of which stain the mouth black when chewed—the very thing for which I had specifically sent him so far. I responded quickly with profound joy, promising upon his return to make crowns with the flowers he would bring back, to adorn the heads of the priests of the temple of FLORA and the altars of the goddess. I pledged to him also that his name would be inscribed on substances as durable and indestructible as diamonds, and that I would be pleased to dedicate to him some very rare *Osbeckia* that would be enrolled in FLORA's army. In closing my epistle, I commanded that he hoist his sails and tow with all his might; but bade him heed not to return to Sweden without the choicest spoils, or I would invoke NEPTUNE to hurl him and all his company into the depths of the Taenarum. I was later to be amply rewarded as a result of my warning, for whence in summer 1752 he did grace my place again, he delivered to me an extraordinarily rich Chinese herbarium of some six hundred specimens, among which was a most beautiful Javanese orchid that I later named *Epidendrum amabile* and described in my *Species Plantarum* of 1753.

Finally, and not to dwell any longer on the more successful of the rest, there was LARS MONTIN who went to Lapland in 1745. Then there was OLOF TORÉN who in 1750 explored Malabar and Surat, and who, like OSBECK, went as chaplain aboard a vessel of the Swedish East India Company, which position he owed solely to my recommendation. BERGIUS went to the Island of Gotland, and KÄHLER to Italy, both in 1752, the latter returning heavily laden with plants. DANIEL SOLANDER, my most favorite, went to Russia, Lapland, and the Canary Islands between 1753 and 1756, and later in 1768 sailed with COOK and BANKS round the world aboard HMS *Endeavour*. I sent MARTIN to Spitzbergen in 1758. KÖNIG went to Siam, Ceylon, and India in 1767, and for reasons fully unknown to me, he decided to remain in Tranquebar until his death in 1785, for which reason I got little out of him in return for all my efforts. ALSTRÖMER traveled through Europe in the 1760s. NIEBUHR accompanied FORSSKÅL to Arabia in 1761, being the only one to survive that ill-fated expedition. THUNBERG went to the Cape in 1771, continuing on to Ceylon, Java, and Japan in 1775, sending back most invaluable information about Japanese medicinal plants. He is at this moment still in that country, gone from me these past eight years; I am desperate to live long enough to witness the joy of his return, to be present on that great day, and to touch with my hands the laurels that will crown his brow. Finally, there is SPARRMANN, who traveled longer and farther than most, venturing to China and several times to Africa, joining COOK's second circumnavigation of the globe in 1772, and returning to Sweden in 1776, thoroughly exhausted and, I dare to say, almost dead.

These and many others not mentioned filled the ranks of my army of devoted naturalists and thus it was that I had pupils in all parts of the world. In this manner my herbarium increased at a rate beyond compare, quickly rivaling any other such collection in the world. And whom to thank for this rich bounty but our Almighty God? Each time upon their leaving, in fear for their safety, my heart went out to these my gentle adventurers. Yet, each time too, I did not hesitate, from the comfort and security of my chair in Uppsala, to console them as to the task ahead. I instructed them, in all sincerity, not to have fear of exposing themselves to some degree of danger, for anyone who hopes to attain a glorious goal must take risks. I assured them too, in my fatherly way, that, in all truth, these journeys are not as perilous as some people here would have them believe. Always sick with worry, I eagerly awaited news of these disciples and, somewhat more impatiently, for the arrival of plants. In my many letters, sent to them in far-away places, I gave them every encouragement that I could muster, praying to God at the same time for their safe return, and begging that I might not be forgotten. It was this last worry that I feared the most, the horrible thought that my gentle confessors and apostles of the faith might forget their good master, the father who made everything possible for them. Thus, I implored them in my letters, and I beseeched them in my dreams at night, to think of me, to "think of me as often as I think of you, which is whenever I touch your plants; when I study them it is as if I were talking to you."

*   *   *

Though he was not the first by any means, KOULAS, the young German medical student whom Dr. STOBAEUS had taken into his house as a secretary, was surely one of the more important to me. I, of course, was living there as well, that kindly doctor, who later became Professor of Medicine and Physician to the King, having offered me lodging during my early days at the University of Lund. KOULAS resided there like a son and had ready access to the doctor's excellent museum and library. Well aware of my uncontrollable desire to see that precious and delightful cabinet of curios, the minerals, shells, stuffed birds, and dried plants glued onto paper that had been so lovingly assembled by my host—permission for which I was loath to request on my own— KOULAS most obligingly allowed me secret access. Knowing also that

I had no money to buy books and that I was eager to examine those things to which I was not privy—for the library was otherwise always kept well locked—he began, on that pretense, to bring books to me in late evening. This, KOULAS did every night, until STOBAEUS's mother, who was very old, and a bad sleeper, became aware of a light constantly burning in my window and warned her son that I often went to sleep with my candle still lit, thus seriously endangering the house, which like all dwellings were made of wood and thus highly susceptible to fire. She, being deathly afraid of fire, a fear not at all unreasonable, desired her son to chide me severely for my extreme carelessness. Two nights later, at eleven o'clock, STOBAEUS burst into my apartment, expecting to find me soundly sleeping, with my candle still flickering, but to his astonishment he discovered the gentle KOULAS and me in bed diligently pouring over his books, the works of CESALPINI, the brothers BAUHIN, TOURNEFORT, in addition to others. So it was in this way that we were duly found out and, alas, the sweet nightly visits ceased abruptly.

In the spring of 1728, I went on a botanizing expedition with my young brother botanist MATTHIAS BENZELSTIERNA, to a most pleasant location at Fågle-sång, where, the two of us, having taken off our clothes because of the heat, took, for our afternoon remission, to lying in the meadow. There I was most violently bitten in the right arm by a worm—some want to insist it was instead a kind of fly, but in this claim they are quite emphatically in error—which insidious parasite I later named *Furia infernalis*, causing the most discomforting pain and swelling. My arm, in fact, became so full with vile inflammation that my life was severely endangered. But, thanks to Dr. SCHNELL, who attended to me in STOBAEUS's absence, the latter having set off to rest in the mineral waters of Helsinborg, I was cured by the rendering of an incision that extended the full length of my appendage. My confidant BENZELSTIERNA, having apparently interpreted this calamity as a sure sign from God of wrong doing, quickly packed up, never to be seen by me again.

Then there was ELIAS PREUTZ. At Uppsala in early 1724, when old RUDBECK was given leave of his public teaching duties so that he might further pursue his study of philology and thus complete his ill-fated

Thesaurus, his lectures were taken over, but not very well, by his son-in-law Dr. PETRUS MARTIN, who unfortunately died rather suddenly in 1727. MARTIN was replaced by NILS ROSÉN, RUDBECK's capable assistant, of whom we shall soon hear more. But ROSÉN, who had been appointed *Adjunctus* to the Faculty of Medicine at Uppsala, was abroad at the time, in Holland to be exact, for the purpose of obtaining a doctor's degree and doing what he could to improve himself in his profession. In the meantime, his place was supplied in turn by PREUTZ, who, by almost universal agreement, was conceited and wholly incompetent. Although he was somewhat older, I, perhaps alone among our colleagues, found a liking for him and made it be known to him that I was a friend in whom he could confide, and he often came to me in confidence for this comfort. But, there was no helping it: being a person for whose abilities the students entertained a most marked contempt, many of them—and I can list in this category LETSTRÖM, ELVIUS, SOHLBERG, VOIGTLENDER, and RUDBECK's son JOHAN OLOF, not to mention several others—turned elsewhere for instruction, putting themselves under my own private tutoring. Thus, in this way, I most seriously caused the position and authority of my despised friend to be undermined. In the end, however, I was brought forward and, having been duly examined by the faculty, was judged worthy—despite the strong objections of Professor ROBERG, who thought it rather hazardous to give a teacher's job to a lad who had not yet been three years a student—of being placed in that very situation, in PREUTZ's stead. I must say, the monetary remunerations of this new and wholly welcome arrangement were quite beneficial, allowing me to assume a more decent appearance in my dress, not to mention other things. But on the bad side of it, strong resentment, might I say jealous hatred, grew in PREUTZ, it becoming acute to the point that our friendship was ended.

In this same way, and only shortly thereafter, my relations with NILS ROSÉN were all but extinguished. Soon after his return to Uppsala from his sojourn abroad, medical degree in hand, we embarked on a close friendship, a quite delightful but brief interlude that was soon broken too by his uncontrollable jealousy of my meteoric success. Only one year older, but provided abundantly with opportunities that I never enjoyed, he had, even by this early time in his career, shown himself to be a brilliant doctor, destined to make his name especially in the field of pediatrics, and later even to be ennobled as ROSÉN VON ROSENSTEIN. Taking over Professor RUDBECK's lectures on anatomy and, I must admit, bringing welcome new life to the Medical School, he made it rather clear to all that he hoped to eventually succeed the old gentleman in his post, as there was no other competitor so highly qualified, unless, of course, consideration was given to me. In so working toward his primary goal, and observing that I came forward more and more, and fearing lest I should become a dangerous competitor, he did his best to wrench away the public lectures on botany and the associated demonstrations in the Botanical Garden, which both at the time were under my sole purview. But, to his good credit, old RUDBECK, who still had the authority to say so, would not hear of it, unwilling to trust this department to ROSÉN who had never studied it. Once then rebuffed, ROSÉN came to me directly to do his best to persuade me to give up to him spontaneously those duties that I so loved, asking that I lend him my lecture notes on botany that I had composed myself and which I valued more than anything else that belonged to me. To this, in part, I consented, in all good faith, but learning shortly thereafter that ROSÉN had copied the first set, I was loath to lend the remainder. When pressed by him to give him more, I agreed to bend to his unworthy intimidation, but only if RUDBECK thought it to be appropriate—and of course he did not. So, once again, a closeness was lost forever for reasons that seemed trivial to me.

Looking back from old age now, it seems I scarcely surmounted poverty before I became an object of envy—a passion that oft played me too many tricks, which are of no use to mention further here. But no matter this last departure of ROSÉN: I hardly had time to grieve my loss, for very soon thereafter I had ARTEDI, who quickly became my best and most faithful companion, my brother in flesh, and my best friend on earth. Nothing so comforted me like his presence—we loved like DAVID and JONATHAN.

CHAPTER 3

Our Friendly Rivalry

> It is a sad truth that, in science as elsewhere in this world, the mediocre man in higher position must hate and if possible persecute the superior man in lower station, and that for his very superiority, if for nothing else.
>
> —EDWARD LEE GREENE, *Carolus Linnaeus*, 1912

I HAVE, to date, enumerated the many similarities between the two of us, a remarkable sameness of background, history, and early circumstance; but in divers other ways we were as different as continents separated by a vast ocean, both in person and disposition. ARTEDI was of a more tall and handsome figure; whereas, I was rather short in stature, yet stout, neither fat nor thin. He had a more retiring and quiet disposition than I, more seriously minded and logical, more attentive to details, slower in observation and in everything he did, but, on the other hand, often more accurate. As for me, I was, some might say, boisterous and more likely to be overexcited than not. I never ventured to procrastinate, for I considered time as the most uncertain thing in the world. I did not linger, but walked quickly and did everything promptly. In fact, I was decidedly quicker and more deliberate in the actual doing of any piece of work, ARTEDI being somewhat sluggish and prone to postpone to an ample extent. It did not seldom happen, however, that he had the laugh of me, by reason of my having to begin my work all over again because some important fact in my haste had escaped my memory. He was an individualist, living a quiet and lonely life—as a habit, he went to the tavern from three to nine, was at work from nine to three in the night, and slept from three till noon. I, in contrast, was marked by a quick and easy friendliness, eagerly seeking engagement with my fellow men, always wanting and requiring the company and attention of others. While ARTEDI was never one to tell a joke, I was blessed with a dry droll humor, always of ready wit. He pursued his favorite studies, chemistry and especially alchemy, with the same ardor as I devoted myself to botany. Neither of us, however, was altogether ignorant in the other's branch of pursuit, but, with a noble spirit of emulation, as soon as one found himself unequal to the progress of the other in one department of study, he dedicated himself to another. Thus we contrived to divide the kingdoms and provinces of nature between us. Certainly we both began to study fishes and insects together, but in a very short time, despite my protracted effort to attain a premier position in the department of ichthyology, I yielded to ARTEDI in that aquatic realm—not being personally so particularly partial to those cold and slippery denizens of NEPTUNE's world, but wanting to hold onto them nevertheless—and he, after some struggle, finally acknowledged me, quite rightly, to be his superior in entomology. ARTEDI took to reducing the chaos that then existed within the amphibians and reptiles, and I the birds, under a mutually agreed, regular arrangement. In mineralogy and the study of quadrupeds, we kept fairly abreast of one another. But in spite of all this open congeniality, it was inevitable that a certain degree of good-natured rivalry should assert itself now and then between the two of us. This rivalry encouraged us in our efforts and spurred us on to greater industry and diligence in our work. However, at the same time, there grew in fact a certain steady and creeping jealousy that caused each of us to keep secret the discoveries that we made. This secrecy, how-ever, never lasted for any great length of time, since not a day passed, I eagerly going to him or he coming to me, notwithstanding the great distance between our respective dwellings, without one surprising the other by narrating some newly discovered fact. We made our reports to each other without reservation, whatever our thoughts, whatever per-sonal events took place, whether it was of a happy or sorrowful nature. To this, however, I must admit with some chagrin, I held back a con-siderable amount of my more profound scientific thoughts, but never did I suspect that ARTEDI did the same. He was always naively most forthcoming. Thus, I gleaned from him all that I could.

The daily intercourse we had together derived much of its value from the openhearted way in which we communicated to one another the result of the researches we were undertaking. In this friendly com-petition, I despaired of ever attaining the same degree of familiarity with the lore of the alchemists that he so thoroughly possessed—I reluctantly acknowledged this fact and relinquished from that time forth the pursuit of that study altogether. I was determined, however, to maintain my full sovereignty in the department of botany, and fully expected him to obligingly desist from the keen inquiry he had previously been following up in that realm, and I was almost successful. But after some contentious argument I felt forced to yield to him the umbellate plants, which he strongly reserved the right to study. He had for some time been working—or so he claimed, and I had no reason to doubt his word—on a new method of classifying this difficult assemblage, which includes those plants with umbrella-like flowers, the hemlock, cow parsley, celery, coriander, and the like. He told me while quite excited that he had been studying the works of the well-known French botanist Sébastien Vaillant and had quite by accident come across a review, published in 1718 in the *Leipzig Commentaries*, of Vaillant's book titled *Sermo de Structura et Differentia Florum usuque, partium eos Constituentium* (Discourse on the Structure and Diversity of the Flowers and of the Use of the Constituted Parts), which gave curious indications of the sexuality of plants. This, Artedi said, had pleased him very much, for he began at that time to take notice of the functions of the *stamina* (stamens, the male organs) and *pistilla* (pistils, the female organs) of flowers and of the essential parts of plants in general. He expressed the thought that these parts, varying as they do among species, as much or more so than the petals, might, in fact, be used as a way to order the contents of the Umbelliferae in a new way that would vastly decrease the chaos this group was in at present. I was thunderstruck by these radical suggestions, which no one had thought of or expressed before—by all my reckoning this was a concept completely new, but I strove to keep my enthusiasm from bubbling forth, and retained my thoughts about its possible utility to myself.

That plants, in a way not wholly dissimilar to animals, engage in sexual union was a subject that had been in my mind ever since my early days in preparatory school at Växjö. It was here that I was greatly stimulated in this direction by the private tutoring of Dr. Rothmann, who, in addition to providing instruction on the botanical system of

TOURNEFORT, made me aware that indeed flowers are the sexual organs of plants—a theory completely new in that time, not at all generally accepted nor even widely known. But, I must admit, my thoughts had not progressed so far as to imagine that details of this system might prove useful as a method to reveal order and hierarchy in nature. It was thus at this instant in time, during this quite useful conversation with my friend, that there became aroused in me a desire to apply the same to plants in general. With ARTEDI's kind permission, which he happily gave, he being of a most generous nature, I summarized quickly the salient points of my thesis, conforming in all manner with genuine botanical principles, in a handwritten pamphlet that I titled *Praeludia Sponsaliarum Plantarum* (Prelude to the Espousals of Plants). I then, in 1730, presented the whole to Professor OLOF CELSIUS, who was then my teacher and patron and in whose house I was living at the time, as the customary New Year's Day gift that all students were obliged to give their benefactors on that occasion every year. By describing vessels, fibers, and other anatomical similarities, as well as diseases, hibernation, and other likenesses, I attempted to establish in this small tract the great analogy between plants and animals. And so, with these elaborations, which were quite well accepted by CELSIUS and the others who were made aware of it, I was able to show quite convincingly the ways in which plants are indeed sexual beings. In fact, I am still so pleased by this work, which I came to call my *Systema Sexuale* (Sexual System), even though decades of time have past and I have produced many other things that no doubt surpass it, I feel obligated to return to this subject in due course.

*   *   *

So it was too in matters of method. Early in my schooling, mostly by instruction that I made available to myself personally—for I never met anyone who could provide me with any help in this department—I began to think about a system or method by which the student of nature could accurately and successfully put together the history of each and every natural subject, whether it be a single specimen or a grouping thereof. Much to my surprise, and, might I say, consternation, ARTEDI let it be known to me that he too in like manner had put some ideas of this subject to paper. Much of what he described was of a similar bent to my own direction in this area, but in some ways he was thoroughly ahead of me, a realization that made my head spin, but I was careful to keep this worry to myself. He began first to talk about names and of naming, much of which was not at all new, some of it, in fact, very old, dating back to ancient Greek times, with ARISTOTLE and THEOPHRAS-TUS, and more recently laid down in a more elaborate form still by the likes of GESSNER, ALDROVANDI, and JONSTONUS. But a good portion of what he wrote, now with my assistance, was wholly new, and what was not, was still very much worth our reiteration.

After names, ARTEDI's attention turned to theory, of the thought intended by the use of class, order, and family, of the meaning behind genus, and of the species. And so it was, in this way, that we began a fervent collaboration to set down our rules, which we were wholly confident, would mediate a general reformation of all of the branches of natural science. Bearing the mutually agreed upon title of *Methodus Demonstrandi Animalia, Vegetabilia, aut Lapides* (Demonstration of the Methods to be Applied to Animals, Plants, and Minerals), the final draft commenced as follows:

> Of Names and of Naming: (1) Give the *chosen name*, both generic and specific of a particular author, if there already is such, or give a name oneself, if a new description is required; (2) List the *synonyms* of all the principal specialists; (3) List as far as possible the *synonyms* used by all the ancient and more recent authors; (4) Give the various *vernacular names*, translated into Latin; (5) List the *synonyms* used by various peoples, of all worldly parts where the subject or subjects are to be found, especially the Greek names; and (6) State the *etymology* of all the generic names.

> Of the Theory: (1) Give the classification as to *classes* and *orders* according to all the systems chosen; (2) Give the classification as to *maniples* or *families*, also according to the systems chosen; and (3) State the *genera* to which the subject or subjects in question have been assigned by various and diverse specialists.

Of the Genus: (1) Give an account of the *natural characters*, with a list of all possible characteristic features; (2) Give the *essential characters*, pointing out the one most distinguishing feature or that which is most exclusive to the genus; (3) Set forth also *artificial characters* in order to distinguish the genera treated as units in the system; (4) Explain all *erroneous ideas*, that is, unsubstantiated claims or *idle dreams* of authors, in the sense of anomalies, monsters, and the like; (5) Establish and demonstrate the *natural genus*; and (6) Confirm the chosen *name of the genus*, which must always consist of a *single word* in Latin, and state why other names are to be rejected.

Of the Species: (1) Let the most complete *description* of the subject be set forth, according to all the external parts; (2) Review all the *species* known or discovered of the genus under discussion; (3) Set forth all the essential *differences* between the species under discussion, along with their characters, in a diagnostic phrase in Latin of length not more than twelve words; (4) Establish and retain the primary *differences* and reject the others; (5) Put together the specific *difference* of the subject or subjects and provide an exposition of the reasons for what has been done until every word of it has been fully accounted for; (6) Set out all the *variations* of the species under discussion, as described by the authors; and (7) Subordinate these *variations* to the species to which they naturally belong, with the reason for the action proposed.

In like manner, we discussed at length, and drew up plans on paper to present, in the best way possible, every one of these categories, examining them each in their turn with a certain detail, but wanting the product at the end to remain as simple as possible. It was ARTEDI's suggestion that we set a firm rule that the genus name shall consist of only a single word taken from the Latin language. As this was not such a revolutionary idea, even during that time, I made no real objection to including a statement of this kind in the *Methodus*, thinking it a practical and quite useful convention. In fact, I resolved at this early time to put it down for all posterity in published form, and did so quite explicitly for plants in my *Critica Botanica* (Rules for Botanical Naming), which, as you well know, appeared at Leiden in 1737. In this treatise, I took full liberty to reject many of the generic names used by both my predecessors and contemporaries, which by the latter, as you might expect, was not at all well received. I well remember the stinging rebuke from one of my detractors whose name is not worth giving here, who wrote to me on 15 November 1737:

> You promise to account, in your *Critica Botanica*, for your numerous alterations of my plant names. I presume you have followed the rules laid down in your *Fundamenta Botanica*. Still many of those rules may, perhaps, not be universally approved, any more than your changes of names. I beseech you to consider what would be the consequence, if every body were to lay down such laws and regulations, at his pleasure, or whenever he felt so inclined, thus overturning names, already known and approved by the best authors, for the sake of making new ones. Would it not lead to worse than the confusion of Babel?

Another woefully ungrateful, yet far more savage, attack, which, when I saw it, made me shake with anger and caused me profound illness for several days, was put to paper by one who had been my good friend and colleague for many years:

> The unmitigated dominance which you have assumed in the plant and animal kingdoms must upon the whole be abhorrent to many. You have considered yourself a second ADAM who has given names to all the products of nature according to their features, which you alone deem most distinctive, without the slightest bother about your predecessors. You can hardly restrain yourself to make man a monkey, or the monkey a man.

O, why these painful barbs? Why cannot these men of superior intelligence see it my way? Why cannot they accept that I have made a revolution in the science of nature, if it is not for their insidious jealousy? But, no matter these silly complaints—it was my expressed intention, regardless of who might not agree or might feel unhappy about it, to make the names short, distinctive, memorable, and as pleasing to the ear as possible. Among other innovations, I took the lead from that industrious French monk CHARLES PLUMIER, most famous for his curious work on American ferns—you are no doubt familiar with his *Traité des Fougères de l'Amérique* (Treatise on the Ferns of America), published in Paris in 1705—to commemorate the lives of my fellow botanists by creating names in their honor. Thus, I took great pains, as well as pleasure, to celebrate the fond memory of my predecessors in this science, and the contributions of my teachers, patrons, and close acquaintances, with names like *Tournefortia*, denoting a handsome and most delightful heliotrope for the great JOSEPH PITTON DE TOURNEFORT; *Rudbeckia*, the black-eyed Susan, for OLOF RUDBECK the Younger; *Cliffortia*, a kind of rose, for GEORGE CLIFFORD; *Burmannia*, a kind of lily native to Ceylon, for JOHANNES BURMANN who wrote so elegantly of the plants of that domain; *Halleria*, containing, in addition to other things, the African honeysuckle for my friend ALBRECHT VON HALLER; *Dillenia*, which of all plants has the showiest flower and fruit, even as JOHANN DILLENIUS made a brilliant show among botanists; and, of course, for my dear friend, *Artedia*, a parsley-like umbelliferous plant so deeply loved by him. A great multitude of other patronymics were established by me for worthy people, but also for some unworthy individuals, who for no good reason whatsoever, attacked my work or in other ways did their best to make my life miserable. I offer here only two examples: for JOHAN SIEGESBECK, a strange man, who with spite and arrogance wrote in harsh criticism of my *Systema Sexuale*, I named *Sigesbeckia*, a highly unpleasant, small-flowered weed. In like manner, I did much the same for that well-known French naturalist BUFFON, who very unwisely attacked me as a worthless "classifier" and "nomenclator." On one particular occasion, he reproached me for placing the flying fox in the same genus as the European bat:

> These two species do not have the same number of teeth in the lower jaw, thus, they cannot be from the same genus, according to this author's own method, the latter, in this case, based wholly on the order and number of the teeth. Besides this blunder, the

flying fox is American, thus, this unfortunate author has erred again in forming a generic name that brings together a large number of species, not only different in essential character, but often far removed from one another geographically.

Never did I respond to this inane criticism directly, but I made it so that his name will forever be associated with *Buffonia*, a plant with a particularly unpleasant odor; but also, by dropping out a letter, I cleverly associated this silly man with *Bufo*, the ancient Latin name for toad. Somewhat later, in a lengthy discourse published in the twelfth edition of my *Systema Naturae* (System of Nature), on the Quadrupedia, a group to which BUFFON had devoted much of his life, I did not condescend to even mention any of his many works. But, I have now strayed quite far from my intended purpose, so let us now return.

*   *   *

In sharp contrast to ARTEDI's way of thinking, and this I must admit, I objected rather violently to a similar suggestion from him for the species name; that is, to employ as well only a single word for this aspect of naming. At the time, it seemed ludicrous to me to replace the traditional Latin descriptive phrase to denote a species, which was in wide use then, more or less following the precepts laid down so long ago by ARIS-TOTLE, that ancient who was first in everything. And here it might be useful to provide an example of what I mean. By purely random choice, let us investigate the name of the common buttercup, which in scientific circles is *Ranunculus seminibus aculeatis, foliis superioribus decompositis linearibus*. The first of these words, *Ranunculus*, is the genus name, which, for those of you whose Latin is lacking, means "little frog," providing useful indication that the buttercup grows in wet places where the frog itself abounds. The second part of the name is the species component, intended to provide a description of the primary distinguishing features of the species, which, in this case, when fully translated, refers to a kind of buttercup, "with prickly seeds, the uppermost leaves more than once divided, each narrow, with sides nearly parallel."

Now it was that ARTEDI, if he had his way, would replace this albeit rather long, but very informative, and thus highly useful, Latin descriptive phrase, with a single word, such that the full appellation for a species would become only two words, a single *nomen genericum* (genus name) and a single *nomen specificum* (species name). The combination of both these words would be made unique to the species at hand: *Ranunculus seminibus aculeatis, foliis superioribus decompositis linearibus* would become simply *Ranunculus arvensis* (a buttercup called *arvensis*, the latter appellation derived from the Latin word *arvum*, meaning field or ploughed land, because it most often grows in or near cultivated fields, especially those planted in corn). Thus, the author of a new name would make little or no attempt to describe the species with the name itself, and hence this new system would separate the description of the species from its naming. What an unfortunate loss! How indeed could a single word stand as placeholder for an object so complex as a fern, a snail, or a mineral! I would not and could not agree with this proposal so strongly advocated by ARTEDI and refused with all my might to set it down. But, just in case this unlikely concept might be accepted at some later date, I thought it judicious to lay it out in published form at that time and so have the right to claim priority to it at such later date as needed. I did this briefly and rather discreetly, while standardizing botanical terminology and meaning, in my *Fundamenta Botanica*, this indispensable book published in Amsterdam in 1736. And what great good that I did, for eventually I revised my opinion on this question. What made this gradual change of mind was no doubt my growing need for accurate names that could be easily and quickly applied in the field by students and the amateur. Stimulus for this too was the ever-increasing complexity of names applied to plants by botanists past and present. Of the latter there are many examples, but take for instance the plants of the genus *Convolvulus*, trailing forms of the morning-glory family, having funnel-shaped flowers and triangular leaves. In 1576, the French botanist CHARLES DE LÉCLUSE designated one species as *Convolvulus folio Altheae*. In 1623, the Swiss botanist GASPARD BAUHIN called this same species *Convolvulus argenteus Altheae folio*, which in 1738, I myself expanded to *Convolvulus foliis ovatis divisis basi truncate: laciniis intermediis duplo longioribus*, which by 1753, I had elaborated further into *Convolvulus foliis palmatis cordatis sericeis: lobis repandis, pedunculis bifloris*.

O what joy, to drop this jargon, unintelligible to all but the highly refined and educated among us, and apply instead *Convolvulus floridus* to that woody climber of the Canary Islands, the roots of which serve as a source of essential oil; or *Convolvulus scammonia* from the Levant, an important source of a drastic purgative.

It is not without some chagrin that I am forced now to admit to arriving myself at ARTEDI's way of thinking—but it was not until the mid-1740s and later that I adopted this method. I first applied it consistently and unerringly for the first time to the whole Vegetable Kingdom in my *Species Plantarum* of 1753—in which I provided a two-word designation for all the fifty-nine hundred known species of plants—and somewhat later to the animate world in the tenth edition of *Systema Naturae*, a wondrous two-volume work that appeared in 1758 and 1759. In the latter production, devoted to the animals, a group somewhat less familiar to me than the vegetables, I scoured the Latin and Greek languages in search of distinctive, rememberable, and well-sounding words for thousands of species, sometimes using a term to describe the shape, the color, or the number of a certain set of anatomical parts. On other occasions, I chose a word for the kind of habitat in which the animal lives, or the manner of its growth, or method of reproduction; and sometimes, as you have already seen, I adopted a patronymic for the first discoverer of the animal. In insects, more often than not, I used names that alluded to color, to mode of conveyance—whether, for example, they be of the crawling, walking, or of the flying kind—or to the kind of plant used by them as food. For differentiating the butterflies, I called upon the full breadth of my rather complete knowledge of classical writings in founding such generic names as *Hector, Helena, Ulysses, Agamemnon, Ajax, Nestor, Achilles, Apollo*, etc. At other times, I simply kept ancient and well-used vernacular terms, such as *Rana*, for the frogs; *Coluber*, for the vipers; *Turdus*, for birds of the thrush kind; *Columba*, for the doves and pigeons; *Mergus*, for the diving ducks; *Canis*, for the dogs; *Felis*, to include all the cats; *Ursus*, for the bears; *Elephas*, for the elephant; and so on and so forth.

What a monumental task! When was there ever before such a colossal feat of name-giving since the Creation of the Almighty? And what a glorious gift did I thus present to mankind, a welcomed return to the simplicity and brevity of the folk-names and vernacular epithets used from time immemorial by peasants, woodmen, hunters, herb-gatherers, and the like, across many lands. Understandably, nearly all of my contemporaries, always stubbornly resistant to change when the change is not of their creation, were reluctant to adopt my binomials. But, in all truth, there was no going back to the old ways. Thus it was codified, from this time on, that all living things shall be known and recognized on the basis of a binomial, that is, one word to denote the genus, another to supply the specific epithet. Considering all my many accomplishments, perhaps nothing gratified me more than to have my method, which came to be called the Binomial System of Biological Nomenclature, universally accepted round the world, even during my own lifetime. In fact, it took a briefer time than ever one might expect, fewer than twenty years, before virtually all opposition to my system had disappeared, there having existed no single accepted method of naming of nature's productions up until this time.

*   *   *

In the end, with this *Methodus*, which proved to be one of my most important and perhaps the most widely utilized of my many works (albeit one of my smallest), ARTEDI and I made the decision to add to our approach several additional categories: three to be exact, and these were the *Attributes* of natural objects; their *Uses* for the betterment of mankind; and the *Literature* of the subjects at hand. In the category of *Attributes*, for example, we thought it best to include what is known about the *season* of production, of growth, vigor, and maturity (the time of flowering if it be a vegetable of the flowering kind), with the mode of breeding and of birth or hatching, old age, and death. We thought it important also to give the *place of birth*, that is, the region and province, and the longitude and latitude of the place where the subject resides or was found; to describe the climate and the soil; and to present something *of the life*, including an account of the diet, the manners or habits, and affections, that is, how the subject is affected by circumstances such as climate and soil; and, finally, to describe the anatomy of the *body*, particularly any remarkable things, together with a microscopical examination.

Under *Uses*, we strove to emphasize the importance of listing *economic use*, both actual and possible among various peoples; to state the *dietetic use*, with the effect on the human body; the *use in physic*, with the mode of action and the constituent principles; the *chemical use* according to the constituent substances from analytical separation by fire; the *medical use* in which diseases, and with what results, demonstrated by reason or by experiment; present the *pharmaceutical* information, as to what parts are used, method of preparation, and composition; and *directions for medical use*, with emphasis on the best method, dosage, and necessary precautions.

And finally, under *Literary matters*, we required that the name of the *discoverer*, with place and time of finding, is to be noted; *historical traditions* of the subject, various, pleasing, and grateful, are to be reported; vain and empty *superstitions* are to be rejected; and excellent *poetic references* are to be cited as adornment.

Thus we contrived together to provide some appropriate introduction to the methods and procedures of taxonomy, an approach that had heretofore been entirely missing in our chosen area of science. ARTEDI did his best to conform to this approach as he worked on his fishes, and I the same as I progressed on my plants. And thinking it important and necessary to make this final edition of our *Methodus* available to the wider general public, I published it under my name as an appendix to the first edition of my *Systema Naturae* that appeared in Leiden in December 1735, the tract itself bearing date 1736. Following soon thereafter, I expanded on these principles to good effect, as I mentioned earlier, applying them most specifically and appropriately to the vegetable world in my *Critica Botanica* of 1737.

* * *

And so it went during those early days, a time full of excitement in the sharing equally of our thoughts and discoveries, deriving sweet consolation in the knowledge that each possessed a true and faithful companion, one who would sympathize in every way with the ups and downs of what life brought to each, and share in each other's prosperity and adversity at all times and in all seasons. Thus it came to pass, in an emotional testament of the quality and depth of our love and mutual attachment, that we made a sacred pledge. It came about first, I believe, as I was preparing for my great journey to far-distant Lapland, which I had resolved to take upon myself in 1732 for the primary purpose of discovery of nature's bounty in a remote and unknown land, the plants from this far north region being especially very poorly known. This undertaking would be long and arduous and fraught with many dangers, and I, unable to give any guarantee of my safety, duly ordained and appointed ARTEDI to be my sole heir and legatee with respect to all those my manuscripts and collections of natural history specimens. And he most solemnly countered with a heartfelt promise to undertake to have such of them published and given to the world as might be deemed worthy thereof, in the event of the enterprise I was about to embark upon proving one from which I was not destined to return alive. In like manner also, some few years later (it was, in fact, September of 1734)—despite a falling out of sorts, to which subject I shall return shortly—upon his leaving Uppsala for England, he directed to be handed over into my care, and for my use, those of his manuscripts and books that he could not conveniently take with him on his journey. At the same time, he implored me to take charge of the said manuscripts and books, and that they were to become my property, if Fate ordained that he should never come back to his native land again. Thus, we were each in unassailable trust of the other: that the one of us who should survive the other would regard it as a sacred duty to give to the world what observations and investigations might be left behind by the one who was gone. Only God had knowledge then that I alone would be obliged to make good on this solemn promise in only one year's time.

CHAPTER 4

Artedi's Fishes

As to Pisces, indeed, our excellent Artedi had written
on them with great ingenuity, but his method was difficult
and insufficient.

—Linnaeus, *Carl Linné*, Vita III, 1769

Fishes not being very much to my liking, I was quite pleased to pass the
chore of working in this department to my friend who was eager to take
them on, and who, from early interest, had already made an excellent
start. As he divulged to me on several occasions, he had acquired a keen
predilection toward these animals while still in his tender youth, not yet
quite a dozen years of age, when his family took up their new residency
in Nordmaling on the coast of the Gulf of Bothnia. Here, water was
everywhere, the briny Baltic to be sure, where sea fishing with rod or
net was best at Kronören and Järnäsklubb; the rivers Öre and Lögde,
whose mouths opened nearby; a myriad of lakes, the largest and most
productive of these being Torrsjön and Sunnansjön; and streams in
large numbers, the sprightly trout most plentiful at Leduån and Präst-
bäcken. All of this was close at hand and on all sides, an abundance of
watery places to find fishes, to learn their kinds and study their ways.
Here our young naturalist whiled away his summer days—and I dare
to guess the spring and autumn as well, the harsh frozen winter making
this all but impossible. In the freshwaters and on the seashore, amid
the rocks and sand of that most abundant coast, he searched for fishes
and other things of God's creation. And just as I put myself behind the
bramble bushes at Växjö to hide from my tutor and masters—thus to
avoid the torture of formal learning, and provide for myself the free-
dom to walk along in solitude among the nearby hills and glades in
search of plants—so too did Artedi, at every possible chance, devote
his daylight hours to the discovery of nature's truth.

Fishing too, with net, and with baited hook and line, awaiting the
return of fishing boats at first light, and examining the catch at the
public market of Nordmaling, begging often a specimen or two from

kindly mongers; thus ARTEDI began, on his own, without books or schooling of any kind, to know the species. He came to understand the pike, the perch, the salmon, and the trout. The whitefish and the grayling became his own, as did become the sprat, the shad, the herring, and untold numbers more. He took to inspecting each and every specimen that came his way, able to put a name to every creature, with unheard of curiosity for a boy of his ilk and age. He studied, and put to paper, in long and detailed lists, the number and position of their various parts, counted whatever could be counted, the silvery scales and scutes on their heads and along the sides of their bodies; the hard sharp spines and soft rays of their various finny appendages; the bony struts on their throats, behind and below their gills. But not at all stopping there, he soon took to dissecting them and describing their internal anatomy with a remarkable detail and exactness. Never have fishes been subjected to such close scrutiny.

Some few years later, as it was told to me, my friend, as a result of his mastery of the Latin language—such knowledge acquired by him rather early, commencing at the school at Härnösand—began to acquaint himself with the contents of the published works of that science of fishes that we call ichthyology. Such books, most of the better and more costly productions, were kindly made available to him by old Professor RUDBECK at Uppsala, whose library was extensive in all departments of natural history. Thus was opened further the expanse of this watery realm to ARTEDI. Of these many works—including the various *Historia Animalia* of the ancient writers; the compendia of the Renaissance naturalists BELON, RONDELET, and SALVIANI, and of the somewhat later ALDROVANDI and GESSNER, of which the latter two authors gave to posterity those great encyclopedic monuments to natural history—only one book proved to be of any worth in deciphering the chaos in natural history that then existed within the fishes. And here I speak directly of that splendid volume in folio, *De Historia Piscium* (The Natural History of Fishes), so diligently prepared by FRANCIS WILLUGHBY who, like my dear friend, died far too early, at only 37 years of age. His extraordinary work, further in curious parallel with that of my friend, was published in 1686, after WILLUGHBY's death, by his close and dear colleague, the venerable English theologian and naturalist JOHN RAY.

Now it was that this WILLUGHBY, with advantages of intellect and circumstance that do not concern us here, was the first to compose an ichthyology in which the fishes were clearly described from nature and arranged according to characteristics taken only from their anatomical structure. He was, in fact, quite original in excluding, in his accounts of their natural history, all those unlikely and unintelligible, might I say mythological, passages of which the ancient writings are so full. While this was a greatly welcomed improvement to be sure, the classification of fishes put forth by WILLUGHBY was full of faults, the rules for arranging the various groups not at all applied consistently throughout. Of great distraction and disappointment also, WILLUGHBY's work was devoid of any definite and precise nomenclature. The various groupings, the divisions and subdivisions, within which the animals were placed, were not provided with definite names, the various categories being identified instead with long, rather clumsy, and impractical Latinized phrases. Thus, when time came for ARTEDI to apply to this muddle our universal *Methodus Demonstrandi* (Demonstration of Methods)—which I have already and so well described to you—the field of ichthyology was quite ripe for remedy.

He began, in a rather small way, to correct the many failings of those earlier authors, those of our predecessors who were inclined to write about fishes, with a descriptive account of all the fishes that dwell in the Baltic Sea and in the lakes and streams of Sweden. This commendable work, based in large part no doubt on observations made by him during those youthful days at Nordmaling, was, as it first appeared before me, penned in a bold hand, with title:

Petri Artedi
Angermannia - Svea
Catalogus
Piscium Maris Balthici
ut et Fluviorum ac Lacuum
Sveciæ
Cum Synonymis præcipuorum Ichthyo-
logorum

PETER ARTEDI of Ångermanland, Sweden, *Catalog of the Fishes of the Baltic Sea and of the Rivers and Lakes of Sweden, with Synonymous Names from the Primary Ichthyologists.*

With quite the same vigor of intellect with which I applied myself to botany, ARTEDI applied himself to fishes, but, and I make this criticism as almost a fatal flaw in his personality, he was ploddingly slow, an attribute of his nature that caused me much annoyance and anxiety. He was never satisfied with what he wrote. Afraid of committing errors, he was overly prone to making multiple corrections and revisions of this or that, and wanting always to add one more thing, and as a consequence no progress toward final completion of his great works was forthcoming. In marked contrast to these unhappy proclivities inherent in him, everything I ever wrote was written briefly and nervously, without going back for a second look, a skill that I acquired without effort from early youth, and which I tried mightily to instill in my friend without any success at all. While ARTEDI was wont to toil over long lines of unrequired complexity, I put down my thoughts in quick, short, lively phrases. When preparing, for example, my synopses of all the many thousands of known plants and animals for my *Systema Naturae*, this concise approach served me quite well indeed. The following may suffice to show the style:

Of the vampire bat, *Vespertilio vampyrus*: at night sucks in the blood of the sleeping, the toes of man, the combs of cocks, the juice of palm trees. Of the manatee, *Trichechus manatus*: lives in American seas, eats vegetable matter, becomes tame, is delighted by music, its flesh edible. Of the sloth, *Bradypus tridactylus*: body very hairy, tenacious of life, climbs easily, walks with difficulty and exceedingly slowly, turns its head as though in astonishment, noise frightful, tears pitiful. Of the cat, *Felis catus*: quiet, purrs, erects its tail, when roused is most agile, climbs, when angry emits an ambrosial odor, the lion of mice, moves its tail when intent on prey, eyes shine in the night, when desirous of prey devours it eagerly, makes love wretchedly with yowling and squabbling, eats meat but disdains vegetables, washes its face with its hand, when thrown from a high place, falls on its feet, does not have fleas. Of the camel, *Camelus dromedarius*: a second chambered stomach for pure water providing for a long time in the thirsty desert, carries burden, makes haste slowly, when weary lies down on its breast.

For the fishes of all the various kinds, ARTEDI could have done much the same, but chose not to follow my lead. And so it was that up until the end, despite a decade of hard labor, ARTEDI's treatise on fishes, to which he aimed to give the simple title of *Ichthyologia*, or *Opera Omnia de Piscibus* (Complete Work on the Fishes), remained unpublished, although left in nearly full and quite acceptable manuscript form, penned throughout in a neat and tidy hand.

I sat those many long evenings, listening to my friend as he read aloud from his papers, often repeating nearly the same content, one revision after another, each only modestly altered, if outwardly modified at all. He once related a curious attempt to outline a system for the mammals, a small tract titled by him *Idea Institutionum Trichozoologiae* (Treatise on the Organization of the Hair-bearing Animals). Although this was a well-meant effort, I was not impressed favorably by these rather few pages, the greater quantity borrowed from the works of previous authors—GESSNER and CHARLETON, and RAY as well—although I must admit it did in some respects show a glimmer of independence, some parts making good use of his own personal observations. Once read to me, I thought little more of it, and if pressed, I would attest to the belief that any remnant of it might now be long lost—certainly no part of it ever reached into print. However, once again I am obliged to divulge, certain good thoughts that I recall about this *Trichozoologiae* made their way into my *Systema Naturae* of 1735.

Minor works on mammals aside, of infinitely greater import was ARTEDI's natural history of fishes, the *Ichthyologia*, of which I have already made brief account. A decidedly heavy manuscript, densely constructed, he had rather judiciously divided it into five quite well-defined sections or chapters, of which I took careful notice, for no one to this time had organized his thoughts about nature in such a way. Heretofore, all authors of natural history, at least those of which I had knowledge—and, I dare say, nothing published in this subject ever escaped my attention—mixed the contents that ARTEDI kept separate in a confusing and illogical way. Here for the first time, was a clean and honest approach, of which again I made thorough mental note, thinking perhaps to model my own botanical treatises along the same lines.

Taking the stand appropriately that any such account ought best to begin with history, that is, with an overview of what had been contributed by others in the past, he called the first section of his Ichthyology *Bibliotheca Ichthyologica* (Library of Ichthyology), or *Historia Litteraria Ichthyologiae* (History of the Literature of Ichthyology). Here, in a full and quite excellent way, he gave a critical and analytical review of all the writings on fishes from the earliest times to the present day. He started with LINUS POËTA of ancient Thebes, ORPHEUS of the Greek myths, the Chaldean from Babylonia ZOROASTES PERSOMEDES, the philosopher PLATO, and ARISTOTLE the Stagirite; and ended with RAY, VALENTIJN, RUYSCH, MARSIGLI, HEBENSTREIT, and CATESBY. As is well to be expected, much good attention was directed to WILLUGHBY, whose work as I have already mentioned contained the only reasonable foundation upon which ARTEDI was able to base his own studies.

Being now well acquainted with this bibliographic introduction to his "Fishes," which was made known to me by my generous friend in early 1730, the whole thing having several times been read aloud before me, I resolved immediately to do the same for plants, for nothing like it then existed for the vegetable world. As ARTEDI's *Bibliotheca* would for fishes, such an analysis of the early writings of botany would supply an essential and basic key to unlock the sources of previous descriptions of a floral kind of which quantity and confusion were then beyond comprehension. As it was, a book of this kind, which I called *Bibliotheca Botanica* (Library of Botany), was indeed published by me with quick dispatch in 1736. It speedily became one of my most popular works.

Next in his sequence, part two of the *Ichthyologia*, ARTEDI proposed the *Philosophia Ichthyologica* (Philosophy of Ichthyology) or *Prolegomena Institutionum* (Treatise on Rules), in which he made a right worthy attempt to correct the chaos in natural history that then existed among fishes by supplying straightforward and precise definitions for the various ideas of this branch of nature. Here he gave due attention to the various elements of the body of a fish, both inside and out, as these structures relate to shape, appearance, function, and other sundry things. In so doing, he provided a firm and meaningful terminology for the parts, thus establishing a foundation for similar descriptions of these curious animals to be applied by students of nature in the future. He was able also to make clever determinations as to what structures ought to be applied to the science of classification—that method by which similar beings are gathered together and dissimilar beings are separated—and what ought better to be set aside. For example, he found such systems as blood vessels, lymphatic ducts, and nerves to be more properly belonging to the purview of that science of comparative anatomy. But, contrastingly, as they apply to classification—thus to construct and define his divisions and subdivisions—he used to good effect such features as the consistency of the skeleton, whether it be soft or of a bony kind, the form of the opercula of the gills, the nature and number of the rays and spines of the fins and the position of the latter on the body, the shape of the scales, the placement of the teeth, and certain peculiarities of the internal parts, as of the stomach, the caecal appendages of the pylorus, the intestines, and the gas-filled bladder. In using only anatomical characters such as these to define his classes, order, families, and genera, ARTEDI was the very first, of all our naturalists who went before, to insist upon the recognition of natural groupings, rigorously rejecting any evidence of classification that be taken from such meaningless attributes as the kind of habitat occupied by the plant or animal, its size or outward shape, the color of the external body, or the number of its appendages. We may recall here the utterly ridiculous notions of that influential professor of Montpellier GUILLAUME RONDELET who divided watery animals into sea-fishes, river-fishes, lake-fishes, and marsh-fishes, a classification that is completely without scientific foundation. One only has to think of the salmon, whose residence at different times includes all of these places, to conclude the complete lack of utility inherent in this proposal. Another equally incredible and entirely worthless proposition, a much older example taken from the vegetable realm, is that of the Greek philosopher THEOPHRASTUS who sought to divide all plants into trees, shrubs, under-shrubs, and herbs.

For our young naturalist, natural genera are those that contain species that are similar in most all particulars. Thus, the species must first be brought together correctly and naturally, and grouped to form natural genera. The genera, in turn, must be grouped correctly and naturally to form natural families, or *manipuli naturales*, as he called them; the families collected to constitute natural orders; and the orders likewise collected to constitute natural classes. Fishes, he proclaimed, form a class that is separate and distinct, and parallel to a class that encompasses all the reptiles, a class of birds, and a class of mammals.

Now, as I suspect that at least for some, this aquatic narrative has been of a somewhat tedious nature, I would fain propose that it was and is of the most profound significance. No one before this time, occupied with fishes or any other subject of nature, whether it be of a vegetable, animal, or mineral kind, had formed such an explicit hierarchical foundation for the classification of all God's creations. I was amazed, might I say disconcerted and rather baffled, to see this great improvement in the progress of our science coming from a fellow student only two years my senior, but I, not to be passed over, quickly made good use of it, as you shall see.

*   *   *

In like fashion to the *Bibliotheca Ichthyologica*, this sort of a *Philosophia* too was completely missing from botany, and so, once again, as this approach had become known to me through ARTEDI's generous sharing of his productions, I determined myself to act accordingly. Thus, in rather quick time, what would have taken years for any other man to complete, I had my botanical version of the *Philosophia* drafted in no less than nine months. In proper deference to my dear ARTEDI, however, not wanting to infringe overmuch on his priority, I reluctantly set my manuscript aside in secret from him, hoping for a better time to make it available to the public. In like manner, and once the opportunity to proceed with it became apparent, I thought it proper also to alter my title to some degree. Thus, the word "fundamental" being of a great enough difference to "philosophy," yet the meaning kept nevertheless rather similar, I titled my book *Fundamenta Botanica* and had it published in Amsterdam in 1736. In this volume, I very cleverly divided the full theory and practice of botany into 365 aphorisms—one for each day of the year—the whole of which was quite acceptable to nearly all who read it. It is true that I had my few detractors—the stupid Medical Faculty of Greifswald, for example, condemned it unreasonably as only fit food for the stove. But, in all truth, praise for this production came to me from all parts and never seemed to cease. In this regard, one of my fondest memories is a letter that I received from Dr. ALEXANDER GARDEN of Charlestown, South Carolina—that gracious man for whom I named the *Gardenia*—penned on 15 March 1755, almost twenty years after publication of *Fundamenta Botanica*, but he being so far and out of the way, a copy had only then reached him:

Learned Sir,

A year ago your *Fundamenta Botanica* and *Classes Plantarum* came to my hands. I have read over and over again, with the greatest pleasure, the *Fundamenta Botanica*, and, if I am not deceived, have greatly increased my knowledge. From that time I have sedulously devoted myself to the study of your sexual system, by which I have, most certainly, made greater progress in the space of a year than in the three preceding ones, following the method of TOURNEFORT. The reading of that inimitable little collection of aphorisms engaged and delighted my mind so powerfully, that, for one whole summer, scarcely a week passed away, without my re-perusing it with the greatest attention. Such neatness! Such regularity! So clear and supremely ingenious a system, undoubtedly never appeared before in the Botanical world. Nothing can be more finished than your works, which will be read with avidity, by those most deeply versed in such studies, for ages to come. I may say I have myself bestowed some little labor and time in these studies; but I freely acknowledge that I, when I read your works, learn from you, not only things of which I was previously ignorant, but even what I thought I had already learned from other teachers. Botany never was placed before in so clear a light. It is not only easier for beginners, but more perspicuous to the learned, appearing in so new and elegant a form, as to be much more attractive. How much you have deserved of all lovers of Botany is strikingly evident; and I therefore earnestly entreat you to accept this testimony of my gratitude, for the benefit which I have received from your writings.

After *Fundamenta Botanica* I quickly followed up with another book, a somewhat different approach to "philosophy" that I called *Critica Botanica*, published in Leiden in 1737, and a work to which I will shortly return. And finally, while on this same subject, a new and, I must say, much better edition of my all-important "Foundations" appeared in Stockholm in 1751, with title of *Philosophia Botanica*.

*   *   *

What next in ARTEDI's sequence of parts, but a *Genera Piscium* (Genera of Fishes), a section with the proposed secondary title of *Historia Piscium Universalis* (Complete Natural History of Fishes). In this he dwelled at length on genera and generic names, with the admirable purpose of setting down for all time a generic nomenclature of all the fishes of the world as known by him through the works of others and from his own personal observations. Here is advanced a quite acceptable classification of the fishes, marked by single-word generic names, detailed generic descriptions, and followed by a list of the species known within each genus. As before, with his other novel offerings, nothing existed like this in fishes up to this time. Thinking it imprudent of me to do anything otherwise, I followed these precepts rather exactly in my *Genera Plantarum* (Genera of Plants), which was published, without time wasted, in Leiden in 1737, a remarkable work that went through six subsequent editions before my fifty-seventh year. In all truth, so great and wonderful was it that the esteemed BOERHAAVE wrote the following to me from Leiden, dated 13 January 1737:

> A scrutiny of the book called *Genera Plantarum* reveals to the astonished reader a work of boundless diligence, of singular devotion, and of incomparable erudition. I myself cannot emphasize strongly enough the usefulness of this very admirable undertaking. Future generations will praise it, able men will imitate it, and it will benefit all men. When you devote all your efforts to it, you will write works that will defy time and ARISTARCHUS.

And so it went also with parts four and five of the *Ichthyologia*: the *Synonymia Nominum Piscium* (Synonymy of the Names of Fishes) and *Descriptiones Specierum Piscium* (Description of the Species of Fishes). Without qualms, and with never a hesitation of any kind, I produced my botanical equivalents of these precious works, and promptly made them available to the public for its edification and pleasure. But, lest you may think me conniving or ungrateful, I, in all good faith, kept my solemn pledge to my friend, to guarantee posterity for his labors, as you shall soon come to know in full as I continue with this narrative. However, with much pressing need for my time elsewhere, I put off the editing of his manuscripts, so that the *Ichthyologia* did not appear in published form until 1738. Of course, this is not to say that his work was ignored by me during this interim of time—good use of its style and method of presentation was made in all my many botanical works published during my residency in Holland, not to mention the contents themselves all well incorporated in my account of the fishes that appeared in the first edition of my *Systema Naturae* published in Leiden in mid-December of 1735.

CHAPTER 5

My Sexual System

> The Sexes of Plants, which have sometimes been maintained
> and sometimes opposed and denied, he proved in so clear
> a manner that all his adversaries were silenced; and who
> could do it better than LINNAEUS? For he had examined all
> known plants—an undertaking that required a man's whole
> time. Nay he went so far as to found on this most essential
> part of vegetables, the whole of his *Methodus Plantarum*,
> or *Systema Sexuale*.
>
> —LINNAEUS, *Carl Linné*, Vita III, 1769

DURING THOSE years of our mutual collegiality as students in Uppsala, beginning in early 1729 and extending through 1734, ARTEDI and I continued our intimate collaboration. He proceeded to work slowly, as was his wont, perfecting his treatise on fishes. This is not to say that he whiled away his time on other things of a trivial nature. It was in fact with him quite the contrary—every waking hour was intensely devoted to his studies, yet nothing was ever completed by him to his satisfaction. I, on the other hand, and in sharp contrast to him, was enormously productive during this time, nearly completing manuscripts for some nine books, and here I list, with no small measure of pride, my *Systema Naturae*, which I published in 1735; my *Bibliotheca Botanica* and *Fundamenta Botanica*, both appearing in 1736; *Genera Plantarum*, *Methodus Sexualis* (Sexual Method), *Flora Lapponica* (Lapland Flora), *Critica Botanica*, and *Hortus Cliffortianus*, all in 1737; and *Classes Plantarum* (Classes of Plants) in 1738. But of all these most valuable works, the one that held the most special interest for me, was the development of my *Systema Sexuale*, which, I had no doubt, even at the early time of its publication, would well prove to be the crowning achievement of my life as a botanist.

You will no doubt recall that I first presented my original notions of vegetable sexuality to my dear patron CELSIUS on New Year's Day of 1730, when I was not yet quite 23 years of age, in the form of a small manuscript of title *Praeludia Sponsaliarum Plantarum*, all bound together with string, within a prettily constructed wrapper:

In my foreword to this brilliant thesis, wishing to show my gratitude to my kind benefactor, to CELSIUS I wrote as follows:

I am not born a poet, but I am, however, something of a botanist. I therefore offer to you this small fruit from this year's little crop that God has bestowed upon me. In these few pages I treat of the great analogy that is to be found between plants and animals, in that they both increase their families in the same way, and what I have, if in all simplicity written, I beg you graciously to accept with favor this humble gift.

In so receiving this elegant present, the grateful CELSIUS—who, by the way, was that same man who made a temperature scale, with the freezing of water set at one-hundred degrees and boiling of that same liquid at zero degrees, but it was I who thought it better to set freezing at zero and boiling at one hundred—was pleased beyond compare. Impressed and flattered that I would honor him in this way, and quite in agreement with my arguments, he passed it to others, old Professor RUDBECK among them, for their edification and reading pleasure. All were delighted with the freshness of its style, and, at the same time, fully persuaded of the truth of what I wrote. RUDBECK especially was generous with his praise, honoring it with the highest approbation, and expressing a fond wish to become better acquainted with the author of so masculine a composition. When I pick it up now, even after the passage of so many years, I am moved by my approach, so much so that tears come to my tired eyes. By way of introduction, I began my dissertation with the following passages:

> In springtime, when the delicious sun comes nearer to our zenith, he awakens in all bodies the life that has lain stifled through the chill winter. See how all creatures become lively and gay, who during the winter were dull and sluggish! See how all the birds, all the long winter silent, now begin to sing and twitter, bursting into song! See how all the insects come forth from their hiding-places, where in winter they have lain half dead, how all the plants push up through the soil, how all the trees, which in winter were withered now become green, breaking into leaf! Yes, even into man himself new life seems to enter. As PLINIUS not unwisely said, "Nothing is more useful than the sun."

Words cannot express the joy that the sun brings to all living things. Now the black cock and the wood-grouse begin to frolic, the fish to sport, and every animal feels the heat of sexual urge. Yes, love comes even to the plants themselves, when amongst them both the males and females, yes, even the hermaphrodites themselves, hold their nuptials—which is the subject that I now propose to discuss—showing by their sexual organs which are the males, which the females, which the hermaphrodites. How they, through the warmth of the sun, which is the life of all things, break out in green leaves and many-colored flowers, decorated no less than ships that everywhere rig up splendid flags on their feast days.

The petals of a flower in themselves contribute nothing to generation, but only serve as the bridal bed, which the Great Creator has so gloriously prepared and arranged, garnished with such precious bed-curtains, and perfumed with so many delicious scents, in order that the bridegroom, with his bride may therein celebrate their nuptials with so much greater solemnity. When the bed has thus been so prepared, then is the time for the bridegroom to embrace his darling bride, and loose himself in her. Watch with me now how one flower breaks out of its calyx and again another buds! Watch further how the one sort of plant can in a thousand ways exhibit likenesses and differences! What brain can be so obdurate, that it does not soften before all this and turn to humble thoughts? And so come thou searching eye, and grant only a passing glance at the gleaming shimmering flowers. See how nature lends them colors of purple and blood, of ivory and snow, of flame and gold! And finally, what perfume, what piercing scent, so that I know not what sort of ethereal air is instilled in them from above! Therefore it is not without reason said by poets that it is from the blood of the eternal gods that many plants have sprung up.

With this prologue well presented, I then proceeded to argue my essential thought, that the various parts so fundamental to the reproduction of plants would naturally be equally essential for their classification.

After all, what are we seeking, but natural classifications, those that discover the true order of God's creation? Thus, in so pressing my case, I began first to identify and describe the various organs of a sexual kind: how the stamens (those structures fully equivalent to the male genitalia of animals) and pistils (those equivalent to the female genitalia) function in the act of pollination, which I equated—in colorful, but altogether tasteful terms—with sexual conjugation between a man and a woman; how, if the anthers are made absent by surgery, in a way analogous to castration, fertilization does not occur; how the powdery pollen, carried by wind or insect, is the sperm, and how the seeds are the eggs, etc., etc. Then, in the form of a simple, but ingenious table, which I titled *Clavis Systematis Sexualis* (Key to the Sexual System), I placed all the then known genera of plants of a flowering kind into twenty-four groupings, or classes if you will, according to the nature of the male organs or stamens, that is, their number, length relative to each other, distinctness or fusion, occurrence in the same flower as the pistil or separation in the case of unisexual flowers, and their perceived absence. Within each class, I arranged the various genera into smaller groupings or orders according to the number of pistils. The names for each group, I cleverly constructed from the Greek language, most of them having sexual and reproductive meanings, drawing on such common words as *andros* (male), *gyne* (female), and *gamos* (marriage). I described, for example, the class *Monandria* as like one husband in a marriage, the *Diandria* as two husbands in the same marriage; the *Polyandria* I portrayed as having twenty or more husbands in the same bed with the female. I sought to show a correspondence of the *calyx* of the flower as a nuptial bed, with the *corolla* acting as a kind of curtain to maintain an imagined privacy. The *calyx* further, I argued, might be regarded as the *labia majora* or the foreskin; the *corolla* could be thought of as the *labia minora*. The earth is thus the belly of the plants; the *vasa chylifera* are the roots, the bones the stems, the lungs the leaves, the heart the heat. The filaments are the spermatic ducts, the anthers are the testicles, the pollen is the sperm, the stigma is the vulva, the style is the vagina, the vegetable is the ovary, the pericarp is the fertilized ovary, and the seed is the egg.

By want of example, we can observe the lily genus *Colchicum*, the flower of which has three pistils and six stamens: three blushing maids the intrepid nymph attend; and six youths, enamor'd train defend. The flower of tumeric, genus *Curcuma*, that well-known tropical plant of the ginger family, which I distinguished by its one fertile stamen and its four sterile stamens, was where,

> Woo'd with long care, *Curcuma* cold and shy
>
> Meets her fond husband with averted eye:
>
> Four beardless youths the obdurate beauty move
>
> With soft attentions of Platonic love.

For convenience of demonstration, and with accompanying diagram— the latter, by the way, designed by that exquisite artist EHRET, who equated my twenty-four classes with letters from the English alpha- bet—my complete system is given here, translated from the original Latin. Of course, those of you not wishing to delve into such details—an attitude, which should it exist at all, is not within my ability to compre- hend—may gloss over as I relate the following:

THE VEGETABLE KINGDOM

Key To The Sexual System

The Loves of the Flowers (the reproduction of the inhabitants of the Plant Kingdom; the flowering)

A. MARRIAGES OPEN TO THE PUBLIC (the nuptials are celebrated openly before the whole world; the flowers visible to everyone)

  I. IN ONE MARRIAGE BED (husbands and wives rejoice in the same bed; all the flowers hermaphrodites, stamens and pistils present in the same flower)

    a. WITHOUT AFFINITY (husbands not related to each other; stamens not joined together in any part)

Clarisf: LINNÆI.M.D.
METHODUS plantarum SEXUALIS
in SISTEMATE NATURÆ
defcripta

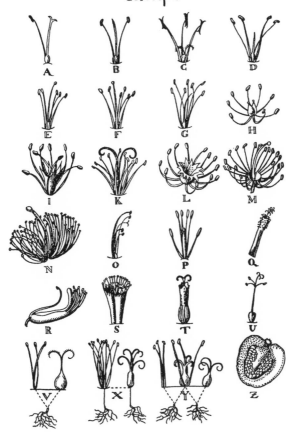

G.D.EHRET. Palat-heidelb:
fecit & edidit

Lugd. bat: 1736

i. WITH EQUALITY (all the males of equal
rank; stamens have no determinate proportion
of length)

1. MONANDRIA (one man), one husband in a
marriage; one stamen in a hermaphrodite flower.

2. DIANDRIA, two husbands in the same marriage;
two stamens in a hermaphrodite flower.

3. TRIANDRIA, three husbands in the same marriage;
three stamens in a hermaphrodite flower.

4. TETRANDRIA, four husbands in the same
marriage; four stamens in a hermaphrodite flower.

5. PENTANDRIA, five husbands in the same
marriage; five stamens in a hermaphrodite flower.

6. HEXANDRIA, six husbands in the same marriage;
six stamens in a hermaphrodite flower.

7. HEPTANDRIA, seven husbands in the same
marriage; seven stamens in a hermaphrodite
flower.

8. OCTANDRIA, eight husbands in the same marriage;
eight stamens in a hermaphrodite flower.

9. ENNEANDRIA, nine husbands in the same
marriage; nine stamens in a hermaphrodite flower.

10. DECANDRIA, ten husbands in the same marriage;
ten stamens in a hermaphrodite flower.

11. DODECANDRIA, twelve husbands in the same
marriage; twelve stamens in a hermaphrodite
flower.

12. ICOSANDRIA, usually twenty husbands, often
more, rarely fewer, in the same bridal chamber;
the stamens attached to the inside of the calyx,
not to the receptacle.

13. POLYANDRIA, twenty husbands or more in

the same bridal chamber, with one wife; fifteen to a thousand stamens in the same flower, with a single pistil.

ii. WITH SUBORDINATION (some males above the others; two stamens are always shorter than the others)

14. DIDYNAMIA (two powers), four males in the marriage, two longer, two shorter; four stamens, of which the two adjacent ones are longer.

15. TETRADYNAMIA (four powers), six males in the marriage, four longer in a hermaphrodite flower; six stamens, four longer, the two opposite ones shorter.

b. WITH AFFINITY (husbands lie adjacent and are related to each other; stamens cohere with each other, or with the pistil)

16. MONADELPHIA (one brother), two males, like brothers, appear from a single base, as from a single mother; staminal filaments united in one bundle.

17. DIADELPHIA (two brothers), males originate from a double base, as from a double mother; staminal filaments united in two bundles.

18. POLYADELPHIA, males originate from more than two bases, as from more than two mothers; staminal filaments united in three or more bundles.

19. SYNGENESIA (confederate males), union of males through their genitals; staminal anthers (rarely filaments) united in a tube.

20. GYNANDRIES (feminine males), males miraculously united with females; stamens inserted in the pistils, not in the receptacle.

II. IN TWO MARRIAGE BEDS (husbands and wives rejoice
     in separate beds; male flowers and female flowers in the
     same species)

> 2 1. MONOECIA (one house), males live with
>   the females in the same house, but in separate
>   chambers; male and female flowers on the
>   same plant.
>
> 2 2. DIOECIA (two houses), males and females
>   live in separate chambers and dwellings; male
>   and female flowers born in different plants.
>
> 2 3. POLYGAMIA (many nuptials), males live with
>   wives and maidens in different chambers;
>   hermaphrodite flowers as well as males and
>   females in the same species.

B. CLANDESTINE MARRIAGES (the nuptials are celebrated
   in secret; the flowers scarce visible to the naked eye)

> 2 4. CRYTOGAMIA (clandestine marriages), the
>   nuptials are celebrated in secret; they flower
>   within the fruit or are concealed from view
>   by their smallness.

When this altogether new classification of the Vegetable Kingdom,
based thus on the "love-life of the plants," was first published at Leiden
in my *Systema Naturae* of 1735, and appearing again in 1737, in full and
glorious flower under title of *Methodus Sexualis*, it was happily welcomed by nearly all. But, as is always the case with lesser men intent on
bringing down their betters, some were more than displeased with my
analogy between plants and animals, not wanting to believe the sexes of
plants. To these helpless doubters, I provided the following irrefutable
evidences of the truth of my convictions: The female of the *Rhodiola*—
which everyone knows is the Rose-root, having lovely yellow flowers
and rose-scented roots—grew in RUDBECK's garden for thirty years
without ever producing fruit. At length he received from the mountains a small male plant, which flowered in a pot, in a considerably

distant part of the garden from the former; and yet the female bore fruit that very year. GLEDITSCH had at Berlin a female palm, which blossomed every year without ripening seed. He obtained, by the post from Leipzig, some male flowers, which were suspended over the females, and ripe fruit was the consequence. The same thing happened with a female *Terebinthus*—which some would call *Pistacia*, the Pistachio—that had flowered for twenty years without ever bearing any fruit, but which became fertile in consequence of the accession of male blossoms. These and innumerable other examples of equal credibility would seemingly have satisfied my detractors, but alas, it is useless to talk to the deaf.

Of greater consequence by far were those infinitely more dangerous critics, who expressed their profound disapproval of my implications of polygamy, polyandry, homosexuality, and incest among the vegetables. Thus, as one might believe, in return for my great efforts, this design received much undeserved criticism in this way, especially from some of my more worthy colleagues residing abroad, which complaints struck me hard and painfully. I thought of these criticisms always to be of a personal affront rather than of a constructive nature. In my daily correspondence—which was not small, I myself having written well over 7,000 letters (to some 570 Swedish and foreign correspondents, the most learned and curious in Europe) in my time, and even now my *corpus litterae* (body of letters) is, I dare say, far from being closed—as well as in letters exchanged between my friends, the contents of which I heard at some later date, I often learned things of a negative nature directed toward me, but never so many as were generated over this. I remember all too well the discomfort felt from knowing that my once good friend DILLENIUS of Oxford was at odds with me, and he said so enthusiastically to all who would listen. Hearing of my justifiable consternation over this affront, he wrote to me directly on 6 May 1737 as follows, a letter, I might add, to which I did not respond:

> You have accomplished great things, and that you may go on and prosper still more, let me exhort you to examine more and more species. I do not doubt that you yourself will, one day, overthrow your own sexual system. You see, my dearest LINNAEUS, how

plainly I speak my sentiments, depending on your candor to receive them favorably.

The sexual differences, in compound flowers, are, in my judgment, altogether useless, superfluous, and mischievous for botanical characters. What is the object of all this apparatus? These are nothing more than showy trifles! It is quite enough that one botanist, VAILLANT, should have had his head turned by them.

And, as if this blast was not enough, the same DILLENIUS wrote to me again on 18 August of that same year, this time to complain again, but on a subject somewhat different. Thinking as any reasonable man would, that I might gain favor from it, and assuming too that anyone would rejoice over so great and fine a gift, I, with elaborate and perhaps somewhat exaggerated praise, dedicated my *Critica Botanica*—which contained the essentials of my *Systema Sexuale*—to this physician and professor of botany, but alas without his prior knowledge or permission. To this he was unreasonably overwrought with anger:

> I feel as much displeased with your *Critica Botanica* as I am pleased with your Lapland *Flora*, especially as you have, without my deserving such a compliment, or knowing of your intention, dedicated the book to me. You must have known my dislike of all ceremonies and compliments. But worse, I am angry at finding my name used in apparent sanction of a system that I consider frivolous, superfluous, and even harmful. I hope that you have burdened but few copies with this dedication. Perhaps only the copy that you have sent me—if that be true, than I am glad of it. But if there are more, I beg of you to strip them of this vain parade, or I shall take it much amiss. At least I cannot offer you my thanks for what you have done, though I gratefully acknowledge the favor of the copies you have sent me of the *Critica* as well as the *Flora*.

But returning now to the strange and unexpected, and I might say wholly unwarranted, criticisms of my newly designed sexual system, there was the sharp sting that came from JOHANN AMMAN, the well-recognized professor of botany from St. Petersburg, who, quite behind my back, in a letter dated 6 September 1737, wrote to HANS SLOANE in London, saying that he "doubted very much if any Botanist would ever follow the lewd and wholly distasteful method given by Dr. LINNAEUS in his systematical tables of a sexual kind." Somewhat later, this same Professor AMMAN, upon learning of the knowledge I had obtained relative to his hurtful insults, wrote to me begging my understanding in a letter dated Petersburg, 15 November 1737:

> I perceive you take somewhat amiss what I wrote to SLOANE, and to GRONOVIUS and DILLENIUS as well, about your new method founded on the stamens and pistils. I was merely joking, in my letter to GRONOVIUS, if I mistake not; and I could not suppose you would seriously be displeased at my remarking the great concourse of husbands to one wife, which often happens I suppose, but which is so wholly unsuitable to the laws and manners of our people here. I was not speaking of those natural laws of the vegetable kingdom, instituted by the Creator of all things. I observed to DILLENIUS that your system was excellent for establishing and defining genera of plants, though scarcely of any use as to class. I continue of the same opinion; for according to your method, plants that agree in the number of their stamens and pistils, though totally different in every other particular, are placed by you in the same class. What affinity is there, pray tell, except in the number of their stamens, between *Valeriana* and *Cyperus*, *Persicaria* and *Campanula*, *Gentiana*, *Ribes*, and *Angelica*, etc.?

AMMAN ended his letter of contrition with a plea for my forgiveness: "I beg you, kind Sir, to please believe that I write with candor and sincerity, not from a spirit of wrangling or contradiction." But, in all truth, I found his apology impossible to accept.

Again, in that same year, I was attacked most harshly, perhaps with encouragement from AMMAN, by another academician from St. Petersburg, JOHANN SIEGESBECK, a man of singular character, of whom, you will remember, I spoke earlier in reference to my naming of a detestable weed in his honor. This horrible person was quite incapable of civil behavior. He was, in fact, so lacking in courtesy that he could not converse directly with my person, but chose to address himself to my method in a book having the not so pretty title *Verioris Botanosophiae Specimen* (Proof of the True Philosophy of Botany). In this treatise, he set aside some pages to a severe and decidedly negative judgment on my writings. From what I gather, having been informed at third hand by a friend whose name shall remain untold, it was a passage contained within the pages of my *Flora Lapponica* (a book, which, you will recall, I published with elaborate celebration in Amsterdam in 1737) to which Siegesbeck objected most strongly. Describing the Rose-root, which plant fits quite reasonably well within my Class 23, the Polygamia, the damning words, which I wrote as diagnosis for the latter, are as follows:

> Sexual relations here show peculiar phenomena. The princely nuptials are celebrated in the home of the one family of flowers, in a splendid bed with five, parted, golden bed curtains, by husbands and wives lying beside each other. But the latter are as barren as Sarah. While in the other family the nuptials take place in an open room without hangings. And there are to be found five women who lack husbands, but these like Hagar are impregnated by the husbands of the legitimate barren wives, and thus they propagate a family.

What pray is incorrect here? To my mind it is an analogy quaintly and charmingly told. But, never mind my thoughts about it, my detractor pressed very hard upon me. He sought to attack me harshly on the grounds that "such loathsome harlotry, such detestable vice, as several males to one female, would never have been permitted in the garden of the Vegetable Kingdom by our God the Creator," and asking, with unmitigated stupidity, as he was so wont to do, "who would have thought that bluebells, lilies, and onions could be up to such immorality?" And, moreover,

> how could anyone, save that Swedish botanist, profess to employ or to teach without offence so licentious a method to studious

youth? In all truth, I am embarrassed at the gross prurience of his mind. A literal translation of the first principles of Linnaean botany is enough to shock female modesty. It is possible that many virtuous students might not be able to make out the similitude of *Clitoria*."

With this harangue SIEGESBECK denied the sexes of plants. He charged my system with indelicacy, and yet I had not written more about polygamy of plants than SWAMMERDAM has about the bees. He laughed at my characters, and called upon all the world to say if anybody understands them. I am said to be ignorant of scientific terms. He judged me by the principles of hundreds of the vilest scribblers!

From this I was filled with woe, wishing that SIEGESBECK and others like him had written these things when I was first about publishing. I might have learned when young, what I was forced to learn at a more advanced age—to abstain from writing, to observe others, and to hold my tongue. What a fool I had been, to waste so much time, to spend my days and nights in study that yielded no better fruit, and made me the laughing-stock of all the world! SIEGESBECK's arguments were nothing, but his book was filled with exclamations, such as I never before met with. Whether I answer him or keep my silence, my reputation must still suffer. Yes, it was true, SIEGESBECK had annihilated me, and no one could know or care how many sleepless nights and toilsome hours I passed incapacitated by fear that all, with but one voice, agreed with him and not with me.

Quite thrown off my stance, when first word came to me, by these rude deprecations, and by the loathsome thoughts that followed, I sought counsel with my old correspondent HALLER who, wanting to relieve me of my burden, wrote to me from Göttingen on 7 April 1738:

> Why should you care for SIEGESBECK, who has also, as I hear, written against our friend LUDWIG? Were slanders ever wanting, or will they ever be wanting, to calumniate all who distinguish themselves by their discoveries or their abilities? Are you destitute of those who are more just to your merits? Or did you ever hope to conciliate the approbation of all these SIEGESBECK's

into the bargain? Do but proceed boldly, and strive to adorn still more the science in which you have already acquired so much true glory. And if you will but listen to me as a friend, I would advise you to write no answers to this man or to any others like him. He is not on a level with you; and the more he is your inferior, the more consequence you give a man who would otherwise remain in obscurity, known only to those immediately about him.

Now I must insist that all my life I was anxious to avoid any suggestion of anger, if that be at all possible. I always detested controversy, wishing only to act in kind and pleasing conjunction with my friends and colleagues. Surely, in all disagreements, whether conqueror or conquered, no side can escape disgrace. Who ever fought without some wound or some injurious consequence? Time is too precious, and can be far better employed, than to take up arms, which if once taken, cannot be easily, if ever, laid aside. Saying this, I well remember that good teacher BOERHAAVE who answered to no one whatever. I recollect precisely, as a matter of fact, his saying to me one day, "You should never reply to any controversial writers—promise me that you will not." I promised him accordingly, and having since followed this advice, have benefited very much by it. Thus, SIEGESBECK did not then, nor shall he ever, provoke an angry word from me, though he has poured out thousands on my devoted head.

Once separated by passage of time from this ugly and uncomfortable affair, and learning that all others, in this country and abroad, who tried my system found it more practical and more useful than any other yet devised, I turned myself away from this despair. I bathed instead in the glory now laid upon me by those my botanical worshipers who hailed my tables as a miracle of simplicity, an ingenious method that had superseded all others by its concise and elegant arrangement. Surely, in this way, I had answered the fervent prayers of those who sought to understand the world of plants. Thus, in short order, my method—whose underlying basis contained the true and heretofore secret working-plan of the Creator—was followed universally to the exclusion of all else. By these means, I was everywhere proclaimed—even at this early time, when I was scarcely past thirty years of age—to have written more, discovered more, and made a greater reform in botany than anyone before had done in an entire lifetime.

*　*　*

And so to close this excellent story of my *Systema Sexuale*, thinking that I might protect myself from accusations laid down by jealous rivals who may write that I took these good notions from others, I gave ample space in the beginning pages of my *Sponsaliarum* (Espousals), and later as well in my *Methodus Sexualis*, to enumerate the thoughts on this subject held by my botanical predecessors. I felt I must admit especially that I derived my first inkling of this sexual discovery from Monsieur VAILLANT, that incomparable Frenchman—a man quite full of himself, ambitious of raising his own fame on the overthrow of his teacher, the honorable and excellent TOURNEFORT, yet a most accurate and inexhaustible botanist—who worked on this very subject and who was a good distance ahead of all the others in this department. He had in fact thought to base his botanical system on this premise, when cruel fate in 1722 snatched him all too early from this life—not, however, before he left some rather insignificant information about it in his *Sermo de Structura et Differentia Florum* (Discourse on the Structure and Diversity of the Flowers), published in 1718, but which copy had not then been available to me. While paying my small debt to VAILLANT in this way, it is with some feelings of shame and regret that I failed to remember my poor ARTEDI who, you will recall, provided me much stimulation with his thoughts of undertaking a complete revisionary study of the umbellate plants by employing a close examination and comparison of their genitalia. To him I owe a small debt for this, but I should sing his praises also for the curious notes extracted from him on the Umbelliferae, all of which I incorporated quite satisfactorily, both in my *Systema Naturae* of 1735 and in several other of my more important botanical works that came later.

CHAPTER 6

Our Respective Travels

> He now bethought himself of endeavoring to obtain such
> aid as would enable him to travel and study first hand those
> collections and materials belonging to his science which
> were so essential to his progress.
>
> —Einar Lönnberg,
> *Peter Artedi: A Bicentenary Memoir*, 1905

Now it was that Artedi, unbeknownst to me, had begun to yearn for change, abruptly announcing in the summer of 1734 his choice to take leave of me and, for that matter, of Uppsala as well. He had been my constant and faithful companion just some months short of five years, the two us together sharing daily in all things of a scientific nature and also of a personal matter. Contemplating the reasons for this new direction—thinking back now over all those years—I cannot but feel that part of it might have been my ever-closer attachment to Claes Sohlberg. I well recall that I did my best to keep those assignations with the latter gentleman a private occupation, but word of my activities was no doubt passed along by the gossip-mongers that everywhere follow the more important men in our midst. Be that as it may, my once intimate Artedi, expressing regret that he had lived for ten years in one place, used as excuse for his new intentions a nervous anxiety of getting on in years—though he had not yet reached 30 years of age—with inadequate experience and no clear pathway for future occupation or employment. So too, he argued, Uppsala, that center of learning so poorly equipped as it was for his chosen field of scientific pursuit, had done for him all that it could and he desired to extend his horizons by traveling abroad. He had long been aware, instructed by correspondence and word of mouth from various colleagues who should know, of the large and varied collections of natural objects in England, and it was that country that now became his main object of interest. He was certain that England, and London in particular, would offer more stimulating surroundings and greater opportunities for study. So, having passed successfully on 17 July 1734 the examinations in theology—then obligatory for any student wishing to travel abroad for the purposes of study—and being modestly supported financially through the generosity of family members still residing in Umeå, he took leave for Stockholm, where in the early part of the month of September of that same year, he boarded a vessel bound for England. I fully imagined that prior to his departure he would have put his valuable manuscripts in my care, as he had earlier pledged, but thinking he would have good opportunity to work on them while abroad, he packed them up in a shabby leather case and took them all with him.

I felt somewhat left behind—dare I admit to a certain loneliness and self-pity, it then being some several months since my once faithful Artedi had deserted me?—and a similar urge to remove myself from Uppsala began to take precedence in my thoughts. But, unlike my good friend who had never traveled anywhere all his life, it was not the case that travel was new to me. Everyone knows, for example, about my journey to Lapland, which treacherous ordeal I successfully completed in 1732. Now you may think an undertaking of this kind to be of little consequence, believing this land to be only a part of Sweden. Indeed it is, but it was, at that time—and mostly still is—a strange and unknown wilderness, the natural history of it being as unfamiliar as that of the most barbaric tract in the whole world. I doubt, for example, whether any place on earth can show a greater number of every sort of bird, as in summer they congregate here to lay their eggs and bring up their young in peace. The same kind of thing could be said for certain aspects of all Nature's Kingdoms in this remote land, be they of the mineral, vegetable, or animal kind, not forgetting the Lapps themselves, their domestic life, medicines and nutriment, and so on. Thus it can be readily seen that no place could give more delightful observations. When the thought first struck me that I should undertake such a journey—for the good of science, if not to advance my own future prospects—I could not keep away from the idea with a clear conscience and proceeded forthwith to make application for financial support to the Scientific Society of Uppsala. In this request, which required me to put to paper all that I could to convince those good men of the Society of my worth, I thought it appropriate to express my views as to the personal qualifications required by a candidate for such a journey. In so doing, I proposed the following prerequisites:

Swedish.

Young and light, that he can spring with agility up the steep mountains and down again into the deep dales.

Healthy, that he is able with greater ease and pleasure to carry out his objective daily.

Indefatigable, for here for the most part is required endurance for tramping, bending, heat, and thirst, none of which make a pleasure trip for arrogant city fops.

Unemployed, for if anyone has a more comfortable post, he knows well enough how to choose the best.

Unmarried, so that he might risk himself on rafts to cross rivers, etc., without thoughts of fatherless children, etc.

Natural historian and *doctor*, that in these subjects he may better understand what he sees.

Understanding of all the three natural kingdoms, which knowledge is more difficult to find than a bird-of-paradise, because amongst all the botanists there are few who are at home in two kingdoms, and hardly one who is capable in all three.

Understanding of natural history, in actuality, not only in theory because it is striking how they differ, when it comes to practice, as I, with innumerable examples, can prove.

Draughtsman, the better to explain and note what rare things may be seen.

After laying out this list of requirements, and admitting freely that very few in Sweden could be found having all these qualifications, I declared myself, in all humility, to fully meet nine of the ten: I am Swedish, young, healthy, fearless, free, unemployed, without dependents of any kind, a natural historian and a medical student, with, from my very early youth, a hearty delight in natural history. My only deficiency was a decided weakness in draughtsmanship, and I begged that this inadequacy not be held against me—and here I give for your critique and judgment a good example of my work, showing the close similarity of ANDROMEDA, and the story thereof, to a curious and altogether new plant that I discovered during my Lapland journey.

But despite my insignificant shortcomings when it came to rendering with pen and pencil, the Society agreed to my plan, granting the meager sum of 400 copper dalers, far too small an amount to guarantee success, but, alas, it was all that body could or was willing to give.

And so it was that on 24 May 1732, about a half a day after my twenty-fifth birthday, I departed Uppsala alone on horseback, without encumbrances of any kind, having all my baggage on my back. The small equipment I was able to take with me included my diary, which every day I filled with observations of every kind. But wishing to spare you all the minute, but nevertheless essential, details of this extraordinary adventure, during which I traversed a total distance of 700 Swedish miles (about 5,000 English miles), surviving every deprivation, I made my way home again, reaching Uppsala on 10 October of that same year. Upon my return, I made my discoveries known to the Scientific Society in an excellent account, in which I included a list of 206 observations that I took to be significant, about the objects and conditions within the mineral, vegetable, and animal kingdoms, this along with much good information about economics and the way of life of the inhabitants of that country. Of special import, to which I devoted ample space in my narrative, were three topics that proved to arouse the interest of some members of the Society: "The cause of cattle death in Torneå," "The use of Aconite as a food in Medelpad," and "A makeshift bed in the wilderness." But I was sorely disappointed—might I say angry and humiliated—that these matters were refused publication by the Society, as was my full report in general. I did, however, make good on my observations by sometime later putting together all that I had experienced during that arduous journey in a charming and delightful travel book, for which I chose the title *Iter Lapponicum* (Lapland Journey). Here in this small volume, which appeared in 1737, I provided a host of practical and valuable things, not to speak of the joy of simply reading it. I tell of ways to cure chilblains with toasted reindeer cheese, how to remove boils with a poultice of birch bark, how to cement broken pots by boiling them in milk, how to exterminate house-crickets, and how to castrate reindeer in such a way as to cause them a minimum of discomfort.

*   *   *

But now, to come back to that cold winter of 1735, stark and lonely on account of the absence of my beloved ARTEDI, I began, as mentioned previously, to itch for ways to change my situation. Like my dear friend, I had, at that time, not yet acquired the promotions necessary to make a proper way in the scientific profession. While I had accomplished most everything else, with efficiency and speed that far exceeded all others, one important missing component to my future success was a medical degree. For reasons not worth mentioning here, it was the custom at that time, if not the rule, to go abroad to qualify for the doctorate in medicine, the most logical destination for Swedish medical students being the University of Harderwijk in Holland. Thinking it the best occasion to accomplish this task, and feeling confident of my ability to defend myself under the strain of rigorous examination, I determined to venture forth for this purpose. Thus, in February of 1735, in the good company of my favorite colleague SOHLBERG, we took our leave of Uppsala on horseback, first visiting Råshult, the place of my birth, where my dear sweet mother had died on the 6th of June of the year before, in the forty-fifth year of her life.

From Råshult we continued our journey through Helsinborg to Elsinore in Denmark, from which place we went by sea aboard the *Resande Tobias* to Travemünde and on by coach to Lübeck, and thence to Hamburg. Here in the latter city I found some things agreeable, but much more to dislike. Considerable good could be said of the general appearance of the buildings, the inhabitants handsome, amiable, and polite, but the filth and stench in the streets was too much to bear. It stunk like a privy, for excrement flowed into the gutters like water—it was a miracle to me that the townsfolk were not all ill. More disgusting yet were the innumerable whorehouses from which violas, oboes, dulcimers, trumpets, and music for bawds could always be heard. But, to speak of the softer and kinder side, JOHANN SPREKELSEN, a lawyer in that city, showed me great civilities, for which I later gave him more than thanks by attaching the name *Sprekelia* to a kind of lily from the New World tropics. Excellent hospitality was also extended to me by Professor KOHL, then editor of the *Hamburgische Berichte*; as well as by Dr. GOTTFRIED JAENISCH, the only real friend I met in Hamburg. I employed my whole time in viewing the fine gardens, and everything else worthy of attention, including the fine library of Dr. FABRICIUS, who kindly lent me some books, and the extraordinary cabinet of the Burgomaster ANDERSSON. It was at the latter place, that I astonished the scientific world with my astute revelation of a case of fakery that had eluded the detection of all others. This was a stuffed monster, the celebrated Seven-headed Hydra of Hamburg, so-called by all who knew it, which had come into the hands of this Burgomaster and his brother. It was declared to be the only one of its kind in the world, and all who saw it thanked God Almighty that it had not multiplied. One year before, this serpent was made famous by ALBERTUS SEBA, of whom you will learn much more as this narrative continues. A drawing of this fabulous creature had been sent to SEBA in Amsterdam who, little doubting its genuineness, published it, along with an admirable description, in the first volume of his *Thesaurus* of natural history, which appeared in 1734.

And here I quote from that most respectable work:

Hydra or seven-headed serpent: Here we see a representation of the animal held to be a serpent with seven heads. A stranger, who did me the honor of visiting my cabinet of natural curiosities in 1720, was the first to give me a picture of it. This stranger told me that he had seen the original animal in Hamburg, that it resembled a serpent with seven raised heads, each of which had its mouth gaping wide open to reveal a great assortment of large and small teeth, having, in addition, only two feet and a long tail, such that although it was thought to be a serpent with seven heads, it nevertheless looked more like a dragon than a snake. I do admit that these relations seemed quite paradoxical to me and had more the flavor of myth than truth. But in the following year, Mr. F. EIBSEN, a preacher of the Holy Gospel in a town called Wursten in the Duchy of Bremen, who came one day to see my cabinet, told me the same thing about this hydra and promised to obtain a drawing of this animal for me, which was easily done, since he had connections with the owners of the hydra, the merchants DREYERN and HAMBEL in Hamburg. He informed me that it had formerly belonged to COUNT VON KÖNIGSMARCK and that subsequent to his death it was then inherited by COUNT VON LEEUWENHAUPT. Having heard that the hydra was being offered for sale for ten thousand guilders, which he confirmed, I was inspired by the sheer size of the sum to obtain an authentic illustration. Mr. EIBSEN kept his word and procured me the copy I wished. I do admit, though, that not absolutely trusting it, I wrote to my friend Mr. JOHN NATORP of Hamburg. This very judiciously curious natural historian, who had seen the same hydra with his own eyes, assured me that it was definitely not the work of art but truly that of nature. This friend also sent me a copy in life size and very well illuminated. This latter was used to produce the figure I present here.

Thus, this ridiculous old apothocary went on to further describe the monster:

> It was of a brown color, shaded with ashy gray. Its back was uneven and rugged. On each of its sides were six large tubercles, which were oblong, and hard as horn, under which row seven other tubercles, which were round, and of the same nature, were arranged along the sides from the feet to the tail. The skin of the whole of the trunk, as well as that of the seven heads, was without any scales, and of a color approaching to chestnut, and marbled. The seven necks were encircled in front, as it were, by rings placed across them. All the seven mouths were equally open, and armed with teeth like those of a lion. Its long tail was entirely covered with rhomboidal scales. Each foot—there were but two—terminated in four toes, each toe being furnished with a long and pointed claw.

But, truly, at first glance, any man with half a brain would see the faults! At once I showed, and spoke of it out loud in public, that the jaws and clawed feet were, without doubt, nothing more than those of common weasels, the body itself covered with the skin of snakes, all curiously and neatly joined together and stuck in place with glue. Nature, always remaining true to itself, has never in a natural way produced several heads on one body. As we ourselves have seen, the teeth of the carnivorous weasel, which differ from the teeth of amphibians, have easily revealed the fraud and artifice. No doubt this monster was constructed by mischievous monks some time in the past as a representative of an apocalyptic beast.

When it was about to be sold for an enormous and unbelievable price, my disclosure, which some criticized as tactless and without charity, caused the value to fall to nothing. Thus, SOHLBERG and I were obliged to hasten our departure from that city for fear of the vengeful ANDERSSONS.

   *   *   *

Setting aside the subject of travels for a time, I may diverge here to relate some further observations about monsters, dragons, basilisks, and the like, whether they be mythical or real. You have already seen that SEBA's Hydra, bearing similitude to ST. JOHN's apocalyptic beast, was by me quite easily revealed as fraud and artifice. In a similar way I have revealed the truth about several other beasts once thought by many to represent truth: The myth of the Frog-fish—or metamorphosis of *Rana* into a fish—is very paradoxical, as nature would not admit the change of one genus into another one of a different class. *Rana*, like all amphibians, possesses lungs and spiny bones. Spiny fishes are provided with gills instead of lungs. Therefore this change would be contrary to nature's law. For if this fish is provided with gills, it will be different from *Rana* and the amphibians; if with lungs, it will be a lizard, for there is all the world of difference between them and *Chondropterygii* and *Plagiuri*.

The *Monoceros* of the Ancients, with the body of a horse and the feet of a beast of prey, with a straight, long, and spirally wound horn, is a painter's invention. ARTEDI's *Monodon* possesses such a horn, but differs greatly in its other parts—it is truly a kind of fish. Then there is the fable of the Pelican, thought to wound its own thigh with its beak in order to quench the thirst of its young with the blood flowing out, a mythical tale handed down through the ages by the same people, the origin of which lies in the fluid-filled sac that hangs from its gullet. The tailed *Satyr*, a hairy, bearded creature, with a man-like body, the purported sightings of which are totally fallacious, is a species of monkey, if ever one has been seen. The tailed men, of whom more recent travelers tell much, are of the same genus.

The so-called Scythian Lamb is considered a plant but resembles a lamb. Its stem transfixes the "umbilicus" of another plant as it breaks forth from the soil. It is also said, without any foundation, to be devoured by animals of prey, as it contains blood. It is, however, artificially composed of roots of American ferns. Natural, however, is the embryo of the sheep, which has been described allegorically, but possesses all the characters attributed to it.

About the Phoenix, a species of bird, of which one single individual exists in the world, the fable is told that after having been burned to death on the funeral pile, which it had itself constructed out of aromatics, it revived in order to live the happy period of youth. It is, however, *Palma dactylifera*, the date-palm. Bernicla, the brent or barnacle goose (*Branta leucopsis*), is believed by the Ancients to be born from decaying wood thrown in the sea. But, in actuality, it is *Lepas* (the bivalve mollusk we call triton) that has deposited its penniform entrails on *Fucus* (seaweed) and, because of its way of adhering, it really is as if the barnacle goose originates from it. *Draco*, with an eel-like body, two feet, and two wings like a bat, is *Lacerta alata* or, if not the latter, a kind of ray artificially shaped and dried as a monster.

The Death-watch, producing the sound of a tiny clock in walls, is in all truth, a kind of insidious bug called *Pediculus pulsatorius*, which burrows into wood and lives in it. But so much for monsters and dragons, whether they be genuine or false—let me now return to the subject on which this part of my narrative began.

*   *   *

As I learned some time later, ARTEDI made good work of his time in England, where his various wonderings in that place were in large part confined to the city of London. The details of most of his sojourn are now lost to me, but I do recall, from direct conversation with this traveler, several points of interest. He described to me in full a rare opportunity to examine a large whale that in November 1734 had been transported into London, a curious mention of which, by the way, under the name of *Balaena*, was found by me entered into ARTEDI's manuscripts for his great work on fishes. Of a certain importance also to the preparation of the latter treatise were the numerous and for him hitherto unknown forms of fishes that he found in fresh condition in the London market places. So too, of even greater significance than these common local kinds, were the several rare exotic species, the *Ostracion, Tetraodon, Diodon*, and the like. Many such as these, ARTEDI was able to see in museums and cabinets, strung up as ornaments in private possession. But coffeehouses, public houses, and taverns, the latter to which ARTEDI was especially partial, served also in this way—many a beer and strong drink was had by sailors who, returning from far-off tropical seas, their money spent, had nothing else but a dried fish to give in payment. These mementoes, then as now, were a common sight in such establishments, they being hung by innkeepers and landlords as items of decoration and attraction. As proof of this with respect to ARTEDI, I found mention again in the manuscripts left behind by this naturalist, several species discovered in this way, of boxfishes and porcupinefishes, to which he gave the generic name *Ostracion*. His *Ostracion quadricornis* and *Ostracion triqueter*, for example, were observed in the company of LARS LILJA—owner himself of the King of Sweden in the harbor district of Shadwell—at the Nag's Head tavern in the borough of Chelsea, both nailed by string to the high beam; his *Ostracion bicaudalis*, at the White Bear; and *Ostracion reticulatus*, with Sir HANS SLOANE at the Green Dragon in Stepney. In his manuscripts too is mentioned a kind of monkfish or angelfish, *Squalus squatina*, observed also at the Nag's Head; and a pufferfish, *Tetraodon laevigatus*, witnessed with SLOANE at Spring Gardens, a well-known place of amusement in that city. Many more specimens of similar ilk were found at DON SALT-ERO's coffeehouse in Chelsea, which establishment was very curiously adorned with objects of natural history of every kind.

But of greater import still were the individuals he met. With letter of introduction from JACOB SERENIUS, the paster of the Swedish parish in London, he, on Sunday, 15 May 1735, called upon HANS SLOANE at Chelsea. It was this SLOANE who well beyond all others of his time constructed an enormous and extremely varied collection of natural objects, which became the most famous, most extensive, most visited, and most admired in all of Britain. My own dear student PETER KALM, who I consider to be my very best and favorite pupil, once availed himself of the opportunity to examine this assemblage of curiosities and wrote about it later in his *Account of a Visit to England*, which book he published in 1748. Thinking it of general interest, I hereby take this occasion to present some description of the cabinet of SLOANE as observed first-hand by this most excellent of observers:

In the morning I went up to Chelsea where we spent some time in looking at Chelsea Garden, but afterwards went to see Sir HANS SLOANE's collections, in all three Natural Kingdoms, Antiquities, Anatomy, and many other Curiosities. We saw here a great collection of all kinds of stones, partly polished, partly such as still lay in their matrix as they are found in nature. We saw all sorts of vessels, tea-cups, saucers, snuff-boxes, caskets, spoons, ladles, and other small instruments, all manufactured out of agates and jaspers, etc.; a number of different kinds of pearls, several learned men's contrefaits, amongst which we particularly devoted ourselves to the study and admiration of the great botanist and student of natural history, JOHN RAY. A very large collection of insects from all parts of the world, all of which were now preserved in four-sided boxes, with clear glass glued on both over and under, so that one could see them quite well, but these boxes or cases were also so well stuck together and so tight that no worms or other injurious insects could get at them, and spoil them. Some of the East and West Indian butterflies were far showier than a peacock with its matchless variety of colors. A very large number of all kinds of corals and other harder sea plants, a multitude of various sorts of crystals, several head-dresses of different races of men, musical instruments, etc. Various stuffed birds and fishes, where the birds often stood fast on small bits of board as naturally as if they still lived. Skeletons of various four-footed beasts, amongst which were particularly noticed that of a young elephant, the stuffed skin of a camel, and an African many-striped ass. Several human skeletons larger and smaller, and the head and other parts of a frightfully large whale. This whale was said to have been 90 feet long. The length of its head bone was nearly 18 feet.

Humming birds from the West Indies, which there made a show with their many colors, and set in their nests under glass as though they had been living; the bird's nest which they eat in Asia as any other food which they eat in the East Indies. It was white and looked almost as if it had been made of white wax. A great collection of snakes, lizards, fishes, birds, caterpillars, insects, small four-footed animals, etc. all put in *spiritu vini* in bottles, and well preserved; dried skins of snakes from the East and West Indies, of many ells length and proportionately broad; very many volumes of a herbarium, amongst which we particularly examined those which Sir HANS SLOANE himself had collected in Jamaica; 336 volumes of dried plants in Royal folio; on each leaf there were as many plants stuck on as there was room for. Sir HANS SLOANE's library, which probably has few like it amongst private collections gathered together by one single man, and consists of somewhat more than 48,000 volumes, all bound in superb bindings. To describe all this great collection in detail, would fill several folios: for any who has not himself seen this collection would probably have very great difficulty in picturing to himself that it is so large. In another room were several of such books as consisted of colored pictures of all sorts of natural objects. Such were MERIANA's, CATESBY's, SEBA's, Madame BLACKWELL's, etc., costly works, Egyptian mummies, Roman, and other antiquities, etc. In the garden we saw Sir HANS SLOANE's chair with three wheels under it, and a little one behind, in which he was drawn about in the garden. Afterwards the most costly stones were shown us, which were arranged in a box made in a particular manner. The box was quadrilateral, a little more than six inches long and not quite six inches broad, and nearly six inches high. On the top it sloped from all sides together, so that it resembled a monument on a grave, or a house with an Italian roof. It consisted of a great many boxes, which are not drawn out as usual, but the upper box was always a lid to the under, so that the lowest box had for a lid all the boxes above it. The gems were small and lay in small round holes turned or cut in the boxes. It was said that in this box there were 1,300 different kinds of gems.

As this cabinet was described to me some years earlier by that personage to whom this narrative is dedicated, ARTEDI saw much the same things, thanks be to SLOANE who wholly took him in and treated him with every kindness. Numerous fishes of divers kinds were made readily available, all carefully labeled with ink on paper. Some were preserved as dry or stuffed skins nailed or stuck with glue onto wooden plinths or cleverly mounted on wires or sticks, but many others were held in bottles filled with spirits, the tops sealed with round glass plates and ox bladders tied tightly with twine, some closed with red sealing wax. All of these specimens were carefully observed by our able ichthyologist—drawings were made, names were given, and descriptions drawn up, the latter all finding their proper place in the manuscripts for his *Ichthyologia*.

On Whitsunday of 1735, which, if I am not mistaken, would have in that year fallen on 29 May, our ARTEDI went by coach to Stratford, then a small town in semi-rural surroundings on the east side of London, where he made visit to GEORGE EDWARDS. This EDWARDS, a well-known specialist of birds, was only two years before, appointed Librarian to the Royal College of Physicians, under patronage of SLOANE. Also, living in the same vicinity, and called upon by our naturalist on this same occasion, was Dr. JOHN FOTHERGILL of Upton Park. While fishes were not the subject of interest of either man, much good came from these meetings, especially that with FOTHERGILL. This good Quaker and man of science, with whom I myself had ample correspondence, formed a shell collection that, next to that of the Duchess of PORTLAND, came to be, in size and diversity, the best in all of England. Of the greatest interest to ARTEDI was the clever, might I say ingenious, way that FOTHERGILL, quite by his own design, arranged his shells in classes, orders, families, and genera, according to their structure.

Finally, I might add here, that ARTEDI took ample opportunity during the time spent in England to prepare his various manuscripts for the great *Ichthyologia*. By himself for the most part, with many free uninterrupted hours at his disposal, he made more progress than it seems he ever did at home in Uppsala. It was, in fact, with some surprise that later upon my reading the general preface to the project at large, I saw that the last line read

Scripsi Londini **1735.**

which finale I interpreted as indication that the end of the work was indeed in sight.

CHAPTER 7
Our Time in Holland

Herr CAROLUS LINNAEUS, the famous Swedish doctor and
botanist whose renown has more than once been mentioned
in earlier numbers of this periodical, recently passed through
here on his way to Holland, where he intends to stay for
several years in order to frequent the famous men there, and
in particular Herr BOERHAAVE with whom he has already
carried on a scholarly correspondence, and thus still further
perfect his already outstanding knowledge of medicine,
physics, and botany.

— *Hamburgische Berichte*, 10 June 1735

WHILE MY long-lost and well-missed ARTEDI was so occupied in England, SOHLBERG and I paid our last good-byes to Hamburg, with some
haste as you will remember, fearing vengeance from the Burgomaster
and his brother. At dawn on the morning of 28 May 1735, we went on
board the *Couffert*, a small, rather uncomfortable boat, with two masts,
of the kind the Dutch then called a "kofschip," thus making our way
from Altona to Amsterdam at a quite reasonable cost of only one ducat
each. As we were taking good advantage of the ebb-tide to sail down
the river Elbe, the weather suddenly and without forgiveness turned
very bad so that our first night was passed miserably in storm and rain.
The weather being somewhat improved the next morning, we sailed
past the town of Glückstadt, but eventually by mid-day, due to contrary wind, we were forced to stop and seek our shelter in the mouth of
the river Stör. Here we found some relief from our sea sickness—my
dear companion, in particular, being unable to keep down any item of
food or drink—by going ashore at Wewelsfleth, where we passed what
remained of the day visiting the church and collecting plants. And so
it was the same nearly the whole of the voyage, some sixteen days at
sea, which, I can say without hesitation, were some of the worst of my
memory. But we soon grew tired of complaining of the wind and ever-

lasting rain, and began to occupy our time with buying and describing fishes that were daily brought aboard the boat by fishermen for our sustenance. On the ebb-tide of Friday, 3rd of June, our spirits rose as the weather improved and we sailed by the island of Langeoog. Here we took time to collect and describe many various kinds of sea animals, which were found here in great variety and abundance. With favorable winds on the 7th and 8th of June, we passed by the coast of Groningen on the left, and on the 9th of that month, West Friesland. The next day we visited Schiermonnikoog, where we were forced, once again due to bad weather, to remain inshore, protected by the elevation of the land. This wait finally over, we were required now to enter the open sea. Sailing along past the coast of Ameland and Terschelling, we encountered such high seas that we, on several occasions, took on water in quantities that even our hardened crew feared might engulf our little boat and us with it. And yet even this was not the end of it: on the afternoon of 11 June, there came the most terrible storm, such rain, wind, thunder, and lightning that we could not see land nor anything else in any direction. Finally, in the afternoon of Sunday, the 12th of June, a much needed calm in the air allowed us to continue our travel unhampered and next morning as the first glow of early morning fell upon us we found ourselves in the roadsteads of Amsterdam harbor.

Not wanting to waste a moment, we immediately, that same afternoon, made our way to the *Hortus Medicus* (Medical Garden), even then famous among botanists, by far the oldest scientific gardens in the world—an extraordinary collection of plants to which I would return many times during my sojourn in Holland. The next day—it was Tuesday the 14th of June—I called upon the wealthy botanist Professor JOHANNES BURMANN, a kindly man of about my own age, who had a most sumptuous library containing every book on plants of any importance. Bestowing every possible courtesy upon me, this professor took me into his confidence, promising use of his books and manuscripts whenever I should need them. Later, when preparing my own works for publication, this generous accessibility would benefit me beyond measure. Dining that evening with BURMANN at this house on the Keizersgracht near the Vijzelstraat, I met his young son, NIKOLAAS, who would later make a good account of himself as one of my dedicated disciples in Sweden.

With a gracious letter of introduction in hand, kindly provided by BURMANN, I called the next day at the museum of SEBA located on the north side of the Haarlemmerdijk near the Brouwerstraat, in a grand, five-storey house—which, I might add here, was originally named the *Vriesse Pijnas* (Frisian Pinnace), but which SEBA called *Die Deutsche Apotheke* (The German Apothecary)—marked above by two "ox-eye" windows and on top by a pair of recumbent horses. This letter from a man of BURMANN's reputation was thought to be needed to counter the negative reception much expected for my having shown the Hydra with seven heads to be a fake, but described by SEBA as real. But these fears proved to be an exaggeration, and so, by these means, after some initial, but weak rebuff, I was soon allowed full access.

SEBA, of whom I have made mention previously, was a famous apothecary, German by birth, who even then was very old, having recently passed into his seventieth year. Having observed previously the handsome portrait of this man—an engraving by the eminent JACO-BUS HOUBRAKEN after a painting by JAN QUINKHARD—said to have been made only four years previously, and as engraved on copper and printed in the first volume of his *Thesaurus*, I must say, I was wholly unprepared to behold him. Instead of the vigorous and healthy figure I fully expected, I found myself standing before a far more elderly man, yet still with all his mental faculties in good working order. In very early youth he acquired an unusual interest in stones, shells, insects, plants, and all other sorts of natural curiosities. Later, and for a good part of his adult life, he spent much of his ample money and leisure time collecting these various things, thus bringing together a large volume of objects that had no equal for quantity and richness of variety. Everyone knows the story of how SEBA sold his cabinet in 1717 to Czar PETER of Russia for the extraordinary sum of 15,000 guilders, and only after that started a second collection that was soon better than the first. It was in fact this second collection that was the subject of his great *Thesaurus*—the beloved objects of his attention here described in great detail and lavishly illustrated in two thick folio volumes just now published in Amsterdam, this pair the first of a projected set of four, the remaining two then still in preparation. These books, which I was allowed to examine during my visit, the first dated 1734, the second just freshly delivered from the bindery, with all its brilliant hand-painted color, were laid out on a great table in the library, together with other volumes of great interest to me. Among the latter, I noticed in particular and took a fleeting glance at the works of ALDROVANDI, JONSTON, RUMPHIUS, and MERIAN. These volumes and everything else were placed at my disposal by this most generous of scholars. I delighted in seeing the many things that were hitherto unknown to me. Of great interest was a cabinet of East Indian cypress wood having 72 drawers with shells; another cabinet of similar wood, only red in color, with a door, the panels of which showed landscapes painted on glass, and containing 400 bottles with animals in spirits; and yet another containing many animals stuffed in life-like pose and fixed on wooden boards. And down the corridor, yet many more cabinets, one of 32 drawers with about 1,000 European insects, another devoted to foreign insects; a Chinese cabinet inlaid with tortoise and silver containing minerals and fossils; a box of birds-of-paradise and other curious winged creatures; a crucifix of coral from a Spanish temple; and more than 60 tea-cups made of twisted bamboo fibers, the inside lacquered, unbreakable, very curious. Figures of steatite from China, of sandal wood, ivory, and coral. Seaweeds from the Red Sea, a box with curious medicines from far countries, eggs of birds, of ostrich, emu, and cassowary, and well-preserved crocodiles, snakes, lizards, and the like. Truly this collection was infinitely more beautiful and much richer than any I had ever seen before. I vowed then to return to that treasure of objects, gleaned from all parts of the world, to learn everything from it that I could.

* * *

But turning my head now toward the principal object of my journey to Holland, I took myself the next day, it being Thursday, the 16th of June, by boat to Harderwijk. There being favorable winds, I sailed the 35 miles to that town, with SOHLBERG ever by my side, arriving by three o'clock the next morning and making my way at first light to the university.

Having well prepared my thesis long before this time—the whole thing ready-written and brought with me from Sweden—and having sound knowledge of its subject and all related phenomena, I went with confidence to my defense. Presenting this worthy document, which had for title, "A new hypothesis as to the cause of intermittent fevers," to my sponsor Professor JOHANNES DE GORTER, I had not long to wait for response. He was fully satisfied with my irrefutable proof that these fevers were caused by or resulted from living on a clay soil, and I received on Saturday the required signature of approval and was made Candidate of Medicine.

While preparing now for the public debate that was to follow, I was obliged the next three days to attend a number of lectures given by DE GORTER. These being rather of a simple nature and somewhat beneath my level, I took time to entertain myself as best I could. I cannot help but recall that during that interim, feeling quite relaxed and satisfied with myself, I made the acquaintance of DE GORTER's young son DAVID, a beautiful boy who became for me a life-long friend. Though a good ten years younger than I, he had already received his doctor's degree the year before. Soon after my departure from Holland some years later and when my fame had advanced before me in all directions, DAVID DE GORTER became a great follower of my system of nomenclature and, in imitation of my many examples, he well described and published some local floras, the volume called *Flora Belgica* (Belgium Flora), published in 1767, being most widely praised.

The final defense, perhaps more properly called a debate, came on Thursday morning. It began with my presenting a somewhat brief oral discourse of the theme of my disputation and the general conclusions arising from it. This being very well received by most, there followed an open and most penetrating examination of my topic, during which I easily cast off contrary arguments posed by some of the doubters in attendance. After this exercise of several hours' time, I was then asked to prepare a written elucidation of two Aphorisms by HIPPOCRATES: his number 14, "A patient suffering from dropsy will be cured when the water will have flown off to the bowels along the vessels"; and his number 15, "In a patient suffering from chronic diarrhea a fit of vomiting stops the diarrhea." Finally, after I diagnosed and prescribed treatment for a case of jaundice, my ordeal was terminated. It was thus on this Thursday, the 23rd of June, after the full set of requirements was met with satisfaction, and all duly approved by the examining committee, I was made Doctor of Medicine, giving me the right to advance to the upper chair of that profession, to justify medical treatises publicly, to teach the craft of a physician, to visit the sick, to prescribe for them, to hold disputations, etc., etc. So successful, in fact, was my defense and my whole demeanor in general that my scholarly examiner Professor GORTER wrote of me as follows:

> With a prayer for his success in the care of the sick, I have not hesitated to add my name to his already long list of advocates, so that it may be universally known that I have found in CARL LINNAEUS, the learned Swede and now a Doctor of Medicine, a unique skill and knowledge, not only in all the fields of medicine, but also of botany, and so that he may stand among the foremost doctors of medicine.

I had already been a full week at Harderwijk and wanting not to waste more time, and anxious also to make further acquaintances in Amsterdam, I returned with SOHLBERG to that fair city on the evening of Friday, the 24th of June. Here I renewed my acquaintance with BURMANN, who once again took me graciously into his care, providing for my every need, both daily victuals and most excellent sleeping accommodations. While dining on Sunday at the house of this latest of my benefactors, the suggestion was made that I journey to Leiden where I might have good opportunity to meet more of the great scientific men of Holland, in this case, namely, the great HERMANUS BOERHAAVE. Holding professorships in three fields, medicine, botany, and chemistry, he was said to be a most gifted speaker in all these subjects, attracting students to Leiden from every country on the continent and beyond. Medical knowledge for him was based on a thorough comprehension of all the other natural sciences, such as physics and chemistry. Instead of fiddling with powders and pills, he strongly encouraged his students to research the cause of disease first hand, attaching large importance to instruction in the hospital itself. When he died on 23 September 1738, at 69 years of age, he well knew it was coming, but accepted it willingly, and with much dignity. I give evidence of the truth of this by recalling, with much pleasure, a letter from the great man, addressed to me from Leiden, with date 16 March 1738:

> I labor under a vomica, or a kind of tumorous amplification, in the lungs, which for the last three months has greatly oppressed my breathing, on the slightest exertion, and has been hitherto increasing daily. If it goes on enlarging, without bursting, it must suffocate me; if it bursts, the consequences are uncertain. Whatever may be the event, it is at the disposal of the Supreme Governor of all things. What therefore can I have to fear or to desire? We must submit to the divine will. Yet I am not the less desirous of neglecting no probable remedy that may alleviate my pain or bring the abscess to maturity, though I am perfectly easy as to the final result. I have lived more than 68 years, with unabated cheerfulness. May you also, my worthy friend, enjoy a long and happy life!

So stimulated by my delightful conversation with BURMANN, I went by towboat—the kind of conveyance the Dutch are wont to call *trekschuit* or simply *schuit*—to Leiden on the following Tuesday. SOHLBERG still with me, that faithful companion, I went by way of Haarlem, which latter place lies some halfway between, all to the southwest of Amsterdam. And what a pleasant journey this was. The canals or waterways, within which the towboats ply, are surprisingly narrow, but made more narrow still by the rapidly growing sedges, waterflags, and lilies, which laborers forever do their best to remove. Almost as fast as it multiples, the cutting and removal of this vegetable material and carrying it from the banks in trough-shaped carts, is an activity everywhere to be seen along the way. What pleased me most were the myriad pure white water-lilies expanding their florescence to the morning sun, intermixed with the yellow-fringed water-lily, both species common in those parts. The smoothness and absolute silence that so pleasantly is a part of this Dutch mode of traveling, so different from the rough jostle and grueling clatter of horse and carriage, increases immeasurably the pleasure of the journey.

Upon my arrival at BOERHAAVE's house—then situated on the Rapenburg Canal—unfortunately without letter of introduction in hand and not realizing an inducement to the maidservant was required to gain audience to the grand old man, I was soundly sent away. You can imagine my indignation at this rough and unseemly treatment. But, as I later learned, this most rude reception was not unlike that received by other men of importance. Even VOLTAIRE, that well-known French writer and philosopher, once arriving while BOERHAAVE was at table, was refused entrance, the doctor declaring that he was not prepared to rise for someone who did not rise for God.

Angry and disgusted at this unworthy rejection, I turned away, resolving to seek out other residents of that town who might be of interest to me and who might treat me more in the way I was accustomed. One of these personages was Professor VAN ROYEN who entertained me very well by demonstrating the Botanic Garden of Leiden University. It was in fact this same VAN ROYEN who, only a short time later, begged me to stay in Leiden over the winter of 1738 to classify the plants in the Botanic Garden according to my sexual system, an offer that I could not and did not refuse. Later still, in gratitude for his kindness to me, I named for him the genus *Royena*, part of a larger assemblage of woody plants that includes persimmon, ebony, and the like.

Also during those initial days in Leiden, I made the acquaintance of young Dr. LIEBERKÜHN, a German physician and anatomist who spent his time on curious studies of the intestine. He had a most magnificent collection of microscopes. With one fine instrument, he demonstrated to me and others what he took to be living spermatozoa in the semen of a dog—innumerable little bodies swimming about, and seemingly endowed with vital motion. But I quickly made the correct determination—what we viewed was nothing more than particles put into movement by the warmth of the fluid.

But more important still, I encountered in Leiden JOHAN GRONOVIUS the Younger, a rich and distinguished doctor of that town who dedicated himself mostly to city politics, but made botany an all-consuming hobby. With this occupation, he also, as you might recall, edited a fine edition of AELIANUS and published several quite acceptable dissertations on fishes, the most acceptable of which was his "Pisces Belgii Descripti" (Description of Belgian Fishes) published in *Acta Societatis Regiae Scientiarum Uppsaliensis* for the year 1742. It was to this GRONOVIUS also that I give thanks for discerning the greatness of my early works, which books then existed only in manuscript form, carried with me by hand from Sweden. Of special example here was *Systema Naturae*—my plan to reveal, in an orderly manner for the first time, the works of the Creator in all three kingdoms of nature—a rough outline of which I showed to GRONOVIUS in late June 1735. So thoroughly impressed was he with my erudition that he wrote the following to a friend residing in England: "Not since the time of CONRAD GESSNER was there a man so learn'd in all parts of natural history as he; and that not superficial, but to the very bottom."

My confidence renewed by this substantiation of my worth, I requested from GRONOVIUS a letter of introduction to BOERHAAVE, which he most gladly agreed to prepare. Thus, with letter in hand and money for the maid, I took myself again to the town house of that giant of intellect. But, as it was, he kept me waiting impatiently for an entire week, before giving me audience. In fact, it was not until 5 July that I was allowed to enter that rich portal. And I must say, what a surprise it was for me to see this rather strange, sickly old gentleman; he was then in his 66th year, with only three more years to live before departing this world. Hoping not to sound too unkind, I later wrote of him in my diary as follows:

> Corpulent, tall, curly-haired, hook-nosed, going bald. Had not visited his nearest neighbors or his relatives for twenty years. Saw patients daily from 9 to 11 a.m., lectured in public at 11, from 1 to 2 in private, and again at 3 publicly. Slept without a nightcap, never had a fire in his bedroom, drank no wine, tea, or coffee, and never smoked. He said that if he dressed before a fire when he got up, he was very soon tired, but if he dressed in the cold he remained brisk.

These first impressions aside, mine of him and his of me, an initial coldness on his part was soon replaced by warmth and acceptance, he being quick to recognize my great merit. In due time, he took a strong liking to me, and brought me on several occasions to his large country estate not far by horse from Leiden, where his well-tended gardens were a love of his life. Here I marveled at the diversity, for the gardens were stocked with all kinds of plants that would bear the climate, some of which I had never seen before. On the very first of those visits, I had an opportunity of manifesting my skills in the science and history of botany. In fact, I was able to add, with much self-assurance, to his knowledge of his own trees. So surprised and impressed was he by this display, from so young a person as I, that he afterwards made everything available to me. In addition to other niceties, he strongly encouraged me not to leave Holland immediately, as I had intended, but to take up my abode and remain there with him in Leiden. But at the time, I could not be persuaded, being determined within the week to visit Amsterdam on my way back to my well-missed Swedish homeland. This decision was soon to change, however, upon my receiving other offers that were impossible to ignore. Be that as it may, and despite my rejection of him, old BOERHAAVE and I became the best of friends, I learning much from him of very great value. It would later prove that this gentleman was very greatly instrumental in furthering my reputation, far beyond what could have been imagined at that time. He was, as it later proved to be, the means by which I was brought into connection with GEORGE CLIFFORD, a Director of the Dutch East India Company, and owner of a princely domain called Hartekamp—the deer pasture— with splendid gardens, lying halfway between Leiden and Haarlem. But more of CLIFFORD and Hartekamp at a later time.

*   *   *

Let me now relate a most extraordinary and unexpected event that occurred that year in early July, not three days after my first meeting with BOERHAAVE—it was a Friday, 8 July, to be exact. While at the Black Adder taking midday food and drink with SOHLBERG, the latter in company with CARL TERSMEEDEN, who was in Leiden for reasons of business, I turned to take notice of none other than PETER ARTEDI.

Quite suddenly and wholly by coincidence, there was my old friend, just returned from England. Thrilled as I was, I put my arms around him, pulled him to me tightly, and sweetly kissed his face. O grateful day—how good it was to see him. We sat and talked together till half past three, hearing of his many adventures abroad, and learning also of his desperate financial situation, which gave us all, his dear close friends, great concern. Promising to help him as best we could, we then said our farewells as SOHLBERG and TERSMEEDEN together took their leave aboard the towboat headed south to The Hague.

Once alone, ARTEDI and I openly rejoiced—nothing more delightful could have happened to either of us, and our tears showed what joy we felt. I told my story, and he his; what kind of life he had led in London; the many splendid observations that he had made in the company of the ichthyologists; how he had enjoyed the favor of various scholars, especially that of the illustrious SLOANE, the kindness and generosity of whose reception he lovingly described; the many museums he had visited; the affection and high opinion therefore entertained by him of England and the English. He now spoke of wanting to take a doctorate in medicine, to follow my path to Harderwijk. But he had been made penniless by the expenses of his journey and was worried about how to get clothes, food, and all the books he needed for his work. He was therefore thinking of returning home to Sweden. But, as we shall soon discover, providence intervened to alter this determination.

CHAPTER 8

My System of Nature

O Jehova
How ample are Thy works!
How wisely Thou hast fashioned them!
How full the earth is of Thy possession!

> —Psalms, 104: 24, quoted by Linnaeus, *In*: *Systema Naturae*,
> Editio Decima, Reformata, 1758

Of all my wondrous works, it was the very first that was of greatest consequence—a publication like no other, which sealed my place in the pantheon of philosophic men. It was, in fact, that which made me equal to the immortals, those who have gained the praise of the learned world, of which I list only four, Galileo, Newton, Leibnitz, and Boerhaave. A rather thin thing it was, only seven extra-large folios when printed, but of explosive import—I called it *Systema Naturae*, my System of Nature. It was in this earth-shaking publication that I took on the task of revealing the works of the Creator in an orderly manner—no one before me had ever done anything like it. In that part of it devoted to botany, for example, I overthrew the old systems, and formed a new one based on the sexes of plants, as I have already described to you. This was done with such perfection as to the genera and species that no other system can be compared to it—in fact, as we have already established, it still stands today. I abolished and rejected more than half the number of genera of other authors, but made up for this reduction by introducing twice as many more, from the plants that I got from Africa, the East Indies, and America; so that in the end I discovered more genera than had all other authors put together, by more than double the number. Before me, everyone formed characters as he pleased, all unstable and insufficient. But I undertook to examine with care number, figure, situation, and proportion in all known plants, and in all the parts of fructification, even to the smallest, and the heretofore neglected stamens and pistils. I am here wont to boast also that through my efforts, all the various parts of plants, whether they be of good use in differentiation or not, were defined by me, in which case, no other terminology of any worth was available. Of good example here are the many different forms of the leaves, which I drew up in great detail, affixing witty terms to them of my own design and classifying them into three general groupings, the *Folia Simplicia*, *Folia Composita*, and *Folia Determinata*.

As to zoology, it was before my time an Augean stable, filled with tables and nonsense, and far from being a science or a system. I entirely reformed it, as well as I did botany. I constituted six classes and distinguished the worms (*Vermes*) from the insects (*Insecta*). I created genera and species where there were none before and gave to each the respective synonyms and differences. Insects seem innumerable; in fact, nature seems exhaustless in her invention of new forms of this class. Others have complained that knowing it is quite beyond the cognizance of any one man, but I collected and described every Swedish species, and procured thousands of others from both the Indies, nay, even from the southern hemisphere, from which part of the globe not ten had been seen before. I described every one, constituted new genera, affixed generic names, specific differences, and trivial names, and ascertained on what vegetable they respectively lived. I made intelligible that which before me was not to be comprehended.

Shells had been arranged by many persons, but none of their methods were good for anything. I found out nature's own key, in the hinge, that part that allows for the opening and closing of the valve. I made genera and specific differences, and with incredible labor determined synonyms, so that even this branch of science became plain and perspicuous. Zoophytes were by some stated to belong to the mosses, by others to the animals, but I decided that they were in between vegetables and animals—vegetables with respect to their stems, but animals with respect to their florescence.

In fishes, I followed ARTEDI's way of thinking in my earlier editions of *Systema Naturae*, but later—despite these slimy creatures belonging to that branch of zoology that I liked the least—I discovered an entirely new way and a simple mode of distinguishing them, namely by the situation of their pelvic fins. I classed the cartilaginous fishes (*Pisces*

Chondropterygii) with the amphibians (*Amphibia*), and the mighty whale (*Cete*), formerly thought by most to be a fish, with the mammals (*Mammalia*). Of regard to the latter, I must agree fully with that prosperous English physician EDWARD TYSON, who in 1680 published a charming treatise on the *Anatomy of the Porpess*, in which he gave emphatic warning of the dangers of systematizing animals by their outward appearance alone:

> If we view a Porpess on the outside, there is nothing more than a Fish, but if we look within, there is nothing less. The structure of the *Viscera* and inward parts have so great an Analogy and resemblance to those of Quadrupeds, that we find them here almost the same. The greatest difference from them seems to be in the external shape, and wanting Feet. But here too we observed that when the skin and flesh was taken off, the fore-fins did very well represent an Arm, there being the *Scapula*, an *os Humeri*, the *Ulna*, and *Radius*, and bone of the *Carpus*, the *Metacarp*, and five *digiti* curiously jointed. I am thus persuaded that the Porpess is in fact of the Mammalian class, similar to land-dwelling Quadrupeds, but liveth instead in the sea, and hath but two fore-fins.

Continuing on with this subject of quadrupeds, I showed how well they could be classified by their teeth, the birds by their bills, and the insects by their antennae, their wings, the joints and spiny protuberances of their legs, etc. To the shock of some, I presented the apes as companions to man—in an order of their own, isolated from others, called *Anthropomorpha*, which I ranked under the quadrupeds, as having hairy bodies, a viviparous and lactiferous female, and four front teeth. The ape-like sloth differs from these only in the number of digits, for it has two or three on each foot, differing front and back. Beasts of prey have six front teeth. Of these beasts, the bear is regarded as more closely related to the anthropomorphic order since it walks on its heels, with big toes turned outward; the rest are characterized by one designation in each case, according to the number of nipples, state of the digits, form of the claws, size of the tail, and so on. In this, I was severely criticized again by none other than BUFFON, who made silly and derogatory comments wholly gratuitous about my method in the first volume of his *Histoire Naturelle* (Natural History): "It really is necessary to be obsessed with classifying to put such different beasts as man and sloths together, all because of the arrangement of their teeth." But of this I took no outward notice.

Having now spoken of the *Anthropomorpha*, I think it of benefit here to speak somewhat of the place of man in my System of Nature. I must confess, and try as I might, I could not discover the difference between man and the orangutan; in fact, in all my later studies I never did find a single generic character to distinguish man from the ape. It is remarkable that the stupidest ape differs so little from the wisest man, that the surveyor of nature has yet to be found who can draw the line between them. After having given it some special thought, I made the choice to enter man into my system as *Homo sapiens*, a name originating from the ancient Latin word *Homo*, meaning man; and *sapiens*, meaning of good taste, mighty, wise, and sensible. In this action, I differed widely from all my predecessors in classifying man as simply another kind of animal, a bold step for which I was later criticized by a few non-thinking personages whose names shall not be repeated here. I then placed this species within the Class Mammalia in my order of Primates, the genus *Homo* itself defined by having "fore-teeth cutting; upper four, parallel; teats two pectoral." The human species, thus placed within this genus, I differentiated by it being "diurnal, varying by education and situation." I then thought well to distinguish the following varieties:

Wild Man. Four-footed, mute, hairy.

American. Copper-colored, choleric, erect. Hair black, straight, thick; nostrils wide, face harsh; beard scanty; obstinate, content free. Paints himself with fine red lines. Regulated by customs.

European. Fair, sanguine, brawny. Hair yellow, brown, flowing; eyes blue; gentle, acute, inventive. Covered with close vestments. Governed by laws.

Asiatic. Sooty, melancholy, rigid. Hair black; eyes dark; severe, haughty, covetous. Covered with loose garments. Governed by opinions.

African. Black, phlegmatic, relaxed. Hair black, frizzled; skin silky; nose flat; lips tumid; crafty, indolent, negligent. Anoints himself with grease. Governed by caprice.

In the kingdom of minerals too, specialists in that realm of science ought not to be ungrateful to me. I tried in an ingenious and pleasant manner to explain the stratification of mountains. I was one of the first and most eminent men who contended that the sea is decreasing, and that the continents are increasing; and I went as far back as the existence of Paradise. I would willingly have believed the earth to be far older than the Chinese assert, had the Holy Scriptures allowed me. I clearly enumerated four orders of earth (*Terrae*), and thought it impossible that there could be more. It is beyond controversy that all rocks, with hardly any exception, derive from soils; for example, schists come from vegetable boggy soil, whetstone from sand, marble from clay. I ascribed the origin of lime to the Animal Kingdom, mold or humus to the Vegetable Kingdom, clay to the slime of the sea, and sand to salt water. I deduced the composition of fossils. Flint I affirmed to be produced from chalk and not *vice versa*. Lapidose crystals, I said, consisted of salt and earth. The history of calculi I explained in a plain and obvious manner. All fossils can be reduced to seven genera and no more are possible. Fossil corals I described and figured very distinctly. I was, in fact, the first to introduce system into the Mineral Kingdom by defining classes and genera, on which mineralogy was afterwards grounded and improved. A whole set of new and curious descriptive terms—crust, surface, composition, texture, hardness, color, and the interactions of the various species—were used by me quite successfully to circumscribe all earthy substances.

Even beyond these revelations within the three kingdoms, which contributions rise far above those of all men before me, I brought the mineral, plant, and animal realms together in grand and all inclusive ways. Take for example, my small treatise of 1744, titled *Dissertation sur l'Accroissement de la Terre Habitable* (Essay on the Increase of the Habitable Earth). Here, I showed myself to be among the very first of men to propose a grand scheme by which living beings came to inhabit the earth. If we believe that, in the infancy of the world, a single sexual pair of every species of living thing was created by the Almighty—and who, pray tell, does not subscribe to this truth?—it is reasonable to hold to the idea also that the habitable earth was no more than a small island of land, in the middle of a vast sea, the surface of which provided space comfortable enough for all living things. This unique place was, of course, the Garden of Eden, where ADAM subscribed names to each being that the Holy Spirit produced before him. Now as these beings came together in sexual conjugation and multiplied their numbers abundantly, each holding to its own kind, they soon came to require more space. It was then that the Creator caused the sea level to subside, the solid land thus increasing gradually and offering boundless room for ever-expanding numbers of plants and animals. And if you think this pure guesswork, I invite you to consider the precise and exact observations of ANDERS CELSIUS, uncle of OLOF CELSIUS of whom I have spoken before. This ardent observer, well fond of experimentation, placed markers at several places along the coast of Finland, and by examination of these markers at various intervals, showed clearly a lowering of the sea. This, then, is the certain proof of what I speak. Not only was this watery decline precisely observed during the time of CELSIUS, but well recorded by others by those same markers, and at those same places, for many years after his death.

*   *   *

Thus, all together, by drawing up very large charts or tables of the minerals, vegetables, and animals—which a person might well put up on the wall for easy inspection—and by attributing a distinct characteristic to each of their families, I made these sciences so simple and comprehensible that within only a very few years, all authors of any sense and worth had adopted my system. There is not a single word in it that is not useful. And I do declare that whoever wishes to see my nice discrimination and clear manner of writing ought to read my introductions to the tables of the *Systema Naturae*, which I properly called my "Observations on the Three Kingdoms of Nature." The neat and simple hierarchy laid out here, in my effort to represent the works of the Creator in a regular sequence, I cleverly am wont to compare to a kind of military mapping: with LINNAEUS as the self-appointed general of FAUNA and FLORA's army, nature, like society, consists of kingdoms, provinces, states, districts, and individual small-holdings, from which the individual soldier is collected. Read and let yourself decide who has composed anything similar.

In revealing this essential hierarchy to the learned world, I thought it important to put a stop, once and for all, to the ridiculous proposals of several of my colleagues, whose names shall not be given here, of the mutability of species. The idea that one species may, under certain circumstances, change in such a way as to give rise to another is an utterly improbable and blasphemous concept. If we observe God's works, it becomes more than sufficiently evident to everybody, that each living being is propagated from an egg and that every egg produces an offspring closely resembling the parent. Hence no new species are produced. Individuals multiply by generation. Hence at present the number of individuals in each species is greater than it was at first. If we count backwards from this multiplication of individuals in each species, in the same way as we have multiplied forward, the series ends up in one single parent, whether that parent consists of one single hermaphrodite (as commonly occurs in plants) or of a double, that is, a male and a female (as happens in most animals). As there are no new species; as like always gives birth to like; as one in each species was at the beginning of the progeny, it is necessary to attribute this progenitorial unity to some Omnipotent and Omniscient Being, namely God, whose work is called Creation. We can count as many species now as were created in the beginning. This is confirmed by the mechanism, the laws, principles, constitutions, and sensations in every living individual. These facts I thought to be of such great importance that I stated them quite specifically, and gave them proper place in the very first introductory paragraphs of my great work.

*　*　*

Now all of the *Systema Naturae* I had penciled out in near-complete form prior to the early age of only 27, even when still at Uppsala, where, if you will recall, much of it was discussed with and deliberated upon with my faithful fellow-collegian ARTEDI. Bringing it with me to Holland, along with the manuscripts of several other books that I hoped would soon be published, I took occasion one evening when in Leiden to show it to GRONOVIUS who was much astonished. It was, in fact, this wealthy doctor of medicine who, of all the persons I met in Holland, paid me more attention than anyone else. He encouraged me now to publish my work forthwith, but I complained of my inability to do so, for severe lack of funds, all the money carried with me from Sweden, 600 copper dollars, having long been expended. Understanding my plight, he requested my permission to get it printed at his own expense. He thought too, at the time, that his good friend, the wealthy Scottish doctor ISAAC LAWSON might also show great interest, and might help as well to defray the cost. And so publication of that great effort accordingly seemed assured. It was now left up to me to put the last parts of it to paper and deliver the final manuscript.

But, for now, after my short stay in Leiden, where I had been so graced with the kindness of BOERHAAVE, GRONOVIUS, and others, I returned to Amsterdam with my dear ARTEDI—SOHLBERG having by this time gone off. Upon our arrival, it was BURMANN who once again made things right, providing handsome rooms, several servants at our sole bidding, and board at his own table, of which we took full and grateful advantage. Under influence of this ample comfort, and surrounded daily by congenial company, it would be easy for most men to relax and allow time to be frittered away, but I soon, under these idyllic circumstances, became nervous from want of applying my mind to scientific pursuit. BURMANN was quick to see this in me, and being a highly respectable botanist himself, asked if I might give some assistance in the preparation of a treatise on the plants of Ceylon, his so-called *Thesaurus Zeylanicus*. This flora—the writing of which had only just begun and which was in much need of help—was based in the main on a herbarium that had been brought together in the middle 1670s by that resourceful Dutch medical officer PAUL HERMANN who later in 1679 took up the Chair of Botany at Leiden University. How these materials, comprising four bound volumes of pressed plants—along with a curious smattering of similarly preserved insects—and a fifth volume of clever drawings, came into BURMANN's hands, I did not know. But, be that as it may, with this request from BURMANN, I was made more than happy by having the opportunity to see many tropical plants that heretofore had been unknown to me. With this new occupation before me, and realizing the good that BURMANN's library—not to speak of the rich and various collections of natural productions to be had in Amsterdam—would offer to the completion of my *Systema Naturae*, as well as to that of my many other works then in manuscript, I vowed to remain with BUR-MANN through the winter. As to the plants of Ceylon, I dare say that my generous host wanted to publish it himself, but I procrastinated with its completion and finally wrenched it from him altogether, presenting it to the public solely under my own name in 1747, under title of *Flora Zeylanica* (Ceylon Flora). Of course, it should not be dismissed entirely that my fine colleague managed an inferior summary called *Thesaurus Zeylanicus*, printed in Amsterdam in 1737.

Determined now as never before to finish my *Systema Naturae*, to make it ready for the press and thus to satisfy my new patrons GRO-NOVIUS and LAWSON, I applied all my concentration to the task. I soon completed the first of my "Observations," which was a list of twenty statements of generalities, meant to serve as a universal introduction to the work—upon which, for all posterity to note, I signed my name,

Car. Linnæus
Equ.

with the date of 23 July 1735—and then turned to questions of the arrangement of parts. Early I had determined that the text of the great work was best given in tabular form, but just how the information should be displayed had somewhat eluded me until now. Then I quickly decided that each major group of objects, be they mineral, plant, or animal, should bear an appropriate heading, with the names of the orders set vertically up the page in the far left-hand column. The second column would be devoted to the names of the genera, the third to con-cise and easily comprehended definitions or diagnoses of the genera, and the fourth to trivial names, for which latter notation, I tried where I thought appropriate to use but a single word. All of this was naturally to be given in the Latin language. Here is a good example taken from

III. AMPHIBIA.

Corpus nudum, vel fquamofum. *Dentes molares*
nulli : *reliqui* femper. *Pinnæ* nullæ.

S E R P E N T I A.	Teftudo.	*Corpus* quadrupedium, caudatum, tefta munitum.	Teftudo teffulata. . terreftris. . . . marina. Lutaria.
	Rana.	*Corpus* quadrupedium, cauda de- ftitutum, fquamis carens.	Bufo. . Rana arborea. . . aquatica. . . Carolina.
	Lacerta.	*Corpus* quadrupedium, caudatum, fquamofum.	Crocodilus. Allegator. Cordylus. Draco volans. Scincus. Salamandra aq. . . terreftris. Chamæleo. Seps. Senembi *Mrg.*
	Anguis.	*Corpus* apodum, teres, fquamo- fum.	Vipera. Cæcilia. Afpis. Caudifona. Cobras de Cabelo. Anguis Æfculapii. Cenchris. Natrix. Hydrus.

AMPHIBIORUM Claffem ulterius continuare noluit benigni-
tas Creatoris ; Ea enim fi tot Generibus , quot reliquæ Animalium Claffes comprehendunt , gauderet; vel fi vera effent
quæ de Draconibus , Bafilifcis , ac ejufmodi monftris *of*
τειραλόγοι fabulantur , certè humanum genus terram inhabi
tare vix poffet.

the Order *Serpentia*, of my Class *Amphibia*, in which I properly place the
turtles and the tortoises (genus *Testudo*); the frogs and the toads (genus
Rana); the crocodiles, alligators, lizards, skinks, salamanders, chame-
leons, etc. (genus *Lacerta*); and the numerous different kinds of snakes,
of which I include the vipers, asps, cobras, sea-snakes, and those snakes
commonly found in various freshwaters (genus *Anguis*).

The treatment of minerals was no problem, my having worked out
a classification long before while still at Uppsala, based on no one's
prior thoughts but my own, there having been, up till then, not a single
qualified person in that realm of science—unless one might mention
the name of JOHANN JACOB SCHEUCHZER, who had produced a barely

passable treatise in 1718 called *Meteorologia et Oryctographia Helvetica*
(The Meteorology and Geology of Switzerland). There is little question but that my approach differs fundamentally from that of the latter.

This was true for plants as well. I applied my altogether new sexual
system for the first time to all members of that Kingdom, having only
some difficulties yet to overcome with the Umbelliferae. The latter
group, you will remember, I had ceded to ARTEDI long before and it
was now on this that I badly needed his instruction. In animals, too, I
was quite well along, but here too I was missing a large assemblage, the
fishes, which again, you will recall, I gave up to my learned colleague
at his insistence, who was now the recognized authority. Though I had
learned much from ARTEDI about these inhabitants of the aquatic world
during our former days together in Uppsala—he taking much of my
time with lengthy reading from his manuscripts—I knew that he had
made extensive and recent revisions, partly stemming from all the new
things he had seen and heard in London. It was his latest thoughts on
this subject that I needed badly for my *Systema Naturae* and for which
I sought his cooperation. So, having carefully drawn up on large folios
that part of it that I thought reasonably finished, all penned in my best
hand, I figured now to seek out the help I could only get from ARTEDI.

*   *   *

You will remember that my old friend had returned from England in
near wretched condition, with not a farthing in his pocket and no more
than the clothes on his person. My friend was in very serious need of
help, and I remembered that SEBA had earlier been looking to pay a
naturalist to put the fishes in his collection in some kind of systematic
order and in other ways to make preparations for the ichthyological
part of an intended third volume of his *Thesaurus*. Because of increasing
age and a feebleness of hand that made it quite impossible to perform
the task himself—not to speak of his total lack of talent for this kind of
endeavor—SEBA had, in fact, inquired as to my own interest in doing
this work. But I, needing all my time to devote to my own projects, and
being supported quite well at that moment by way of the generosity of
BURMANN, I respectfully declined his offer. It struck me now that this
opportunity would serve as excellent employment for ARTEDI—and

who better than our ARTEDI to take on this assignment? At first chance, and declaring that no better collaborator could be found anywhere, I posed this idea to the old man, who at once responded in a most positive way. Naturally assuming that SEBA, being extraordinarily well off, would pay handsomely in return for this work—in fact, a promise was made for a fair and honorable remuneration—and with fine quarters made available to ARTEDI on the Haarlemmerdijk, the latter readily agreed to this proposal. Thus, on 17 July 1735, I took ARTEDI to SEBA's house for the purpose of formal introduction and to make final closure on the proposition. And so it was done—ARTEDI was made content, at least for now, knowing that his talents as a naturalist would be used in a productive way and that too, the resources he needed to complete the requirements for a medical degree might soon be in hand. As for me—in return for my sincere kindness in arranging this situation, but not openly voiced at the time—I hoped that ARTEDI might lend his assistance in dealing with the fishes for my *Systema Naturae*.

Another startling and unexpected event now took place, which made me think, as I often did, that the Lord favored me above all others, that he made things happen for me as a person singled out of the crowd—in this case, making a dream come true, the very one that, above all others in the world, I had wished for. It happened like this: While ARTEDI was busily employed with SEBA's fishes, and after I was at BURMANN's only some few weeks, that enormously rich merchant and banker GEORGE CLIFFORD, having heard much good about me, came to dine with us in Amsterdam. This evening of fine congeniality, at which I did my best to make a good impression, ended with an invitation that I should soon visit Hartekamp, his private country estate, which lay not five miles from Haarlem on the way to Leiden. And so it was that BURMANN and I went there on 13 August 1735, where we were delighted with the splendors of that place. Never had I seen such wondrously rich gardens—masterpieces of nature aided by art, interspersed with shady walks, topiary, various statues, fishponds, and artificial mounds and mazes. And then there was the zoo, full of beasts of every kind—tigers, apes, wild dogs, deer and goats, peccaries and African swine, with many different kinds of birds that made the garden echo and re-echo with their cries.

Still more unbelievable to me were the hothouses for tropical plants purely constructed of glass: I was amazed when I entered these abodes of ADONIS, so full were they of such a variety of plants that they bewitched a Northerner, who could not imagine into what foreign land he had been led. In the first house, one could see the plants of southern Europe—the flora of Spain, southern France, Italy, Sicily, and the Isles of Greece. In the second, treasures from Asia such as cloves, poincianas, mangosteens, and coco-palms. In the third, the plants of Africa—forms whose structure was unique and their nature indeed monstrous, such as mesembryanthemums and aloes of many different kinds, carrion flowers, euphorbias, crassula, and protea species. In the fourth, all of our beloved progeny of the New World: innumerable cacti; orchids, passion flowers, magnolias, and tulip trees; the calabash tree, acacias, tamarinds, and peppers. Among these were arranged the earth's strangest wonders: bananas, exquisite hermannias, silver-leaved protects, and valuable camphor trees.

When finally I entered his truly regal house and splendidly equipped museum, where the collections spoke no less of their owner's renown, I as a foreigner felt quite carried away, for I had never seen their equal. I desired above all things that he might let the world have knowledge of so great a herbarium, and I did not hesitate to offer to lend him a helping hand. But my tactful and subtle suggestion passed by him and was not taken up.

I came away from Hartekamp completely enthralled, wanting then with all my being to devote myself in service to CLIFFORD and to the Almighty Creator, to become keeper of that most marvelous domain. The thought of tending to those gardens and hothouses, and having unfettered access to CLIFFORD's sumptuous library and handsome herbarium, burned in my brain. And so I devised a clever way to make it happen. Taking my good friend GRONOVIUS aside some days later, I asked if he might intercede for me, to suggest to CLIFFORD that I might be given the charge to live at Hartekamp, and to put forth this idea as if he, my intermediary, thought of it all on his own. With this suggestion also, I implored GRONOVIUS to advance the further notion that I might be employed to wait on CLIFFORD as his personal physician, while also serving as superintendent of his gardens. It was said that CLIFFORD had a tendency to hypochondria and would thus no doubt be pleased to have a doctor of proven skills on his doorstep.

Incredible as it was, this bit of deception resulted in complete success. CLIFFORD was, from the start, enamored of the plan, almost to the same extent as I. And so it was that I moved out of my quarters at the house of BURMANN and took myself to Hartekamp, where I, as it were, lived like a prince. In addition to having everything of a scientific nature put at my disposal—more, in fact, than I would ever need—I was paid a thousand florins a year and given free room and board. In return for all this, I was obliged to supervise the gardens, to curate the vast herbarium of dried plants, to publish botanical accounts, or books if you will, describing the plants, and to see after the health of my host.

There at Hartekamp, with plenty of opportunity also for my own studies, I continued to work that summer on my *Systema Naturae*, soon thinking to call on ARTEDI for his assistance. Having now full access to a coach and four, thanks to the kingly status I enjoyed through CLIFFORD's generosity, I used this conveyance to make my way to Amsterdam in late August. By this time, ARTEDI being of a quiet nature, much reserved in his ways, not at all liking the hubbub of excitement at SEBA's place, with its constant stream of visitors—for this collector was glad to show his museum to almost anyone and it was not seldom that it took more than one day to see everything—had chosen to take up quarters of his own along the waterfront, a short distance by foot from the house of his employer. After some difficulty, my driver, winding his way through the narrow and unsavory streets of that part of the town, we found his place at the sign of the Arms of Overijssel, a tall narrow house owned by one HENDRICK WILLEM JÜTTINCK on the Warmoesstraat near the Nieuwebrugsteeg. There ARTEDI lived alone, in a small, poorly furnished room at the very top of a narrow staircase, the whole place a dark and gloomy affair, with only one small window to provide but feeble light. He offered some wine, which I accepted, and we sat and commenced to talk of our respective studies.

With very little difficulty I managed to extract from him what little I needed to complete that part of my systematic table that included the umbellate plants. As it was, he gave me from his notes what I had already supposed, so in this I learned nothing new. With fishes, however, things were somewhat different. As I suspected, I learned from him at least that he had revised extensively the several thick manuscripts on these animals that he had read to me some years before, which he, if you will remember, envisioned as chapters of a proposed five-part mono-graph to be called the *Ichthyologia*. While he was quite willing to show me the texts of his introductory bibliography (*Bibliotheca Ichthyologica*) and the philosophy that he proposed to apply to the study of fishes (*Philosophia Ichthyologica*), he was not of a mind to make me privy to the real meat of his work, a denial which surprised me very much. Hoping then to receive an oral survey of his system of classification, including perhaps a list of the genera and species that he recognized, along with descriptions, I was further astonished to witness ARTEDI's reluctance to offer up even this rather small information. This was not the gener-ous ARTEDI whom once I knew. He instead expressed his desire to hold on to these original ideas for his own. I learned later that in London, a colleague—perhaps it was SLOANE himself—had advised him to hold things closer to himself; otherwise, he would have nothing to show for it in the end. Quite disappointed by his rebuff, I did well at that moment to hide my outrage, thinking that more gentle coercion at some later date might better get me what I wanted. But several days later, in pri-vate conversation with SOHLBERG, my anger rose again, such that, in a moment of weakness, I intimated to this friend my wish to see ARTEDI removed from my midst.

Still sitting in that dismal room, with wineglass again refilled, I did my best to set aside my bitter disappointment for the time and sought to turn ARTEDI's attention to another work that had occupied much of my time that summer, and which I had brought with me to his quarters that same afternoon, hoping to receive his advice and suggestions. This was my manuscript for what I thought to call *Bibliotheca Botanica*, which I described to you earlier. As I was reading my text aloud, I soon saw in him an ever-increasing annoyance and lack of interest that greatly intensified my anxiety, thinking that perhaps he saw in it too much that was his. Interrupting me more than once, he finally took over the purpose of my visit by reading out loud to me a revised version of his *Philosophia Ichthyologica*. This total reversal of my intentions left me aghast. Though now quite anxious to leave that place and get to work at my other tasks, I was not allowed to depart until he had read his Philosophy from beginning to end. I, in return, did my best to communicate to him those criticisms that occurred to me concerning the laws of systematization—surprisingly and dangerously similar to my own—which he had there proposed. In every particular case, however, where I had any suggestion or criticism to offer, he seemed prepared to vindicate his own opinion to my entire discomfort. He mentioned also, after the reading was done, that he meant to publish in collected form all the works on fishes that he had up till that time written, and that he was only waiting until his labor for SEBA should be completed to put the final touches on them to make them ready for the press. And so in this way I was held there in that dingy space, listening to his banter, far beyond the time I had intended to stay. Our discussion had far exceeded my limits of attention and my patience had long begun to fail. I did my very best to swallow my repugnance and made my good-byes in the most cordial way possible considering the difficult circumstances. Though it may appear that I reacted without charity to a person whom I once so deeply loved, in all truth, until such time that I could be satisfied of my needs, it was his selfish attitude that caused a cold and painful rift between us. But had I known at the time that this would be my last sight of him alive, I may well have behaved quite differently.

*   *   *

Stymied for the while, not knowing quite how to proceed, and realizing I could not readily go on with my work without accurate characterization of the fishes—such knowledge of which only ARTEDI could provide—I turned to several other of my manuscripts, which I thought could be completed in the interim. Later, as it turned out, under circumstances never expected, but of which I will soon relate, I acquired, in mid-November 1735, full and personal possession of all of ARTEDI's writings. Upon close examination of these treasures, for which I had yearned so long, I was startled to see what good he had done with the fishes. His index of synonyms was astonishing, as was the detail given to his orders, the genera and their characters, the species with their names and definitions, etc. I quickly incorporated all that was needed to complete my manuscript for the *Systema Naturae*. After presenting the finished result to my patrons GRONOVIUS and LAWSON, and receiving their enthusiastic approval, I presented the final copy in late November 1735 to the publishing house of THEODOR HAAK in Leiden, where, incidentally, it was to be sold at 2 ½ guilders per specimen. After I had waited impatiently for another several weeks, the delay being the result of undisclosed problems at the printing office of JOHAN WILLEM GROOT, the thing finally appeared. Receiving word that the printing had been completed on 9 December, I hurried to Leiden, where on 13 December I saw my first copy. O happy day—what a grand culmination to my many years of hard effort! Countless well-deserved accolades came to me from all directions, but I specially remember the fine letter to Sir HANS SLOANE, dated 19 December 1735, one of several sent to learned men in civilized societies everywhere, penned jointly by GRO-NOVIUS and LAWSON to accompany presentation copies of my work:

> Some months ago came to this city Dr. CAROLUS LINNAEUS from Sweden, a person very well known by his knowledge in Natural History, for which reason he was sent by the *Societas Regiae Uppsaliensis* to Lapland, where he hath discovered several things not before known, which possibly ere long will be published. He was so kind to communicate to us his *Systema Naturae*, which we sent to the press at our own expense, with an intention only to have a few copies; but at the request of several friends we were determined to communicate it fully, judging that it might be agreeable to the Learned World. Wherefore we take the Liberty to represent you a copy, and request you will also make the other acceptable to the Royal Society, of which you are deservedly president.
>
> We are, Sir, your most obedient and humble servants
>
> JOH. FRED. GRONOVIUS
> ISAAC LAWSON
> Leiden, 19 December 1735

You may think this but muted praise, but from the likes of these two highly esteemed gentlemen, it was glorious tribute indeed. A small start also it may seem to you, but it was this single minuscule publication that changed the world. There have subsequently appeared no less than sixteen editions of this work. While some of these have been stolen by unscrupulous authors and publishers, at least twelve of them, each enlarged and improved over the last, have been produced under my own personal supervision. The latest edition was printed in three octavo volumes from 1766 to 1768, containing altogether some 2,300 pages. I am content in the certainty that many more printings will follow after my earthly demise. Full of sincere gratitude to Lawson—who, by the way and most unfortunately, died in 1747 while still quite young—I later named in his honor *Lawsonia*, the henna of the East. To my other patron, for whom even greater appreciation was due, I described *Gronovia* as a climbing plant that grasps all other plants, being called after a man who had few rivals as a collector of nature's bounty.

In closing this part of my story, I address the following passage to those of you who would question the importance of my *Systema Naturae*. Hoping not to repeat what has already been said, I hereby take liberty to leave you with this summary of my contentions:

> Wisdom's first step consists in knowing things in themselves. Knowledge consists in a true idea of objects, and, by the properties with which the Creator has endowed them, to distinguish the similar from the dissimilar so that this knowledge can be communicated to others by affixing a name to each thing to distinguish each from the others; for if the name be lost, the knowledge of the thing is also lost. For these shall be the basis of literacy without which none can read, for, in ignorance of the particular subject, no accurate description can be transmitted, or accurate demonstration made but only errors committed. Method is the soul of science.

CHAPTER 9

Supper with SEBA

I do remember an apothecary,
And in his shop a tortoise hung,
An alligator stuff'd, and other skins
Of ill-shaped fishes; and about his shelves
Green earthen pots, bladders, and musty seeds,
Remnants of packthread, and old cakes of roses,
Were thickly scatter'd to make up a show.

—SHAKESPEARE, *Romeo and Juliet*, Act 5, Scene 1, Lines 37 ff

OUR BRILLIANT ichthyologist had, for some two months, been working in the employ of SEBA at the latter gentleman's house on the Haarlemmerdijk where all the best resources required for zoological study had been made available to him, including, of course, an extraordinary and sizeable collection of preserved fishes. It was the identification and description of these watery animals that formed the subject of the work toward which ARTEDI was directed. You will recall that this well-to-do amateur had just published two great volumes in folio, his so-called *Locupletissimus rerum Naturalium Thesauri*, abbreviated by most as simply the *Thesaurus*, but which, on the whole, might better be called *An Exact Description of the Principal Natural Curiosities in the Magnificent Cabinet of* ALBERTUS SEBA. It was here in these two books that the animals in his collection were described and illustrated, the first volume appearing in 1734, the second in early 1735. Though still quite fresh from the well-respected publishing house of JANSSONIUS VAN WAESBERGE, WETTSTEIN, and SMITH of Amsterdam, the work had already received wide acclaim, so sumptuous, luxurious, and costly was the design. It can quite easily be said, in all truth, that no other composition up to that time gave such a full and all-inclusive indication of the variety of earthly living things. A good measure of its worth and the profound influence it had on learned men everywhere is the large quantity of references made to it in the works of others. I myself, especially in my later editions of the *Systema Naturae*, have used these excellent books to my very good advantage.

The first volume of the *Thesaurus* contains the greater quantity of the plants, the quadrupeds, birds—the latter including some rather curious flying creatures of the bat genus *Vespertilio*, a kind of animal that I showed rather well in my *Systema Naturae* to belong not to the bird class, but with the mammals—and most of the amphibians and reptiles, especially the frog, lizard, turtle, and crocodile kind. Of greatest interest among these latter groups is quite elaborately and accurately displayed on Plate 78. Here is shown the extraordinary change, or should we say metamorphosis, of a kind of South American frog, from eggs to sperm-shaped off-spring, each of which eventually, by sprouting arms and legs, takes the form of a four-footed amphibious creature, after which it later becomes a fully formed fish—presented by SEBA as a miraculous truth of nature never before made public but, in reality, certainly a baseless fable. Also well worth taking note of here is a rare fetus of an Indian elephant, *Elephas maximus*, shown on Plate 111, which is placed next to a fetal human being of the fair gender, with her tiny hands out front, almost as if in prayer, and suspended by a narrow thread in a sealed jar of spirits.

Looking now at the second volume of SEBA's great masterpiece, it is quite easy to see that Serpentologia, the study of Serpents—or *Slangen* as the Dutch call them—takes up by far the most space. Wanting to know the full extent of this enormous collection—at least the part of it that was displayed so elegantly in the *Thesaurus*—which must truly have been one of the largest of its kind in the world, I counted 325 of these wormy and phallic creatures shown so beautifully slithering over those folio pages. Surely old SEBA must have had a strange and inordinate fondness for these animals that put such fear in the hearts of men and, I dare say, our women, even more. Especially interesting here among these many serpents is the skeleton of a very large snake of the constrictor kind shown on Plate 108, demonstrating well the parts of the backbone, the head, and the jaws, with their strong and numerous toothy fangs. It was claimed by those in a position to know that SEBA got this and other beautifully preserved skeletons by feeding the animals to hordes of tiny insects that he allowed to grow and multiply in a large wooden barrel in his cellar. Of further interest in this regard is a curious paper published by our collector in the *Philosophical Transactions of the Royal Society of London* for 1730—that highly esteemed serial that devotes itself to valuable treatises on medicine, natural philosophy, mathematics, and other such important subjects as these, but strictly rejects any theological nonsense (by the latter, I, the most religious of men, refer only to vain cavils, or doctrines supported from interest, or party spirit, certainly not conviction). It is here that SEBA gave away the secrets, once so tightly held by FREDERIK RUYSCH, of how to make skeletons of leaves and fruits. It was RUYSCH, you will remember—that celebrated physician and professor of anatomy at The Hague—who made himself so famous by acquiring ways to preserve human bodies in such a fashion as to keep them soft and pliable, as well as attractive to observe, for many years after their death. His collection of human and animal corpses was indeed marvelous. The finest tissues of organ and muscle, and of capillary vessels of blood and lymph, were perfused and precisely filled by needle injection with a waxy colored fluid so as to represent the tone, the luster, and the freshness of youth, and to imitate sleep rather than death. The carcasses, with all their viscera, were far from having a nauseous smell, as one might guess, but instead took on a rather pleasant perfume, this too in cases where they smelled very strong before the procedure. In this way, assisted by his wife and children who greatly shared in his interest, RUYSCH preserved entire bodies of infants, as well as those of young and adult specimens, in a flawless state of mummification. His museum in Amsterdam, situated on the south side of the Bloemgracht only six houses from the Prinsengracht, was thus filled with cadavers arranged in amusing and agreeable attitudes, often to express dramatic gestures—a perfect necropolis, all the inhabitants of which were asleep and ready to speak as soon as they were awakened. This display became the desired destination of visitors of every sort, from generals and ambassadors to princes and even kings. Everyone was made happy by the opportunity of examining it. But, unlike his secrets pertaining to the anatomical preparation of vegetables, his confidential recipes for making corpses seem as if alive he took with him to the grave when he died of a fever on 22 February 1731, in the ninety-second year of his age.

Well before the time of my arrival in Holland in June of 1735, RUYSCH's museum had been closed and his collection widely dispersed. Some of the objects had been purchased at auction by Professor GAUBIUS—of whom you shall hear more later—but a much greater part was acquired by JOHN SOBIESKI, the King of Poland, who, it is said, paid 20,000 Dutch florins and had it removed to his native country. Unable then in Amsterdam to personally examine any part of it—to thus judge for myself the quality of its contents—you can well imagine my surprise and joy to later come across a small bit of it during my visit to England in July of 1736. Upon personal invitation of Sir HANS SLOANE himself, I had the pleasure to examine, on the 28th day of that month, the artifacts in the museum of the Royal Society of London. Among the large number of cabinets filled with natural objects of every sort, was a side table bearing the weight of a large wooden box. Contained within was a well-preserved assortment of parts of the human body, which, as told to me by SLOANE—who, in fact, went out of his way to make certain that I knew of these precious things—had been presented to the Royal Society by RUYSCH on 23 October 1718. With the collection was a document copied from the *Journal Book of the Royal Society* for the years 1714-1720 that read as follows:

> From Dr. RUYSCH of Amsterdam, Nine several specimens of parts of the Human Body very curiously prepared, by filling up with a sort of wax or other Balsamine substance, the most minute filaments of the Arteries and Veins:
>
>> *First:* A small piece of a Man's skin, Exhibiting the smallest Ramifications of the blood vessels on the inner and outer surfaces; these require a Convex Glass and the Beams of the sun to be seen to advantage.
>>
>> *Second:* A portion of the *Placenta Utorina* so prepared and ordered that the whole appears vascular without Glands.
>>
>> *Third:* A part of the *Intestinum Rectum* of a Man lively Represented.

Fourth: The Head of a Child curiously preserved, seeming better to represent the life than wax-work.

Fifth: A Human Testicle wholly resolved into its filaments, which seem like a lock of Wool without any glandulous substance therein.

Sixth: The *Pia Matter* of a Boy in which the Number and minuteness of the vessels is very Remarkable, all filled and Distended with a Balsamick substance whence a judgment may be made of the penetration of this Matter and of the Art of injecting it.

Seventh: A portion of the *Intestinum Duodenum* of a Man, with its Wrinkles and Valves preserved after the same manner.

Eighth: The Ear of a Woman, Appearing as if alive.

Ninth: A Bit of the Membrane in which innumerable vessels shew themselves; By it the curiosity of the Art by which these Injections are performed is very manifest.

Ordered that a Box be provided with a Lock and Key, to preserve these great rarities from Dust and other Damages that they be shewn with care so as not to be injured.

Ordered that Dr. HALLEY in the Name of the Society Do give Dr. RUYSCH their humble thanks for this Noble present.

With great interest, I carefully examined each piece, expressing to my generous host my wonder at the delicacy of their manufacture and vouching for their exquisite beauty. But with this talk of old Dr. RUYSCH and his anatomical preparations, I have once again strayed widely from my main purpose—let me now return to SEBA's *Thesaurus*.

Scattered between both volumes of this most delightful *opus*, in a rather haphazard way, are to be found various insects—of which I remember mostly butterflies and ants, but also a grasshopper—spiders, millipedes, scorpions, mollusks, and some crustaceans. Also pictured is a quite good collection of those strange lumps of uncertain function that people are wont to call bezoars, or what the learned more properly refer to as *lapides animantium variorum*, those stones or concretions often and variously found within the alimentary organs of certain ruminant quadrupeds and which are generally but falsely believed to have magical properties.

But these two large books, as thick and weighty as they were—all together consisting of some 366 pages of text and 225 plates, each of the latter showing numerous objects, all very precisely drawn and beautifully colored—did not contain even half of the curiosities in SEBA's collection. Thus, as you may well imagine, the author of these volumes, getting on in years and not knowing how much time was left for him—and, indeed, feeling quite fortunate that he had lived to see the first two books—was very eager to see the remaining in print. Two more volumes of approximately equal size were now proposed and efforts toward completion of volume three were well along: nearly all the copper plates, including twelve devoted specifically to the fishes, were at this time finished and what little more was needed as to text was to be supplied by ARTEDI. Alas, the old man, gray-faced, gross and stumbling of body, but still jovial and sharp of mind as ever, was, at this time in the early winter of 1735, close to his end. But no one then gave a moment's thought that he would succumb to the pull of death so soon, in little more than half a year.

On 30 April 1736, after suffering for some weeks from colic, SEBA, at age 70 years, made his last testament, and on 2 May, with great dignity despite his near intolerable pain, he departed this world—six days later he was buried in the Westerkerk. This unexpected demise led to such profound difficulties among his heirs in the settling of his estate that publication of volumes three and four were considerably delayed. In fact, if rumor proves truthful, even after the estate was finally settled some six years later, the daughters—of whom SEBA was blessed with no less than four, by way of his youthful and comely wife ANNA LOOPES, daughter of ENGEL LOOPES from the Egelantiersgracht—and their husbands fought bitterly over the publication of the *Thesaurus* not able to decide on who should pay for what part, etc. In fact, it seemed for a time that the remaining volumes were not likely to ever appear, and that these heirs, quarrelling for SEBA's purse as they were, cared more about money than the fame of the deceased. But, in the end, this was not the case, a result for which we can only thank the Lord. Yet, still, the third of this series, containing the fishes, worms, mollusks, testaceans, lithophytes, and zoophytes, was not made available to the public until 1759; and the fourth, which pages encompassed the insects, minerals, and fossils, in 1765. I well recall my infinite pleasure upon seeing those newly produced works, which were by far of a significantly higher quality than the initial two. This improvement was obviously due to the fine editorship of AERNOUT VOSMAER, who you will no doubt recall was then employed as director of the cabinet of natural and other valuables of his Highness the PRINCE OF ORANGE. It was this VOSMAER who in 1752 was given charge to finish the task of production. The changes that he made for the better are best seen in the descriptive text, which is considerably less replete with accounts of the wonders of the color pattern, and which is without undue reliance on the use of superlatives in an attempt to portray the beauties of the different forms. So too, the individual drawings on the plates are ordered according to systematical principles in a way that is largely missing in the earlier volumes.

*   *   *

But returning now to *Die Deutsche Apotheke* on the Haarlemmerdijk, during that ill-fated summer of 1735, our ARTEDI occupied himself with the undertaking that I have described, working during day-light hours, but also deep into the night by the light of flickering candles, plodding along slowly, but meticulously, as was his style. He devoted himself fully and intently to this task, with old SEBA doing his best to push him along in the work. Annoyed by this unwelcome and continual poking into what he considered to be his personal territory, and not liking also the constant interruptions of inquisitive visitors, ARTEDI began to take specimens away to his own quarters on the Warmoesstraat, where he could conduct his lucubrations in silence. Here he sat day by day in the semi-darkness, quite alone, but seemingly happy with his books and specimens. And, other than this, when not sleeping, he occupied his time at the Unicorn some few doors down the street, or more often at the tavern of JAAP DE KREEK—which public house, by the way, had been in that same business under various other names since 1619—on the nearby corner of the Warmoesstraat and Nieuwe-brugsteeg, just across from the sign of the Lompen. I might mention here also—if it is truly to be believed, and something tells me we should not—that our ichthyologist had once been observed at the establishment of Madame TRAESE on the Prinsengracht, where one could find every kind of earthly pleasure regardless of gender.

ARTEDI's blatant abandonment of the comfortable space provided by SEBA, and the consequent circumvention of oversight that was the main cause of his move, became a growing irritation for the old man. As the days and weeks went by, he saw less and less of ARTEDI, the latter visiting the big house on the Haarlemmerdijk only to leave off specimens and to pick up new ones. By making this change, however, ARTEDI's efficiency, not surprisingly, increased somewhat, but still, for anyone looking on, the work was decidedly slow, yet ever coming closer to the final goal.

In all, there came before him some 200 fishes, some dried, stuffed, and mounted on wooden pedestals, but most in tall, slender glass bottles of spirits, each sealed with a tightly fitting red top. By far the majority of these specimens were said to have come from Amboina and Surinam, which localities should be of no great surprise to us, both places being Dutch colonies, the first in the Molucca or Spice Islands of the East Indies, the second in Dutch Guiana in the northeastern part of South America. Objects of natural history such as these, as well as all sorts of unnatural mementoes and curiosities that made up his collection, were often given to SEBA as gifts to gain his patronage. But more usually these things were purchased by him from sailors or merchant-travelers returning from distant, mostly tropical parts of the world. In fact, it is said that he, upon learning of returning vessels, would hasten aboard these newly arrived ships, selling and distributing his medicinals among the crew, who were invariably exhausted and sick. By these means, it was rather easy for him to get from them at very good prices the curiosities they had brought from the Indies, from Africa, and from the Americas. It was generally well understood also that he was always careful to sell his duplicates at much higher prices than he paid, so that his hobby was not an occupation that cost him much money—rather it was a good source of happy profit. And so it was, in this way, that over the space of time, with his excellent aptitude for business, joined with a great veneration for the Creation and an inexhaustible enthusiasm for collecting its curiosities, our SEBA was able to bring together such a vast and diverse assemblage of objects.

Early in his investigation, ARTEDI found that some of the specimens laid before him were duplicates of one another, forms representing the same species, but still, from it all, he was able to distinguish no less than 107 different kinds—in fact, this is the number that he reported to me as resulting from his tedious examination, and the quantity later verified by me by my own consulting of the manuscript of his work left behind. By far most of these various kinds were then new to science and without names. Thus it was that our determined ichthyologist—with the drawings of the fishes, numbering a total of 141, already engraved and printed on twelve folio sheets, and made available to him for his easy comparison—closely examined each and every specimen. He carefully measured lengths, widths, and diameters; counted spines, rays, and scales; made note of the shape of the body, of the head, and of the tail; recorded the position of the fins, the placement of eyes, the relationship of the bones of the upper jaw, the presence or absence of teeth, whether there was but a single nostril on each side of the snout or two. With great intensity he worked to analyze the pattern of pigmentation, as well as it could be done on such long-dead fishes, bleached and dehydrated as they were from the effects of the strong, odorous fluids by which they were preserved. So too did he look inside the body of every fish, taking notice of the presence or absent of a gas-filled sac, whether the liver was of one piece or divided to form two or three separate parts, the shape and position of the urinary bladder, the size of the ventricle of the heart, the length of the intestine, the number of pyloric caeca, etc., etc.

While he applied himself diligently to this necessarily initial part of the work—and by this I mean the purely descriptive and comparative analysis—he labored to assign well-meaning and pleasant sounding names to each kind, as he understood them to apply to the various orders, families, genera, and species. To every genus, he gave a single name. For example, whereas before there were more than fourteen names attached to members of the herring genus, he brought them all together under the name *Clupea*, the original Latin appellation applied to those oily fishes by the ancients. Of added benefit to nomenclature, he was careful to substitute new names for all those that then referred to other kinds of animals, thinking that no two unrelated groups of objects in nature should share the same generic name. He was scrupulous also in his choosing of names, adopting only those that were of Latin or Greek origin and being ruthless in rejecting all others.

Resulting from this hard and painstaking labor was a draft of a manuscript, some 85 pages in length, to which he gave for title *Manuscriptum Ichthyologicum quod Petrus Artedi elaboravit in Usum Thesauri Sebai* (Ichthyological Manuscript Compiled by PETER ARTEDI For the Use of SEBA's Collection), in which he laid out everything in a clear and concise order: an ichthyological treatise describing more than a hundred of the principal fishes of Amboina and Surinam, which are arranged according to the natural method, with their distinct genera and new specific differences, and with the principal synonyms used by authors in previous descriptions.

All of this was very well and good, and altogether acceptable to SEBA his employer, but how well I recall ARTEDI's woeful complaints about the figures of the fishes, already engraved at great expense, and surely not to be done over! While the species described on paper by ARTEDI were neatly and accurately arranged or grouped, each within their own proper genus—and likewise the genera, such as they were, arranged in like manner, within maniples or families—the individual drawings themselves were scattered haphazard over the page, the position of each on any one plate determined not by natural order or relationship, but purely by the available space at the engraver's disposal. And so it was, for example, that the fishes given by Plate 23 were shown in rather good order, with porcupine fishes and spiny puffers arranged together in a neat and tidy way, but Plate 24 was, by our friend, referred to as a wild abomination: nineteen fishes, mostly of the boxfish and cowfish kind, floating over the page as if dead in a stagnant pond, some drifting up, others down, one upside down completely, and some, in fact, overlapping each other. Quite the same he said of Plate 29, which contains a host of meandering catfishes, but also a butterflyfish, several gobies, and a sturgeon shown with its belly up. This strange juxtaposition of species—so declared ARTEDI, and I am quite ready to agree with him—defies all natural order. But knowing that the plates could not, under any circumstance, be made right, and with extreme effort to think away what some might call petty details, ARTEDI put all his concentration into making perfect that which he said about each species. And what glorious consistency and perspicuity did he then bring to each and every account! What beauty of arrangement and precision did he bring to the porcupinefishes, boxfishes, cowfishes, and puffers, of which he gave good proof of no less than sixteen species. All of these forms he assigned to *Ostracion*, a single genus of his own naming, but an amalgamation of species that I would have surely divided among three genera: *Ostracion*, *Diodon*, and *Tetraodon*.

Well differentiated and described by him too were the triggerfishes, surgeonfishes, and butterflyfishes of the genera *Balistes*, *Teuthis*, and *Chaetodon*; the scorpionfishes, wrasses, and the shark-sucker, placed within *Scorpaena*, *Labrus*, and *Echeneis*; the gobies, porgies, and the zebra shark, assigned to *Gobius*, *Sparus*, and *Squalus*. All of these above mentioned fishes were inhabitants of the salty domain, but there were also many from the sweet waters of the rivers tributary to the great Amazon: whiskered catfishes of divers kinds, belonging to *Silurus* and *Loricaria*; numerous attenuate and tapering eels of the genus *Gymnotus*; and a most peculiar fish having four eyes that ARTEDI called *Anableps*.

ANABLEPS. *Arted. Gen.* 20. *p.* 25. *n.* 1: *Synon. p.* 43. *n.* 1

About this last mentioned fish, it is truly one of the most curious of all aquatic animals; nay, might I say of all animals, whether they be watery or land-dwelling by habit. It is quite true that this fish has four eyes, and, for all to see, ARTEDI gives the evidence for it. While giving clever drawings of the ocular parts, all finely labeled—which artwork was later made available to SEBA's engraver for the making of small additions to the final rendering of Plate 34, and which, fortunately, fit rather well between the large fishes already engraved on the copper—he explained in his text that this animal likes to swim on the surface of the water, the upper two eyes protruding into the air above, giving clear sight of possible enemies, while the lower pair looks down into the depths, watching for things to feed upon. Now, if this story had been told by some traveler, claiming to have seen it even with his own eyes, I would be loath to believe a word of it, but here is the real proof: ARTEDI's admirable description, together with the specimen itself, so well preserved in SEBA's cabinet.

Laboring long and hard through the summer and into the autumn of 1735, ARTEDI's work was coming to completion by late September—in fact, as rumor had it, only six specimens were yet to be included in the whole. It was at this time, that SEBA, as he was wont to do, announced a dinner party for friends and business associates at his house. It was to be, at least in small part, a celebration of the near completion of the enormous manuscript for the third volume of his *Thesaurus*, which, so he thought, would soon be ready for the presses. To this social gathering, reserved for Tuesday evening, 27 September, invitations were extended to a rather select few. Some of those favored were already then living in the big house on the Haarlemmerdijk, which residence was always full of people, or so it seemed. There was, of course, the old man and his wife ANNA, but also, at this time, the youngest of their daughters, JOHANNA—then 25 years of age, the other daughters having left their parents to live with their husbands some years ago—and her husband of less than a year ROELAND WILLEM VAN HOMRIGH, who, by the way, after the death of SEBA, got the house as part of his inheritance. In addition, there were always two or three resident apprentice apothecaries, not to mention the servants, all of whom required space. But the great house, with its five stories, provided quite ample room to lodge them all in good comfort. Of these apprentices, two were in SEBA's employ at the time, both Germans, natives of the country that was more favored by SEBA than any other. The first was PHILIP KEERSEBERGH who had begun his employment in January 1726 and stayed on till SEBA's death in early May 1736; the other was JOHANNES GÜNTHER who joined in November 1733, contracted for a period of two years. Invitations were extended to both these able gentlemen, but only the former accepted. GÜNTHER begged to be excused to meet prior obligations to a lady friend, who, as I later learned, was of rather questionable character.

Another on the list, who quickly replied in the affirmative, was Dr. HIERONYMUS GAUBIUS, professor of medicine and chemistry at Leiden, and just about of my own age, who was in Amsterdam that week for the purpose of calling upon that wealthy but ridiculous amateur CHRISTOFFEL BEUDEKER to seek permission to examine certain coccionellid coleopterans in the latter's cabinet. While in no way rivaling that of SEBA, GAUBIUS himself maintained an extensive cabinet of natural history in which anatomical preparations took precedence over the rest. A good part of his collection had been purchased by him at the public sale of the property of RUYSCH—to whom quick reference has already been made—which took place on 15 August 1731, some six months after the death of the latter. It was this same GAUBIUS who assisted with the *Thesaurus* by translating SEBA's Dutch text into Latin, a service for which the former received little thanks, for an acknowledgment of such is not to be found anywhere in those great volumes.

Graciously accepting the offer also was the French newsmonger LOUIS RENARD who was then living on the Herengracht at the corner of the Reguliersgracht. This last mentioned fellow had early been in the book trade, but later established for himself a curious and highly lucrative business as joint agent for His Britannick Majesty and for Hannover at Amsterdam. In this capacity he had been over the years engaged in numerous clandestine and surreptitious negotiations, so secret that nothing whatsoever is known about them. But more curious still—and of special interest to the old chemist—was RENARD's occupation with the selling of certain medicinals, the recipes for which had been held in strict concealment. One of these products was a *Tincture de Tartre*, the claimed effect of which was the immediate elimination of boils, pustules, and other eruptions of the skin. Another one, more valuable still, was called *Beaume de Réunion* or *Beau Céne*, said to heal thoroughly all sorts of fractures in children within eight weeks, and in older people within a slightly longer period; a bottle sold for eight guilders, or one could agree to pay for the entire cure with a money-back guarantee: you apply a plaster, which in the evening is moistened with only ten to twenty small droplets. Now it was that SEBA, for many more years than he would want to admit, had sought unsuccessfully to learn of the contents of these therapeutic curatives and thus RENARD was a frequent guest at *Die Deutsche Apotheke*, where the wine was never enough to pry loose the facts of those closely held ingredients.

I too was graciously put on SEBA's list of dinner guests, but, con-cocting a quite believable opposing offer for that same evening at CLIFFORD's house on the Hartekamp, I gave my most profound apol-ogies, suggesting instead that my tender mate SOHLBERG be invited in my place, which proposal was accepted after some subtle coercion on my part. Finally, there was ARTEDI, who was happy to accept, not because of the social intercourse, for which he was not especially eager, but rather for critical need of a good meal, not to mention the ample drink that was sure to be made available.

Early on that fateful day, Tuesday, 27 September, my dear SOHL-BERG made me an unexpected visit to Hartekamp. I took this occasion to show him around the splendid gardens. We spoke at first of trivial matters of no special import, but as we strolled among the epiphytic orchids in the hothouse next to the orangery, I turned the conversa-tion abruptly away from the former drivel to the subject of my *Systema Naturae* and my inability to complete that section pertaining to the fishes. I feel required to admit that I blamed this conundrum on the unreasonable and thoroughly unwarranted selfishness of ARTEDI, and I sought to put the problem in the larger context of how this genius, in his slowness and lack of self-confidence, was a serious deterrent to the advance of science. Later that afternoon, as we took food and drink together, I sought to reinforce my criticisms with good examples of what could be accomplished in the way of publication if certain obsta-cles were removed. SOHLBERG, thoroughly in love with me still, just as he had been since we first met as students at Uppsala, kept his silence on this subject, but it was then I knew there was nothing he would not do for me.

Having occupied SOHLBERG at Hartekamp considerably longer than I had intended, I sent him off on the 4 o'clock towboat, which got him back to Amsterdam and to SEBA's place by 8 that same evening. His arrival was somewhat late, a serious and unwarranted irritation for the old man, but it was well before the social gathering had reached its climax. As SOHLBERG sat himself down at the big table at his place reserved next to ARTEDI—where in the center lay a large platter of fresh oysters made more elegant by an array of parsley and quartered lemons—RENARD was speaking with enthusiasm of a demonstration of a curious electric machine, around which, only two days before, thousands of Amsterdammers crowded together to witness. RENARD himself had been electrified, so he said, and I have no reason to doubt his story, though it seems rather incredible: holding the machine with one hand, he could set fire with the other to a spoonful of brandy; when another person took his place he seemed to be able to draw sparks from RENARD across two pairs of stockings, without burning them or causing him any pain whatsoever. Thinking these results to be of delightful entertainment for the naive and uninformed, but of nothing else at all of any good to society, he spoke disparagingly of those who would pretend otherwise. But it was at this point that GAUBIUS interjected, disagreeing heartily with this presumption and describing some electrical experiments told to him by letter received recently from Mr. CROMWELL MORTIMER, Medical Doctor and Secretary of the Royal Society of London:

> Take a small iron globe of an inch or inch and a half diameter, which set on the middle of a cake of rosin of about seven or eight inches diameter, having first excited the cake by gently rubbing it, clapping it three or four times with the hands, or warming it a little before the fire. Then fasten a light body, as a small piece of cork, or pith of elder, to an exceeding fine thread, five or six inches long, which hold between your finger and thumb, exactly over the globe, at such a height that the cork, or other light

body, may hang down about the middle of the globe. This light body will of itself begin to move round the iron globe, and that movement always being from west to east, the same direction that the planets have in their orbits round the sun. If the cake of rosin be circular, and the iron globe placed exactly in the centre of it, then the light body will describe an orbit round the iron globe, which will be a circle; but if the iron globe be placed at any distance from the centre of the circular cake, then the light body will describe an elliptical orbit, which will have the same excentricity as the distance of the globe from the center of the cake. If the cake of rosin be of an elliptic form, and the iron globe be placed in the center of it, the light body will describe an elliptical orbit of the same excentricity as the form of the cake. If the iron globe be placed in or near one of the focuses of the elliptic cake, the light body will move much swifter in the apogeè part of the orbit, than in the perigeè part, contrary to what is observed of the Planets.

Somewhat overly excited by his own recitation of these experiments, GAUBIUS did his best to contradict RENARD's cynical conclusion by making known to what useful purpose these findings may be applied. He did not doubt, for example, that MORTIMER, with continued study of such phenomena, would be able, but in a short time, to astonish the world with a new sort of planetarium never before thought of, and that from these experiments might be established a certain theory for accounting for the motions of the grand Planetarium of the Universe.

GAUBIUS was about to rattle on further about this when SEBA, the excellent host that he was, interrupted with another offer to fill the wineglasses all around—which good attendance he had been proficient in throughout the evening—paying particular attention to ARTEDI, knowing how much he enjoyed his drink, and seeing how often and how quickly his glass was emptied. Being a right practical man, curious, but moderate in his thinking, and knowing well the world, the old gentleman doubted aloud that small balls of iron and suspended bits of cork would or could improve man's knowledge of cosmology. But he did not hesitate to tell then of another curious series of electrical experiments made some years past at the house of Mr. WHELER on the Heilige Weg. It seems that this WHELER had procured silk lines strong enough to bear the weight of his footboy, a good stout lad who had been in WHELER's employ some six months. Despite strong objections from the boy, he was then suspended above the floor upon the lines and, for all to witness, a strongly electrified tube of glass was applied to his feet or sometimes to his hands, the result being that when the finger of anyone who stood by was held near the hands or face of the boy, the observer found himself pricked or burnt, as it were, by a spark of fire. At the same time, a loud, sharp crackle or snapping noise was heard. But these same reactions did not occur when the observers applied their hands to any part of the boy's body through his clothes, except upon his legs, which touching caused the boy some considerable pain through his stockings, although his stockings were very thick. Similar experiments were then tried upon several species of animals, including a large white cock, still living, both whole and with its feathers stripped, producing the same general results. Again using a large sirloin of beef that came from an ox that had been killed two days before, fingers held near any part of it resulted in the same snapping, but the sound was thought not to be quite as loud as when the experiment was made on the cock.

And so it went throughout the evening, a convivial time for all, when at half-past midnight ARTEDI, who had hardly uttered a word until then, and by this time was well along toward a state of drunken incapacitation, turned the conversation away from electrical physics to an altogether new and unusual method of castrating fishes, about which he had heard tell at the fish market only that very morning. Several at the table, wanting to understand the utility of such a practice, prompted the following explanation, well told by ARTEDI: fishes with their gonads removed, whether they be male or female, have been shown quite conclusively to grow much larger than their usual size, adding a considerably greater amount of fat, and doing so in much quicker time. In England, for example, where in many parts sea-fishes are in great plenty, the fishes of rivers and of ponds are less esteemed, and thus improvements, either with regard to their bulk or increase, are less attended to. But in other places, southern Germany, for instance, remote from the sea, where pond-fishes are a great article of commercial traffic, castration, and this proven method for accomplishing it, may be of important use. He then explained in detail how it is done: the fish must be held firmly in a wet cloth, with its belly upwards. Then, with a pen-knife exceedingly sharp, its point bent backward, or other adapted instrument, the operator cuts through the integument, while he carefully avoids wounding the intestines. As soon as a small aperture is made, he carefully inserts a hooked pen-knife, and with this he dilates this aperture from between the two fore-fins, almost to the anus. He then, with two small blunt silver hooks, of five or six inches long, by the help of an assistant, holds open the belly of the fish; and, with a spoon or spatula, moves carefully the intestines from one side. When these are displaced, you see the ureter, a small vessel, nearly in the direction of the spine; and at the same time the ovaries, be it female, or the testes, be it a male. After the proper identification, you snip the ducts and holding membranes of the gonads with a pair of sharp scissors, remembering all the while to take great care not to wound, or otherwise injure, the intestines. Once this is performed, you sew up the divided integuments of the belly with silk, inserting the stitches at a very small distance one from the other.

*　　*　　*

At this point, it being nearly one o'clock in the morning, KEERSE-BERGH, overly tired by now and badly wanting to relieve himself—and, I dare say, not interested to hear more of this rather unpleasant, almost nasty account—pushed himself back from the table and, giving gracious thanks to SEBA for a most delightful evening, stumbled to his room upstairs. GAUBIUS followed soon thereafter, extolling the fine meal and brilliant conversation, and promising to reciprocate soon with a social gathering of his own, if only SEBA and the others might see their way to his place in Leiden. Then it was SOHLBERG and ARTEDI who, after expressing similar appreciations to their kindly host, made their departure. Once outside SEBA's door, SOHLBERG, bidding ARTEDI a hearty good-night, turned away, seemingly to abandon his drunken colleague to make his way home alone along the Haarlemmerdijk. But once hidden by shadow and darkness, the former gentlemen reversed his course, following closely and undetected on the heals of his tottering friend.

Now under normal circumstances, in the full light of day, ARTEDI, traversing at a leisurely stroll the short distance from Seba's house to his room on the Warmoesstraat, would certainly have required no more than 15 minutes and, if in a hurry, the walk could be done in perhaps as little as 10 minutes. But in the thick darkness of that late September night, without aid of a lantern—which, some were surprised to learn later, had not been offered by SEBA—severely disoriented by drink, ARTEDI, at a distinct disadvantage, staggered along slowly. Moving east along the Haarlemmerdijk, he took the first left down Buiten Brouwersstraat toward the waterfront, and then right along the Droogbag to the mouth of the Singel and the Nieuwe Haarlemmer Sluys. Had all gone well, he would have continued on along the Haring Pakkerye and Texelse Kay, over the bridge across the Dam Rak, straight on to the Nieuwebrugstraat, taking then the first right onto the Warmoesstraat. But things did not go right. As he approached the bridge over the Nieuwe Haarlemmer Sluys, feeling his way along over the rough cobblestones, he suddenly was hurled into the air, tumbling downward headlong, with arms and fingers out-stretched instinctively to break the long fall, and finally, plunging into the cold, black, fetid waters of the canal. All of this I learned several days later from my ever-faithful SOHLBERG who took great care to keep his wits about him and to watch and to remember every detail.

CHAPTER 10

St. Anthony's Churchyard

> Death is nature's finest invention, it repeals calamities,
> terminates the weariness of old age, removes shackles, provides
> an escape from prison. It reserves its greatest benefits for those
> it visits uninvited. The blessings it bestows recompense me for
> the injuries of life.
>
> —Linnaeus, *Nemesis Divina* (Divine Vengeance)

At first light on the morning of 28 September 1735, passers-by, hastening to begin the tasks of the day, observed a body floating in the Singel near the Nieuwe Haarlemmer Sluys, a discovery not unusual in those days, and, for that matter, just as common now. The unlighted waterways that pass everywhere in that city, their banks without protective railings of any kind, offer treacherous going in the pitch black of night even for the sober and most vigilant wayfarer. Accidental drownings were, and, I dare say, still are, almost a weekly occurrence, especially in those wicked and disgusting parts of town, where every night uncontrolled drinking and whoring are most rampant, and here I refer mainly to the Gelderskade and Boomsloot districts, which are, by the way, only a few minutes by foot in a southeasterly direction from where our Artedi had his lodgings. So too are there numerous cases in that city of suicide by drowning, the canals providing a readily accessible means of efficient self-demise. These happenings are, in fact, so common that no one much thinks about them, unless, of course, the unfortunate person is a loved one or owes you money. But, I do well recall a particular example because it has to do with our Mr. Renard, of whom I have already spoken. This secret agent to His Britannick Majesty was by all indications quite well-off, rich enough to provide his family with a maidservant and a fine house on the Herengracht. It was therefore unexpected by all to learn that at his death in February 1746, he left a very mediocre capital. In fact, as we discovered later, with much surprise, things were so adverse that Jeanne, one of his daughters, too proud to go out and sell herself as a cleaning lady, committed suicide out of despair. She had a beautiful figure and blond hair. She was only twenty-five years old, and was always dressed in white. As she happened to be very proud and haughty, it was difficult for her when her friends told her that she might have to become a charwoman and that when she died, her friends would have to see to it that she got a proper burial. Then she went to the ferryboat on the Overtoom, and, arriving on the Haarlemmermeer, she asked the skipper to indicate where the water was the deepest. The skipper, who could not have been the most intelligent man—otherwise he would have thought about this peculiar question—complied with her request. She came on deck, paid the skipper for the ride, and, waiting a moment until he was just busy enough that he would not be able to help her immediately with his boathook, she jumped overboard and drowned. At home she had left a note in which she wrote that now there was no need for her to go out cleaning and that nobody now needed to pay for her funeral.

The canals of Amsterdam also provide an expedient apparatus for murder—a firm whack on the head from behind, a tripping up with the foot or cane, and perhaps a little push are all that is needed, the flowing water providing a convenient depository for the body, removing it nicely from the scene of the crime. But, in the case of ARTEDI's unhappy termination, no evidence of unlawful death was suggested. Indeed, what motive could there have been? He was a poor man, his costume thoroughly dilapidated, his boots badly worn—gentle and reclusive by nature, he posed no threat to anyone. Besides, he was very much inebriated when he met his death. The fact of the latter was made evident not only by medical report submitted by the coroner, but later by confirmation by those with whom he shared his plate the evening before. The event was duly recorded as accidental, without a second thought.

The body was hoisted from the water, tossed into a wagon designed for that purpose, and conveyed to the City Hospital—or *Binnengasthuis*, as the Dutch are wont to call it, situated in between the Grimburgwal, the houses along the Oude Turfmarkt, Nieuwe Doelenstraat, and Kloveniersburgwal—where, at that time, corpses were usually dressed and prepared for burial.

As you might remember, I was not informed of these incidents until

the late afternoon of the following day when SOHLBERG and TERS-
MEEDEN called upon me at Hartekamp with the dreadful news. By the
time I arrived in Amsterdam, early on Friday, the 30th, to which place
I rushed with utmost urgency to see what I could do for my friend,
HENDRICK JÜTTINCK, ARTEDI's landlord on the Warmoesstraat, had
already made provisions of a sort. Sending his young servant girl, ANNA
MOLENBEEK, to the City Hospital, he instructed her to give notice of
ARTEDI's death and to classify him with the impecunious, that is, as a
pauper unable to pay for his own grave.

SEBA, soon hearing of the news—and strongly prompted by JÜT-
TINCK who certainly did not want to pay anything himself—offered the
sum of 50 guilders to be applied to the expenses of the burial. The small-
ness of this gesture was shocking to me and, I dare say, to everyone who
heard of it. Why such a pitiful small amount? Surely this was indeed a
minuscule quantity for a man as rich as SEBA, to honor the memory of
someone who had served him so well and without complaint. This near
empty token on the part of the apothecary became more astounding
still when it was later revealed that for all the time he had ARTEDI in his
employ, he had paid him nothing, despite the promise to provide a fair
and handsome recompense for the work on the fishes for the *Thesaurus*.
Thus, since mid-July, our ichthyologist had been obliged to eke out a
paltry existence on his own—how he got by during those days was well
beyond my ability to grasp until I learned later that financial aid had at
various times been procured from his relatives in Sweden. The proof
of the latter assistance I discovered in a letter written by ARTEDI to his
mother and siblings, a copy of which was found pasted to the last folio
of an otherwise worthless manuscript left behind in his room:

My Dear Mother, Gentlemen Brothers, and Dearest Sisters,

I traveled from England at the end of the month of June and,
within a rather short space of time, came back here to Holland.
Along the way, my travels took me to Rotterdam, Delft, Leiden,
Harlem, and Amsterdam. Upon my arrival in Amsterdam, I was
privy to much talk about a certain pharmacist who here in this city
is publishing a large work about natural history. It was to this man

that I made myself known. After he noticed that I was familiar with the science of Ichthyology, he persuaded me to remain some time in Amsterdam to produce a description of his East Indian and American fishes, because he himself did not know a single one. I accepted to undertake this task, but only on the agreement that my name be attached to the work in some prominent and forthright way as author of that part concerning the fishes. At this time, I have already described over one hundred of his specimens, and have still about fifty undescribed yet to examine. They are mostly from Amboina in the East Indies and Surinam in America, and all of them rare and curious, so I can say quite easily that I have seen more curiosities in that part of natural history, than any one who has traveled through all of Europe. I estimate that I still have enough work for another three weeks or more.

The published work of which I mention consists of three large volumes in folio: the first two, dealing with the vegetables, mammals, birds, snakes, and turtles, are already complete; the third, which will be about crayfishes, fishes, and shells, has just now begun to be printed. Altogether the work is precious and estimated to cost 300 to 400 Swedish dalers. To provide some further credibility to the worth of what I say, it is rumored that Her Majesty of Sweden has already ordered to buy the first two volumes for the library of Drottningholm.

What I might get in return for my troubles, I cannot say. With people who already sit in credit and reputation, one must not negotiate beforehand, until they themselves or through others hear what the man is capable of, as they often better show their generosity than if one negotiated before. This pharmacist ALBERTUS SEBA is happy that he has met me, and I also him, that I have such a good opportunity to train myself and also, on top of that, to have something for my trouble. Here in Holland there is no one in particular who understands Zoology and, concerning Ichthyology, I will admit no one as my master, neither here nor elsewhere, because I have for almost seven years devoted myself to it. I find now that I lack nothing in particular, except money.

For the allowance that my dear relatives had the kindness to send me, I give thanks with all my heart. I wish nothing more than to come someday into such a position that would allow me to repay this sum as well as the other advances so received. The travels from England to here cost me dearly, in addition to what I then had to pay for accommodation and food, so that now I have nothing. I fear that I cannot live long, much less take my doctor's degree and buy clothes, unless I get something of value from the pharmacist SEBA. It is a difficult thing when one first starts to show oneself in the world, and when one's name begins to become familiar to others, that resources are not there to allow one to take the advantage and rise up further, that is, to become what he well knows he can be. To trouble my dear relatives for any further remittance, I do not dare. I have asked for BRENBOM, who it was thought might help me, but I have not yet met anyone who knows him here in Amsterdam. The accommodations here in Holland are less dear than in England, but food and drink are more expensive. And, I might say also, that the people here are not as nice as those in England.

I eagerly wait for a reply here in Holland from my dear family. The letter can be addressed to Leiden for I have there an acquaintance who can receive it, even if I myself will not be there.

> My most respected and dearest relatives,
> Your most obedient servant,
> PETRUS ARTEDI
> Amsterdam, in the beginning of September,
> new style, 1735

And so it was, in this way, that ARTEDI survived this arduous time, through the kind generosity of his family, though the allowance could not have been much, for he was always hungry and his clothes forever badly in need of mending. So too is revealed herein further evidence of a lack of recompense for ARTEDI's ichthyological labors, but more on this and SEBA's rather bewildering parsimonious behavior later as my story unfolds further.

*   *   *

On that same Friday, the 30th of September, I made my way alone to the City Hospital to pay my respects to that once bright star who was my closest and most intimate friend. Here I found him laid out prone, on a slab of cold stone, his body stiff and gray and looking colder still. Horrible did he appear, not having died well. Bodily corruption was by now already showing its sign, the spirit of his life having been lost some three days ago. And what a loss it was! Too early did Fate pluck this unique genius! In the flower of his age and strength died one who was the ornament and glory of his nation! Thus did the most distinguished of ichthyologists perish in the waters, having devoted his life to the discovery of their inhabitants!

Later on the same day, I, together with my colleagues SOHLBERG and TERSMEEDEN, and with public notary SALOMON DORPER, called upon Mr. JÜTTINCK on the Warmoesstraat for the sad purpose of making an inventory of the goods left behind by ARTEDI. Collectively we climbed the narrow stairs to his dingy room at the top, breathing the stale air as we entered and struggling to see in the near dark of the narrow place. And here, with slow and patient method, we carefully made account, by list on paper, of all his things, even to the minutest of objects. With careful control of my anticipation, for which I was forced to gather all my strength, I had it in mind above all else to locate and to procure for myself, if at all possible, those manuscripts of the *Ichthyo-logica*, the long-sought-after contents of which would allow me finally to complete my great *Systema Naturae*. And, of course, I had it also in mind to procure these great works so as to guarantee their eventual publication in order that the genius of them might be made available to the public. In the end, the treasures were found in a small leather case under his bed, but, as you shall soon learn, I was prevented from taking them by the vigilance of DORPER, but also by JÜTTINCK, the latter wanting to claim them for himself in lieu of payment due him for several months of unpaid rent. But more of this later.

As it was, a detailed account of all ARTEDI's things was prepared for our signatures as witnesses to the facts. And here, for your interest— with various small and scattered annotations by me—the list is given in full, the items presented in the order that they were examined, to show what a man of his place and situation in life might own and what he might think of importance to keep around him:

> Inventory of the goods and estate left by death of the late PETER ARTEDI, who between Tuesday the 27th and 28th of September 1735 came to be drowned in this town, and which were found to rest in a room in "The Arms of Overijssel," where he was lodged, as was given notice by and at the request of the host HENDRICK JÜTTINCK in the Warmoesstraat:
>
> > In a small leather bag: 26 English shillings, 1 twenty-eight ditto, 4 half shillings ditto [the small remains of his travel money, which he had not yet changed into Dutch currency].
> >
> > *Manuscriptum thunusis* in quarto [a superficial and worthless description of a tunny, a kind of mackerel or tuna fish, never published].
> >
> > Another manuscript [untitled and roughly prepared, but certainly this was meant to be the text of ARTEDI's *Praefatio Authoris* (Author's Preface) to his *Ichthyologia*, which he had written during his time in England and to which, at the end, he affixed the words *Scripsi Londini 1735*].
> >
> > Another manuscript [again untitled and containing extracts from divers books on alchemy, botany, zoology, agriculture, etc., showing well the broad interests and extensive reading of its compiler; but of no value save for an appended copy of a curious letter in ARTEDI's hand addressed to his mother, brothers, and sisters, of which mention I have already made].
> >
> > SHAW's *Physic*, two volumes in quarto, printed in English [this is *A New Practice of Physic* by PETER SHAW, the second edition of 1728, wherein the various diseases incident to the human body are orderly described, a publication no doubt acquired by ARTEDI during his visit to England].

Collectania practica, a manuscript in octavo [as everyone knows, ARTEDI was a physician and, although he ministered to very few patients during the time that I knew him, it is here in these pages that he collected notes and memoranda of significance to his medical practice].

The *Lexicon* of BLANCARDUS in quarto [an edition of *Lexicon novum medicum* published in Leiden in 1702 by STEPHANUS BLANCARDUS, that prolific author and physician from Middelburg whose name as written in the Dutch language is STEVEN BLANCKAERT].

A calendar with annotations [of no value].

A small booklet, being a memorandum bound in green leather [also of no significance].

HEISTER's *Anatomicum*, in quarto [the third of many editions of LAURENTIUS HEISTER's *Compendium anatomicum*, or *Compendium of anatomy, containing a short but perfect view of all the parts of humane bodies*, published in Altdorf in 1727. It was, in fact, this same HEISTER who, liking the copy of my *Musa Cliffortiana* (CLIFFORD's Banana Plant) that I sent to him in 1736, pretended to do some research towards a *historia botanica*, but I preceded him with my *Systema Naturae*. I had written in the latter that all botanists acknowledge the fundamental importance of the fructification, except perhaps HEISTER alone, who I mentioned as a botanist—it had appeared to me that this eminent man did not admit to the above principle, as he founded his orders and genera on the leaves. Despite his displeasure at my remarks, we remained the closest of friends, until, when in April of 1742, he naively criticized my sexual system—at one point arguing that because he could not find the stamens in an *Aloe*, the Linnaean system was useless—and complained of my changing of botanical names. It was from this time that I rightly refused any further correspondence with this silly man].

BOERHAAVE's *Institutiones* in octavo [one of the many editions of *Institutiones Medicae in Usus Annuae Exercitationis Domesticos* (Medical Principles in Domestic Practice) by HERMANUS BOERHAAVE. First published in 1708, this book on physiology must be recognized, in my humble opinion, as BOERHAAVE's most influential work].

Manuscript mineraloesis in octavo [a manuscript, never published, intending to lay out the results of ARTEDI's studies of minerals—of some small importance in giving an overview of his early alchemical ideas, but otherwise quite worthless].

Manuscriptum idea institutionum trichozoologiae in octavo [Treatise on the Organization of the Hair-bearing Animals, a manuscript, also never published, containing the results of ARTEDI's investigations on mammals, of which enough mention has already been made earlier in this discourse].

HENCKEL's *De Appropriatione* [a copy of *De Medicorum Chymicorum Appropriatione in Argenti cum Acido Salis Communis Communicatione* (On the Extraction of Medical Chemicals from Ordinary Silver, with the Acid of Common Salt) written by chemist and mineralogist JOHANN FRIEDRICH HENCKEL and published by him in Dresden in 1726].

Manuscriptum de amphibiis in quarto [a manuscript, also never published, containing the curious results of ARTEDI's investigations on amphibians].

MEAD's *De Pesta* [a copy of RICHARD MEAD's *De Pesta* (The Pestilence) published in London in 1723, a discourse—stemming from the great fear felt in London as a result of the horrific epidemic of plague that ravaged Marseille in 1719—concerning pestilential contagion and the methods to be used to prevent it. I did not know it myself, but I had then been told that MEAD was physician to many important personages of that time, including GEORGE I, GEORGE II, NEWTON, and

WALPOLE. I remember having been encouraged by colleagues to call upon this great man during my visit to London in 1736 to see his great collection of paintings and ancient sculpture, which he generously made available to visitors for study at his house in Great Ormond Street. But, having never been partial to pictures and the like, I let this opportunity pass me by].

Gustav van Vasa levensbeschrijving in octavo [one of several biographies of VASA, but in Dutch, a language mostly unavailable to ARTEDI].

Phisiologia humana [a book of which I know nothing].

A small leather bag containing copper coins.

A small box containing dried fishes [without doubt the property of SEBA].

Eight shirts.

Three half-shirts.

Three pairs of sleeves, and an unmatched singlet of the same.

A sanative [that curious piece of underwear that the Dutch call *Een gesondheijd*, a broad abdominal belt-like sash of baize worn by either man or woman and meant to keep the body warm in winter].

Another small box of dried fishes, large and small, together with 30 small bottles of insects, all belonging to Mr. SEBA.

RUYSCH's *Theatrum Animalium* in folio [likewise belonging to SEBA, a fine copy of HENDRICK RUYSCH's *Theatrum Universale Omnium Animalium* (General Survey of All Animals), containing myriad descriptions and copper cuts of curious fishes from the East Indies, and included in the third edition of JOANNES JONSTONUS's *Historiae naturalis*, published in Amsterdam in 1718 by the WETSTEINS. This JONSTONUS tried to arrange fishes according to a method, but it was a very ill-conceived one. He mingled distinctions based on their habitats, with those based on their structure, the latter being ill-chosen and inconsistently followed in detail. The fishes ranked under each chapter do not by any means have all the characteristics indicated in the title].

WILLUGHBY'S *Ictiographia* [this is FRANCIS WILLUGHBY'S *De Historia Piscium Libri Quatuor* (The Natural History of Fishes in Four Books), printed at Oxford in 1686, one volume in folio, with one set of 188 plates dating from 1685. Though the book bears only WILLUGHBY'S name on the title page, it is said that a large part of it is the result of a friendly and fruitful collaboration with the venerable JOHN RAY, a good probability that I mentioned to you in my earlier discussion. This too must have been the property of SEBA, for no one of ARTEDI'S station in life could ever afford to own such a dear volume as this].

VALENTIJN'S *De Amboina* in folio [obviously this is extracted from FRANÇOIS VALENTIJN'S *Oud en Nieuw Oost-Indiën* (Old and New East Indies) of which the second part contains *Beschrijvinge van Amboina* (Description of Ambon) and the third part *Verhandelingen der Dieren van Amboina* (Discourse on the Animals of Ambon), of which *Gemeene en Ongemeene Visschen van Amboina* (Common and Uncommon Fishes of Ambon) was obviously of great interest to ARTEDI. The latter production, printed at Dordrecht and Amsterdam in 1726, and put together by VALENTIJN, that famous Protestant minister of Amboina, contains 528 engravings of fishes. The latter appear all too similar to those contained in RUYSCH'S *Theatrum* and it is quite obvious that they are one and the same, yet, and most shamefully, the one more recent does not acknowledge the other].

Three day-shirts marked with S, belonging to SOHLBERG, with a stock [the latter a kind of tie, to be worn around the neck. I must say that when I recognized this apparel as the property of SOHLBERG, whose faithfulness to me I had not up until this time had reason to question, I became distraught and quite beside myself. When confronted then and there in the presence of TERSMEEDEN, JÜTTINCK, and DORPER, SOHLBERG explained this clothing in ARTEDI's possession as nothing more than a loan of badly needed attire to a near destitute friend. But I believed otherwise and could not be dissuaded. This unhappy discovery added greatly to my ever increasing discomfort as we carefully enumerated those sundry things piece by piece].

An assay book, and a pair of scales for weighing gold, both inscribed by one ANTHONI GRILL, assayer in Amsterdam [why ARTEDI should have these items, I cannot guess, for he certainly had no gold or other noble metal to which this equipment might be applied. The only imaginable thing is that it related in some way to his long-held interest in alchemy, yet I was fully unaware of any experimentations in that regard, with which he might have occupied his time].

An old dictionary also belonging to SOHLBERG.

In a small, hinged, leather case [tucked beneath the narrow and unkempt bed where he slept] the following five manuscripts in quarto [at last, the grand prize for which I had so eagerly waited for so long]:

Bibliotheca ichthyologica, or *Historia litteraria ichthyologiae* [Library of ichthyology, or History of the literature of ichthyology, a full inspection and detailed analysis of the works of all those scientific predecessors who had devoted themselves to the study of fishes, intended by our poor departed friend to form the first part of his *Ichthyologia*].

Philosophia ichthyologica, or *Prolegomena institutionum* [Philosophy of ichthyology, or Treatise on rules, the definitions and set of laws that ARTEDI enforced upon himself and to which he expected all others to adhere in examining and describing fishes; intended as Part 2 of the *Ichthyologia*].

Genera piscium, or *Historia piscium universalis* [Genera of fishes, or a Complete natural history of fishes, in which the deceased proposed a classification of fishes, wherein were provided only single-word generic names, detailed generic descriptions, and an enumeration of the species accepted in each genus; intended as Part 3 of the *Ichthyologia*].

Synonymia nominum piscium, or *Synonymologia* [Synonymy of the names of fishes, a comprehensive scrutiny of all those seemingly countless names used by other authors for each species of fish allowed in his classification; Part 4 of the *Ichthyologia*].

Descriptiones Specierum Piscium (Description of the Species of Fishes, in which ARTEDI provided a most thorough anatomical portrayal of all the fishes he had examined, often including descriptions of their fleshy innards as well as detailed enumerations and measurements; the fifth and last part of the *Ichthyologia*].

What the deceased was wearing:

A shirt, a cloth dress-coat, camisole, and pair of breeches.

A hat and a wig.

A pair of stockings and one shoe.

A sword, with sheath, and a walking stick.

In his pocket, a golden double guinea, nine stuivers, and four duiten [a stuiver being the equivalent of $\frac{1}{20}$th of a guilder, a duit, $\frac{1}{8}$th of a stuiver, stuivers and duiten being somewhat similar to English pennies and farthings; this seems to have been all the Dutch money that poor ARTEDI had to his name].

Thus inventoried in Amsterdam the 30th of September 1735, by me SALOMON DORPER, Notary Public at Amsterdam, admitted by the Honorable Court of Holland, in the presence of the gentlemen CARL GUSTAV TERSMEEDEN & CLAUDIUS SOHLBERG as witnesses:

This list then is the full extent of this man's worldly belongings. What a sad and pathetic thing to contemplate—a life of thirty years now extinguished and what small results to show for its passage. All of these material things brought together could not have been worth more than a few English farthings, save those priceless, fishy manuscripts that I coveted like nothing else. But, alas, I could not have them! Nor was I given the least opportunity to examine them—barely was I allowed enough time to verify their contents and to arrange them in the order, one through five, that was intended by ARTEDI. At least for now, by consideration of the large debt left by the deceased, all of his property was to be held by JÜTTINCK, to keep or disburse at his own discretion, until such time as he might receive full reimbursement of the amount outstanding or as the courts might decide otherwise. And what a large price he was asking! No less than 320 guilders was demanded—an altogether huge amount that was wholly beyond my means to supply at the time.

I did my best to hold my anger, but my distaste for this outcome was made known to those present despite all my efforts. I did explain, as well as anyone might, that those papers contained nothing but arcane things, indecipherable gibberish that would be of no value to anyone but a man of my position and talents. I brought also to the attention of the notary and to JÜTTINCK, ARTEDI's last will and testament—alas, unwritten, but made solemnly and without coercion, just prior to his departure for

England—to grant me as caretaker of all his possessions should anything adverse happen to him. But these arguments fell on deaf ears. In
my disappointment and rage, I lost my composure—an unfortunate
result that I am embarrassed to admit, even now after this long passage
of time—and refused to apply my signature to the document as witness
to that unhappy inventory. I then, with some additional outward show
of irritation, left that dismal place, without the barest valediction.

*　*　*

On Sunday, 2 October 1735, the body of my dear departed PETER
ARTEDI was laid to rest. That he had been classed as a pauper, unable
to pay for his burial, was an extraordinary pain for me. Try as I might,
I could not think of how to procure the necessary funds to guarantee
a proper place for him, a committal that might give him honor as was
befitting of his goodness, his well-intentions, and his stature as a true
man of science and of letters. But, regretfully, I must admit that these
superior attributes, given here sincerely and without exaggeration,
were well known only to those few acquainted with him. He had never
published, nor had he established any correspondence with his fellow
scientists—I am, in fact, unaware of a single letter by his hand, save
the one addressed to his family already mentioned. Once more, he had
never sought to gain favor among the rich, and unlike me, who had been
blessed many times over by generous benefactors, he had no patrons.
Indeed, a rather small circle of friends and colleagues was all that he had,
none of the members of which were especially wealthy. TERSMEEDEN
and SOHLBERG—particularly the latter—were not without means, but
they hesitated in this instance, as did the exceedingly affluent SEBA,
as we have already learned. As for myself, having just commenced my
employment with CLIFFORD at Hartekamp, I had not yet had time to
build up the capital needed for such an expense as this. And so it was—
SEBA unwilling to give more, and JÜTTINCK surely not prepared to
give anything—that the body of poor ARTEDI was handed over to be
interred in the least expensive way, in the churchyard of ST. ANTHONY.

On that gray Sunday morning, a small procession made its way to
that place, a small triangular piece of ground in the southeast part of the
town, reserved as a potter's field, a means of quick disposal of the poor

and forgotten. Located just south of where the Herengracht meets the Muidergracht, and bounded by gardens on the west and a low stone wall on the north and east, it was perhaps a fitting place for ARTEDI only for the small reason that it was also situated just across from the *Hortus Medicus*, a place where he often took pleasure in strolling alone among the plants. Many years later I heard tell that this burial ground had been appropriated to other purpose, part of it allotted to the building of a school and part added to the botanical gardens of the University. Thus, there never was a memorial stone raised to mark where this penniless foreign student was laid to rest, and the place and the event were all too soon forgotten. The only remaining proof of it now is his name duly recorded in the Register of Burials of ST. ANTHONY's Churchyard:

With much regret, I disappointed myself by not attending the burial, but, for good reason, as I was in need of a quick return to my obligations at Hartekamp where I was wanted by an impatient GEORGE CLIFFORD. So too I was in great want of solitude to formulate a plan of how to get those things that I wanted so fervently.

CHAPTER 11

Gratification

Nothing vexes me more than to be suspected of plagiarism.

—LINNAEUS to ALBRECHT VON HALLER, from Hartekamp,
    12 September 1737

NOT KNOWING the exact and best pathway by which I should go forward to reach my purpose, I thought it prudent at the outset to establish myself in some legal way as executor of the things left behind by my old friend. Thus, I took liberty to seek this permission by letter from his family still residing in far away Nordmaling. I well recall his sweet mother HELENA, whom I called upon in that small coastal village in the early summer of 1732—it was the 3rd of June of that year to be exact—while on the first leg of my Lapland journey. I remember too making acquaintance at that time with a brother, and perhaps a sister or two, but their names now escape me. His father, you will recall, passed from this earth in early March 1729. Thus it was to this good household that I made my petition. With all the humility and sincerity that I could assemble, I first expressed my deep sorrow for the loss of this most excellent son and brother who left so abruptly, without a farewell, and in such a cruel and unexpected way. I then made my plea in clear and simple writing from the heart, invoking the wrath of the Highest if I should subtract one particle of those manuscripts for myself. This being done, and knowing that it would be some time before an answer could come back to me—the post to such small and far off places being especially slow—I did my best to turn to other things to occupy my mind.

As I have already mentioned elsewhere, perhaps more than once, I had carried with me from Sweden several botanical and other manuscripts in a variety of stages of completion, thinking that I might find in Holland the occasion to finish them and to have them published. I had already acquired the admiration and, what is perhaps more important, the patronage of GRONOVIUS and LAWSON with the manuscript for my *Systema Naturae*, so I forged ahead to see what I might do with my other productions. The most important of these were my *Bibliotheca Botanica*, *Fundamenta Botanica*, *Critica Botanica*, and *Genera Plantarum*, all fashioned to a large degree on ARTEDI's manuscripts of similar titles, these latter facts being truths that I am not adverse to admitting after all these years. But while attempting to improve and finish them, starting first with *Bibliotheca Botanica*—a work that I began in 1730, a year after I first made my acquaintance with ARTEDI—I found, with acute frustration, that I could not efficiently progress without having those examples of ARTEDI before me. Feeling quite beside myself, I gave up all hope that I could continue, without first resolving this most weighty conundrum—I thus craved mightily for an answer from Nordmaling. But then it arrived, in unprecedented good time, only ten days for passage of my letter there and another week for a return—it was now 20 October 1735.

I was well pleased to be informed by the response that the mother agreed willingly and happily that I should take full possession of her son's papers, but only under condition that I publish them as soon as they could be made ready for the press and that I reproduce them in the same way that I found them to fullest extent possible. With this unqualified blessing of my intentions in writing, I went back to JÜT-TINCK, thinking that I might have my gratification. But he was not to be dissuaded. After making up his account and giving the expenses of the funeral, he exacted no small amount to be paid before he would restore anything to me. The same 320 guilders that he had demanded before, he flung at me again, an amount that I could not possibly pay under any reasonable circumstance. My purse by then had been emptied by extensive travel in so many countries and, though well employed at Hartekamp, I had not yet been paid, having fulfilled my obligations to that position not yet two full months. Moreover, I had no friends in this foreign country who were willing to extend this money to me by loan. When I offered that JÜTTINCK might keep all the movables that ARTEDI had left behind, except the manuscripts, for a sum of 20 guilders, this haughty landlord laughed aloud and again sharply declined. With this rejection, he then threatened in an angry way that he could get much more by selling those things by public auction. Fearful of the latter, that by my hesitation these precious papers might fall into the hands of someone else and thus be lost forever, I went back to SEBA, begging that he might render the defunct this last deed of Christian charity and pay this amount, which for him was indeed a very small quantity. Quite willing to compromise and show my patience, I suggested that he take to him all those things left behind, including the papers, so that they could not be dispersed by the landlord, till such time as I could raise the money to reimburse him. But this unhappy and purse-proud man arrogantly withdrew, not desiring to meddle any further with this affair, saying that it was no concern of his. Rather he advised me that the things might better be put up for auction, as he was sure that he would without any doubt be able to obtain everything at a much more modest price, confident that nobody else in Amsterdam would care for these manuscripts, and who, pray tell, in any case, would bid against him? Once if done and the manuscripts obtained, he promised that he would freely communicate them to me. But, far too shrewd to be taken in by it, I thought this advice ambiguous and dangerous, fearing that he would only keep the manuscripts for himself.

Now feeling quite desperate, and not knowing of other recourse, I went to my employer—the kind and generous GEORGE CLIFFORD— recounting to him those recent events and asking for his advice, but secretly hoping that he might offer the money needed to resolve the problem. Unfortunately, in doing so, I revealed too much of my contempt for the miserly old apothecary, an opinion which, much to my surprise, CLIFFORD did not share. He argued instead that my reaction to SEBA's dismissal had been too harsh. He reminded me that the latter gentleman had willingly come up with 50 guilders for the funeral, when in all truth he was not obliged really to give anything. Certainly, this was not a lot of money, but SEBA as a successful merchant, a German, was very thrifty by nature. And how can one blame SEBA for being so cautious? He was being asked to pay a high price for goods, the value of which had been established by a churlish landlord of obvious low breeding. No doubt also, I was to him nothing but a young, ambitious, and over-enthusiastic foreigner; how could he be certain that I would return the advanced money? In all probability, too, SEBA must have thought the ARTEDI manuscripts to be of no use to him. Most likely he had concluded long ago that what he needed to know about ichthyology was already in his possession, in the form of ARTEDI's notes on fishes for the pending third volume of his *Thesaurus*.

At this mention of ARTEDI's *Manuscriptum Ichthyologicum*, I was suddenly reminded that it had not been discovered along with his other papers—another disappointing result of that survey and inventory made of his possessions back in late September. I was so hoping that I might at least get the opportunity to examine these pages, thinking that they might shed some substantial light on *Classes Pisces* for my *Systema Naturae*. But this important work was not to be found at his lodgings, and the next most obvious place for it was with SEBA. What an unfortunate circumstance! Surely this manuscript contained the most recent of ARTEDI's thoughts about the classification of fishes—information that would have been invaluable to me at the time. And, o, how I longed to see it.

But, when many years later—in 1759 to be exact—the third part of SEBA's great work finally appeared, I well recall my relief when I saw that nothing really new was there. And when, later still, I was allowed to compare the latter with a copy of the *Manuscriptum Ichthyologicum* that had somehow found its way to the library of GRONOVIUS, I saw that much had been changed by SEBA before he died in 1736. The good parts done by ARTEDI that related to genera, families, and orders, information that was of greatest interest to me, had been expunged without explanation. This was a true surprise to me, because, as everyone knew, SEBA was quite ambitious to pose as a man of science—so why leave out the most erudite part of the whole work? The answer to this, I concluded, was that the old man could not distinguish what was good from what was bad. He left out the science to give more room to meaningless anecdotal material, and, in this case especially, replaced the precise anatomical observations that so characterize the good work of ARTEDI, with useless accounts of the wonders and attractiveness of the different species. I was aware myself, and had been told by others, that SEBA possessed many manuscripts of various authors that, in like fashion, he used promiscuously in his publications, without ever mentioning the true source, hoping to direct the credit to himself. And, in this case too, although ARTEDI had nearly finished the identification and description

of SEBA's fishes, he did not see fit even to mention ARTEDI's name anywhere in the *Thesaurus*. Sadly, this was the only condition mentioned by
our ichthyologist in his letter to his mother and siblings, here violated by
this rich man who in the end got all the work done for only 50 guilders,
and reaped at the same time all the fame from posterity.

Be that as it may, I came away from CLIFFORD feeling dispossessed
and not at all convinced of the good side to SEBA's behavior. In the
meantime, to add to my anxiety, the landlord JÜTTINCK was hard at
work, calling on the city magistrate to come to his aid:

> To Their Honorable Lordships, The Aldermen of the Town of
> Amsterdam. Reverently gives notice, HENDRICK JÜTTINCK,
> resident in this city, that some time ago came to stay with him
> a certain PETRUS ARTEDI, that the same PETRUS ARTEDI
> recently passed away from this world, and that the suppliant
> had him buried as a stranger and advanced the money required
> therefore, for which reason as well as for board and lodging and
> money supplied, an amount of 320 guilders is due to suppliant, as
> per account added, that some goods are left by PETRUS ARTEDI
> mentioned and are deposited with him, suppliant, which are
> specified in the annexed inventory [the same as the one quoted
> above]; there appearing no one to repay the advanced money to
> him, suppliant, he, suppliant, is approaching Your Honors with
> the request to instruct someone, who may represent the men-
> tioned PETRUS ARTEDI and against whom he, suppliant, and
> all the other creditors may institute and finally prosecute their
> actions, the which doing, etc.,
>
> Signed: JOHANNES COMMELIN

> Aldermen, having examined HENDRICK JÜTTINCK's annexed
> request, agree that the suppliant summons PETRUS ARTEDI's
> nearest friends on the extra ordinary roll, 25 October 1735.
>
> All Gentlemen Aldermen being present, except Mr. JEREMIAS
> VAN COLLEN,
> Signed: PIETER DE LA COURT

Aldermen, with reference to HENDRICK JÜTTINCK's added request, arranging accordingly, commission JAN MOL ANTONISZ to represent the person of PETRUS ARTEDI, against whom suppliant and all other creditors may institute and finally prosecute their action.

27 October 1735, all Gentlemen Aldermen being present, Signed: PIETER DE LA COURT

But, praise be to God, this effort on JÜTTINCK's part, to press for the full amount of 320 guilders, was, to his great surprise and disappointment, reversed by the court, which by a fair liquidation through the procurators reduced the debt to only 100 guilders. But, this amount still being beyond my means at the time, I went once again to CLIFFORD who instantly made good on my request. But while the latter gentleman proved to be amply generous, even he kept the manuscripts for himself and had them copied for my use.

And so it was, in similar fashion, that SEBA came to recover what was rightly his:

To Their Honorable Lordships the Aldermen of the Town of Amsterdam. Reverently gives notice, ALBERTUS SEBA, resident in this city, that he, suppliant, has lent to the person of PETRUS ARTEDI, a Swede by birth, and staying in this city at HENDRICK JÜTTINCK's house, in Warmoesstraat, where the Overijssel Coat of Arms hangs out, a box with thirty-five bottles of insects, as well as three books, viz. RUYSCH *Theatrum Animalium* in folio, WILLUGHBY *Ictiographia* in a sheaf, and VALENTIJN *Amboina* in folio, for his use in composing a description of the nature and character of Fishes, that, same PETRUS ARTEDI having recently died within this city, he, suppliant, had requested his host, the above mentioned HENDRICK JÜTTINCK, to make restitution of the above mentioned thirty-five bottles and three books to him, suppliant, but that the same HENDRICK JÜTTINCK, though fully aware that same belong to suppliant, as he himself had entered in the inventory of the estate of the above-mentioned PETRUS ARTEDI (made on 30 September of this year 1735 by Notary

Salomon Dorper, at his, Hendrick Jüttinck's request), still persists against right and reason in refusing to return the above-mentioned bottles and books, for which reason suppliant very respectfully begs Your Honors to summon the above-mentioned Hendrick Jüttinck, immediately and forthwith to deliver up the above-mentioned thirty-five bottles of insects and three books to suppliant, unless and in case unexpectedly any objection should be made about this delivery, with provision under caution.

The which doing, etc.

Signed: J.A. Creighton

Aldermen having examined the annexed request by Albertus Seba, resident within this city, agree that suppliant shall have to summon Hendrick Jüttinck on the extraordinary roll, on 26 October 1735.

All Gentlemen Aldermen being present,

Signed: Pieter de la Court

Aldermen further disposing about the annexed request of Albertus Seba, living within this city, ordain Hendrick Jüttinck to deliver up immediately and forthwith to suppliant the thirty-five bottles of insects and three books, mentioned in the request, by provision and under caution.

15 November 1735, all Gentlemen Aldermen being present, except Mr. Van Loon,

Signed: Pieter de la Court

Thus, old Seba got back his possessions, but not without some difficulties; while that mean-spirited Jüttinck received only 100 guilders, far more than what he deserved, but still far less than what he wanted, an amount in any case, that I was able to borrow rather easily from Clifford. Surely, much time had been lost—a deficit not to be taken lightly, for I always considered the time Fate has in store for us to be the most uncertain in the world, for which reason I never ventured to postpone anything—but no better outcome to this quandary could have been expected. Once again I must look to the heavens and praise the good fortune that was mine for this divine gratification! One more favor bestowed upon me by God the Almighty.

Now with those most cherished manuscripts before me, the keys to my kingdom finally in my hands, I turned first to ARTEDI's *Genera Piscium* and there I saw what good work he had done. Indeed, it was much changed from what he had showed to me so long ago back in Uppsala. Here were all the known species of fishes divided into four major groupings, which he designated as orders: I. *Malacopterygii* or soft-rayed fishes, containing twenty-one genera and ninety species; II. *Acanthopterygii*, the spiny-rayed fishes, sixteen genera and seventy-eight species; III. *Branchiostegi*, fishes with constricted or partially closed gill openings, four genera and thirty species; and IV. *Chondropterygii*, the cartilaginous fishes, four genera and thirty species. All of this I quickly entered into my unfinished manuscript for the *Systema Naturae*, but instead of writing it all down *verbatim*—something I was loath to do—I reversed the order of presentation so that *Chondropterygii* came first and *Malacopterygii* last. This clean and simple classification I thereafter used quite successfully in all my subsequent editions of the *Systema Naturae* through to the ninth, which latter work, you will no doubt recall, was published in 1756 under the excellent editorship of my old friend and patron GRONOVIUS.

The genera used by ARTEDI, of which I found he recognized a total of 45, were also quickly copied down, but again, within each order, I reversed his order of presentation. In Chondropterygii, for example, he included *Petromyzon, Acipenser, Squalus*, and *Raia*, but I entered these into my *Systema Naturae* as *Raia, Squalus, Acipenser*, and *Petromyzon*. In Branchiostegi, he included *Balistes, Ostracion, Cyclopterus*, and *Lophius*, but, in like manner, I listed *Lophius, Cyclopterus, Ostracion*, and *Balistes*. Much in the same way, I reversed the order of presentation of the genera of the other two orders. I saw too that he kept several genera that I thought wrong and defunct, among these being *Chaetodon, Scorpaena*, and *Sciaena*, within the Acanthopterygii; and *Anableps, Ophidium, Anarhichas, Stromateus, Exocoetus*, and *Argentina*, within the Malacopterygii. All of these I left out of my system, thus reducing the number of genera to 36. Moreover, I was quite surprised to see in his arrangement the genus *Blennius* classified among the Acanthopterygii—quite rightly, it is a malacopterygian, so I took it from the former order and placed it in the latter, between *Muraena* and *Gadus*.

I then took also his generic descriptions, or diagnoses, if you will, abbreviating them in most cases, and giving much weight to the number of branchiostegal rays. The result was a considerable improvement over the deceased ichthyologist's descriptions, thus presenting a more concise and pleasing whole. Much in the same way, I scrutinized his *Synonymia* and his *Descriptiones Specierum Piscium*. From these I considered his species—of which he included some 228 different kinds—examining closely the basis on which they were accepted, and finding his number to have been grossly inflated. I thus removed 72 kinds, recognizing in my account a total of only 156, a number that I am certain better reflects the true quantity in nature. Thus, very much pleased with these results—and thinking I had made the best use of ARTEDI's work, yet not impinging in any way upon his priority—I made the last and final touches to the manuscript for my *Systema Naturae* and delivered it to the press. There it was printed in good order, with copies made available to the public by mid-December 1735. And soon after the New Year, almost as an afterthought, I caused to have printed the *Methodus Demonstrandi Animalia, Vegetabilia, aut Lapides*, which you will remember, I constructed, with some small help from ARTEDI, during our days together in Uppsala—and appended it to the larger work. With this whole I was quite satisfied.

Having now this enormous accomplishment in hand, any ordinary man would beg for respite from these toils, but I, not wanting to waste a moment, immediately turned my full attention to various other manuscripts, many of which—with ARTEDI's works used as guides to method and design—were quickly nearing completion. By the early spring of 1736, my *Bibliotheca Botanica* and *Fundamenta Botanica* were fully finished and sent to press in Amsterdam, both to be published by July of that same year. Shortly thereafter—just as I was putting the final changes to a magnificent little treatise on CLIFFORD's banana plants, which I called *Musa Cliffortiana*—came, fully by surprise, a suggestion from that generous employer that I journey to England at his expense. For several years, I had corresponded with many of the learned men of that country. It was now an opportune time that I should meet them, to examine their collections, and to bring back, God willing, what specimens I could gain from them to augment those already held at Hartekamp. So too, I had been most intrigued by all that ARTEDI had told me about that place, and perhaps feeling somewhat jealous of his going there before me, I considered these feelings as further incentive to venture forth in that same direction.

And so it was that I left Amsterdam on 21 July 1736, setting sail from Rotterdam and arriving in London a full week later, the weather along the whole way having been very bad. My first duty, which I rather thought of as a most profound privilege and delight, was to call upon Sir HANS SLOANE in Chelsea. As you will remember, GRONOVIUS and LAWSON had already, some seven months earlier, prepared my way to audience with that great man, by their sending of two copies of my *Systema Naturae*—one for SLOANE himself, and the other for the library of the Royal Society of London, of which SLOANE was then president, having succeeded Sir ISAAC NEWTON in 1727—accompanied by a most pleasing letter of introduction. So too did I arrive at SLOANE's door with a letter in hand from BOERHAAVE, which, while seemingly quite pleasing and altogether proper to me, rather put the old English collector out: "LINNAEUS is particularly worthy to be seen by you. Those who see you together will look at a couple of men whose equal can hardly be found in the world." SLOANE was at that time seventy-six years of age, and I not yet thirty. As I later learned, for I was fully ignorant of it at the time, he, whose fame was limitless, was not happy to be thought of by others as my equal. He was therefore cold and unfriendly to me at first, but soon warmed to my charms, as I knew he would.

Now fully in SLOANE's good graces, I thoroughly examined the specimens in his cabinet. Then, just as ARTEDI had done before me, I directed myself to the collections of the Royal Society itself, whose headquarters were at Crane Court in Fleet Street. Next, I proceeded to the Apothecaries' Garden at Chelsea to make my acquaintance with its

Scottish superintendent Philip Miller, that well-known horticulturist and author of *The Gardeners Dictionary*, a small two-volume book in
octavo, first published in London in 1724. Miller, quite kind enough
at first, showed me the garden, and named the plants as he went, according to the nomenclature then in use in that country—for example, to
milfoil, he applied a long and cumbersome polynomial: *Achillea foliis
duplicatopinnatis glabris, laciniis linearibus acute laciniatis*. Although surprised by this old-fashioned approach, I was careful to keep my silence,
which Miller badly mistook for my ignorance. This caused him the
next day to remark to a friend that Clifford's botanist does not
know a single plant. These words were soon repeated to me, and when
I visited Miller again some days later, I suggested that it would be
judicious of him not to name plants in his old-fashioned manner, but to
use instead shorter and more certain names. When I provided a number
of examples to show my meaning, he became annoyed and decidedly
unfriendly, refusing my request for plants for Clifford's garden. But
over time, his ill-humor passed, and in the end he promised to give me
all that I wanted. I was thus able to assemble a fine collection of things
to take back to Hartekamp.

Having got all that I could from my colleagues in London, I went
by coach to Oxford to call upon Dr. Dillenius, hoping to meet him,
of course, but wanting more to glean what I could in the way of plants
from his fine collections. When I arrived, I found him occupied with
Jacob Sherard. As I approached, he greeted me kindly, but then
turned to Sherard, and by way of introduction, described me in his
native tongue as the person who has confused the whole system of
botany. Everyone thinking that my facility to comprehend the English
language was wholly lacking, I pretended not to understand. Then we
walked together, the three of us, in the garden, where for the first time
I spied *Antirrhinum minus*. Upon seeing this plant, a species completely
unknown to me, I asked Dillenius for its name, and he, in reply,
expressed great surprise that I did not know it myself. I admitted that
I did not, but added that if I could only glance at the flower, I would
know it at once. He plucked the flower and passed it to me, upon which
I instantly saw to what genus it must be ascribed. This display of my

ingenuity was well taken by him and he soon after began to warm to me. By the time I left that place, where I remained for some eight days, he had accepted me fully, and in the end gave me all the living plants that I desired for CLIFFORD.

And so it went in similar fashion as I made myself known to others among my English counterparts. But now it was late August, and I having already spent a considerably longer time away than had been expected by CLIFFORD, I made my way back to Holland, burdened with a great bundle of still living specimens. Upon my return to Hartekamp, I was for several weeks sorely bothered by visitors of divers kinds arriving rather continuously to view the many exceedingly curious things brought back by me from my journey. But this parade eventually ceased and I was able then to return to my *Musa Cliffortiana*, a telling, in careful detail, of my extraordinary success in causing the *Musa*—or banana, as you no doubt know it better—to come into flower. In this small book, decorated with two large engravings on copper and published at Leiden in 1736, can be found the very first complete description of this rare plant to be had by botanists. But of greater consequence still, here it is shown, how a plant, which had in Europe never flowered before, can be forced to do so by being nourished in an imitation of its native climate. Even the most distinguished persons, including BOERHAAVE himself, visited Hartekamp to request a demonstration on this plant to be made for the benefit of a future world. The ingenious treatment by which I secured these miraculous results I have no reason to keep secret—it was by establishing the tree in rich soil, keeping it quite dry and unwatered for several weeks, then deluging it with water as if by tropical rains.

Knowing well how to make good use of my time, and working both by day and by night, I soon sent my *Musa* to the press to be printed in late 1736. Following soon thereafter was my *Critica Botanica*, which appeared at Leiden in 1737. Next, in order of their appearance, was a delightful study of the plants of Lapland, much sought after—and assisted in its publication with money given by a small company of friends brought together by BURMANN—titled *Flora Lapponica*, published at Amsterdam, also in 1737; *Genera Plantarum*, with a fine and generous dedication to BOERHAAVE, at Leiden, 1737; a brief, but well-constructed preamble to the wonders and pleasures of CLIFFORD's garden, called *Viridiarum Cliffortianum* (CLIFFORD's Pleasure-garden), Amsterdam, 1737; and finally the great consummation of my extraordinary work for CLIFFORD, a full and detailed description, with 518 pages, and 36 plates beautifully engraved on copper, of all the plants in his garden, called *Hortus Cliffortianus*, Amsterdam, 1737. Thus it was that the years 1736 and 1737 were for me a most glorious and carefree time. There at delightful Hartekamp, I existed in complete fullness, forgetting all my past sorrows and unable to imagine any future troubles that might come my way. Existing like a true prince, it was all I could wish for, living in such splendid lodgings as I had never had before. Nor could I have ever dreamed of anything more grand—such delightful gardens and orangeries, such a complete botanical library, every chance to meet and converse with important scientific men of the age, etc., etc. It was, as well, a time filled with astonishing, might I say, overwhelming, activity. In a space of time considerably less than those twenty-four months, especially considering my five weeks away in England, I had done the work of several lifetimes. My books that bear date of 1737 alone total more than 500 pages in large folio and well in excess of 1,350 pages in octavo. So too, among those volumes of that year, the first of my many editions of *Genera Plantarum* appeared, in which I found it necessary to either change or abolish more than half the number of generic names that had been established by preceding authors; and the prodigious quantity of non-descript plants which had fallen into my hands, obliged me to frame new genera to the amount of more than double the number of those that were left as I found them. In all, this one book by itself demanded that I examine the characters of more than 8,000 flowers. In addition, during these years, I maintained my large and varied correspondence with botanists all over the world, for even by this early time, before I was yet 30 years of age, my fame had reached to the edges of the earth. What man, pray tell, has ever done more good works in a space of time as small as this?

But now, as truth would have it, I had exhausted my obligations to botany. Not another plant book of any large importance, save new and revised editions of my works already published, was produced by me until my *Flora Suecica* (Swedish Flora) of 1745, and *Flora Zeylanica* (Ceylon Flora) of 1747. Thus, with ample time finally at my disposal—it now being early March 1738—I was then able to apply myself to ARTEDI's *Ichthyologia*, a work which I had by no means forgotten. In this connection, however, I am hereby forced to mention, with some embarrassment, my receipt of several letters, all unanswered, from that deceased ichthyologist's dear mother in Nordmaling, inquiring about the fate of those manuscripts and asking why she had not yet been sent a copy of the publication.

In perusing those most excellent manuscripts bequeathed to me by Providence, I had from the beginning realized that they were all in near completed form. It thus fell to me simply to follow the logical order of presentation already indicated by ARTEDI and to make only a very few editorial changes to the text. These things I did quickly, without hesitation, adding only a one-page introduction to each of the five chapters. I saw too that some of the material was not integrated into the whole, but not wanting to break the sequence of ARTEDI's text, I simply added the unplaced text at the end of the chapters as appendices. Finally, just as I was about to conclude the work, I had the thought to preface the whole thing with an historical account of the life of the author, a *Vita Petri Artedi Descripta*. This I also wrote quickly—and all of it completely from memory, for nothing of its kind, up to that time, had ever been put to paper—laying out all that I knew about the good man. I then penned a worthy dedication to the illustrious GEORGE CLIFFORD, signing it with my name, dated 20 March 1738, and carried the whole to the publishing house of CONRAD WISHOFF in Leiden. There it was exceedingly well printed, with copies made available to the public by the end of April. With this effort I had amply fulfilled my sacred obligation to my friend now dead and gone. If it had not been for me and my profound allegiance to duty, nothing would now exist to show for his life. Truly I made the blessed memory of ARTEDI live for all time.

PETRI ARTEDI

SVECI, MEDICI

ICHTHYOLOGIA

S I V E

OPERA OMNIA

de

PISCIBUS

SCILICET:

BIBLIOTHECA ICHTHYOLOGICA.
PHILOSOPHIA ICHTHYOLOGICA.
GENERA PISCIUM.
SYNONYMIA SPECIERUM.
DESCRIPTIONES SPECIERUM.

OMNIA IN HOC GENERE PERFECTIORA,
QUAM ANTEA ULLA.

POSTHUMA

Vindicavit, Recognovit, Coaptavit & Edidit

CAROLUS LINNÆUS,

Med. Doct. & Ac. Imper. N. C.

CHAPTER 12

Walking in the Steps of God

Great and Almighty God I thank Thee for all the good Thou
hast made for me in this world.

—LINNAEUS, *Nemesis Divina* (Divine Justice)

WITH MY work in Holland finished, having got all I could from that
country and having published all that I thought I might, I began to yearn
for my homeland, wanting to return to the place of my beginnings,
where I could speak my own language and be comforted by a climate that
is more acceptable to my constitution. Many of my Dutch friends and
colleagues begged that I stay, but I put them off, giving thanks to them
for their guidance and friendship, but insisting that I must go. So it was
that in May of 1738, I left Holland for Sweden, arriving in Stockholm
in June, where I immediately set up a medical practice, which in time
became extraordinarily successful. It was here that I gained much fame
and fortune by way of my clever and curious remedy for the syphilis,
which fearful disease I clearly demonstrated is caused by the smallest of
worms—animalcules, a hundred times smaller than particles of dust that
dance in a sunbeam, which are disseminated far and wide, and which,
though they are the minutest of creatures, can cause greater devastation
than the largest, killing more people than all the wars.

In June of 1739, I married SARA ELISABET MORAEA, this woman
being even now still by my side, for better or for worse; and in January
of the following year a son was born, to whom we gave the name CARL.
In late April of 1741, I was infinitely blessed with the offer of a medical
professorship at Uppsala. Thither I removed my family in October of
that year, and my inaugural lecture was presented and kindly received
on the 27th of October. In 1743, my first daughter, ELIZABETH CHRIS-
TINA, was born. In the following year, a second daughter arrived, but,
alas, died within the week. In 1748, my dear father died, causing in me
a deep oppression of spirit that subsided only with the birth of another
daughter, LOVISA, in the following year. In 1750, I was appointed by

the Academy of Sciences of Toulouse to their esteemed membership. In 1751, a fourth daughter, SARA CHRISTINA, was born, and in that same year my extraordinary *Philosophia Botanica* was published in Stockholm. Again in that same year, due, in part, to the quality and charm of the latter book, I was summoned to Drottningholm Palace by Queen LOVISA ULRIKA and charged with the description of her zoological collections, where later I also was commissioned to do the same for those of King ADOLF FREDRIK. In 1753, *Species Plantarum* appeared in Stockholm, this publication soon proving its worth as one of my most precious contributions to botany. On 27 April 1753, I was dubbed a Knight of the Royal Order of the Polar Star by his Majesty's own hand, an honor above all others, which had never before been conferred on any Doctor, Archiater, or Professor. Indeed, no Gentleman of the Bedchamber, though of noble extraction, had yet been presented with this Star. I took for motto *Famen extendre factis*, meaning that the task of the brave is to spread his fame by deeds—undeniably the true mirror of my soul.

In the year 1754, on 7 April, at 3 o'clock in the afternoon, my wife gave me a second son, JOHANNES, who, with most crushing grief to all, died in March 1757. Nine months after this ill-fated birth, following a long and hard labor, came another daughter, SOPHIA, seemingly born as if dead. But by means of *insufflatoria medicina*—that is, medication breathed into the body—and deft quickness on my part, she came to life in the space of half an hour, and was duly baptized on 9 November. In 1755, I was offered by the King of Spain a Barony and the post of Chief Inspector of Botany, and invited to settle in Madrid, where I would have everything I needed at my disposal, and not least I would enjoy full liberty of exercising my own religion though living in a Catholic country. But this kind proposal was rejected by me in favor of ennoblement by the King of Sweden, which honor was officially conferred upon me on 20 November 1756, and for which I took the name

Carl v. Linné

In 1758, wishing to remove my family from the noise and general dis-comfort of the city, I purchased the small country estates of Hammarby, Säfja, and Edeby near Uppsala, where, in 1762, we took up our residency there as a summer retreat. The years 1758 and 1759 were marked by the publication of yet another edition of my *Systema Naturae*, this one a two-volume affair, the tenth in that series, which was credited by all as a good improvement over the ninth. In 1766, a most horrific fire destroyed one-third of the town of Uppsala and very nearly took my house as well, a near catastrophe that prompted me at once to begin construction of a small museum at Hammarby to hold my prized col-lections and my books, an ample space that was completed in early 1769. In 1771, my good friend King FREDRIK died, succeeded by GUSTAF III who, like his father, took a sincere liking to me, giving me all the atten-tion and patronage that I deserved. In 1772, my term as Rector of the University of Uppsala ended and I thus settled into old age. But, not yet quite finished as thought by some, I published my *Systema Vegetabilium* (System of the Vegetable Kingdom) at Göttingen and Gotha in 1774.

And so this has been my life up to the present time. In seeming recompense for my labors and all that I have given to the world, the Almighty has allowed me to live well. I have achieved fame beyond mea-sure, doing only the work to which I have been born. I have had more than enough money, a beloved wife, handsome children, and an honored name. I have lived in a fine house, with a most lovely garden. What more could a man desire, who possesses every satisfaction? In my collection are innumerable minerals, in my herbarium and garden innumerable plants, and in my cabinet innumerable insects that I have assembled and pinned myself, in my cupboards innumerable fishes glued on paper as if they were plants: all these things, together with my great library, have kept me busy in full occupation even in my retirement.

So too, throughout my long and blessed existence, the Lord has provided that I am very seldom sickly. In the year 1748, I became much dispirited and suffered acutely from what I imagined was the verge of a breakdown of my nervous system. Later, in 1750, having executed my academical duties with great attention and at the same time given pri-vate instruction to many, mostly unworthy, students, I, in consequence of my great exertions, and the spring just setting in, had a severe attack of the gout. Being brought to the point of death by this disease, I cured myself of the agonizing pain by eating wood-strawberries. From that point on, I have eaten, every season, as much of this fruit as I can, and as much as my stomach will bear. By this means I not only have escaped the gout entirely, but also, I have derived more benefit than others from drinking mineral waters, and have got rid of the scurvy that every year rendered me heavy.

In 1753, owing to my continual sitting, writing, and laboring on the two volumes of my great *Species Plantarum*, one of the most useful of my many works, published in the autumn of that same year, I felt a severe and distressing pain in my right side. This was the unfortunate fore-telling of a habitual malady, the stone, of which, before that time, I had never had an attack. However, thanks be to the Almighty, it passed off in the course of several years, and again by my eating large quantities of wood-strawberries. Then in 1764, I was attacked by a violent pleurisy, but this too was cast off by long periods spent in fresh air.

By early 1772, I began to take notice from many indications that my time was nearly up, and that my fate must be a stroke, for my head often grew giddy, mostly when I bent down. My feet often stumbled as when a person is drunk, mostly on my right side. It seemed to me something not to be wondered at, for I had already arrived at an age that is not reached by the ninth part of a hundred born. I had by that time striven and worked with all desire, strength, and mind, but the very iron itself that I was made of was on the face of it nearly worn out. I was certain then that God thought to take me away very soon, in time perhaps so that I may not bear the misfortune and pain that shall surely come. Thus knowing my time was fast approaching, I prepared the following instructions for my burial and placed them in a sealed envelope:

> Lay me in a coffin unshaven, unwashed, unclothed, wrapped only in a sheet. Nail down the coffin forthwith, that none may see my wretchedness. Let the great bell of the Cathedral be tolled, but not those in other churches in the town or in the Hospital, and in the countryside only the bell in Danmark's church. Let

thanksgiving services to God, who granted me so long a life and so many blessings, be held in the Cathedral and in Danmark's church. Let men from my homeland carry me to the grave, and give to each of them one of the little medals bearing my portrait. Entertain nobody at my funeral, and accept no condolences.

Cause me then to lie under stone in the floor of the Cathedral in a place well seen and visited, and nearby mount a bronze medallion upon which is inscribed my name, the dates of my birth and death, and the words *Princeps Botanicorum*.

Wanting also to give some specific instruction to my wife about my possessions I sealed the following letter in another envelope with note that it should be opened only after my death:

Voice from the grave to her who was my dear wife:

1. The *two herbaria in the Museum*: let neither rats nor moths damage them. Let no naturalists steal a single plant. Take great care who is shown them. Valuable though they already are, they will be worth still more as time goes on. They are the greatest collection the world has ever seen. Do not sell them for less than a thousand ducats. My son is not to have them because he never helped me in botany and does not love the subject; keep them for some son-in-law who may prove to be a botanist.

2. *The shell cabinet* is worth at least 12,000 dalers.

3. *The insect cabinet* cannot be kept for long, because of moth.

4. *The mineral cabinet* contains things of great value.

5. *The library in my museum*, with all my books, is worth at least 3,000 copper dalers. Do not sell it, but give it to the Uppsala Library. But my son may have my library in Uppsala at a valuation.

Alas, I was quite correct about the nearness of my death, for the New Year brought further discomfort. It was then that I began to suffer rather horribly from severe pains in my back and thighs, a condition that I myself diagnosed as sciatica. A single journey to Stockholm after that cost me more fatigue than did the whole of my travels through Lapland. And then it came, quite suddenly and unexpected, on a beautiful sunny day in May of 1774, in the garden at Uppsala. I was in the midst of presenting a most charming lecture on how I had long ago discovered an ingenious method whereby pearls could be caused to grow within the soft, moist, inner folds of a living oyster, when I was seized by a stroke that nearly took my life away right there on the spot. "The egg has cracked," I wrote somewhat later to ABRAHAM BÄCK who had been my dearest friend and companion for many years, "it is not yet entirely crushed, but what is hidden is not forgotten—I have lived my time, and completed the task that fate laid on me."

But, quite paralyzed at first, I rallied somewhat, able even to hobble around, but not without considerable pain. And now I continue weary, have difficulty moving, my speech is slurred, my once neat and well-formed hand now shaky, and, most fearfully, I take notice of my memory failing me. But I take courage in knowing that I have conquered all, with God always and still by my side. He and He alone allowed me to see the wonders and fullness of the Creation as He Himself went forward with it. I tracked His footsteps over nature's field and marked in each one, even in those I could hardly discern, an ineffable wisdom and might, an impenetrable completeness. There I saw how all *animals* were supported by plants, how *plants* were supported by earth, and how *earth* was supported by the globe; how the globe spins night and day around the sun, which gave it life. How the sun rolled as if on its axle with planets and fixed stars to an inconceivable number, each and all of them upheld out of the empty void of the incomprehensible primary movement. He is the Creator of all beings, the impulse and helmsman of all things, Lord and Master of this world. If one will call Him "Fate," he makes no mistake, because all things hang on His finger; if one will call Him "Nature," he errs not, because everything comes from Him; would one call Him "Providence," one is right, because all goes according to His beck and call; He is the consummate Mind, Sight, and Hearing. He is the Soul, and He is His own master. No human conjecture can find His person; it is enough that He is an immortal, eternal, and divine being, who is neither created nor born. A Being without whom is nothing that is created; a Being who has founded and built all this, which shines everywhere before our eyes, without being able to be seen, and *can* only be seen in imagination, because such great Majesty resides on a sacred throne to which none can reach except the soul.

How small a part of the great works of nature is laid open to our eyes, and how many things are going on in secret of which we know nothing! How many things there are with which this age was first acquainted! How many things that we are ignorant of will come to light when the memory of us shall be no more! For nature does not at once reveal all her secrets. We are apt to look on ourselves, as already admitted into the sanctuary of her temple, but we are still only in the porch. I have entered into the thick and shady woods of nature, which are everywhere beset with thorns and briars. I have endeavored to keep clear of them as much as possible, but experience has taught me that *there is no man so circumspect as never to forget himself,* and therefore I have borne with patience the sneers of the malevolent and the buffooneries of those whose vivacity is excited only to molest and give offence to others. I have, in spite of these insults, kept on steadily in my old path, and have finished the course for which I was destined.

And what of that man ARTEDI whom I knew so long ago and loved with all my heart? His life, a small speck of dust indeed in the swirling cosmos of the Universe, was sacrificed without regret for the greater good. For had he lived, I might not have persevered to such an extent to reach my final zenith.

Memories of LINNAEUS and ARTEDI

THE MEMORY of LINNAEUS is everywhere. His name is a household word around most of the world. In Europe he is even better known, and in Sweden he is revered perhaps more so than GANDHI in India, NAPOLEON in France, and certainly more than WASHINGTON in America. His publications, in all their various later editions, as well as those about him, number in the tens of thousands. There have been over the years no less than eighteen societies founded and named in memory of LINNAEUS. Of these the Linnean Society of London is the oldest still in existence (founded in 1788) and, with its three journals concerned with the process of organic evolution (the Biological, Botanical, and Zoological journals), it is the world's premier society devoted to the Swedish botanist. Others include the Société Linnéenne de Paris founded in 1787 and similar organizations at Boston, Bordeaux, Lyon, Caen, Stockholm, Amiens, Berlin, Brussels, Angers, Sydney, Lancaster (Pennsylvania), New York, Ashton-under-Lyne, Marseille, Uppsala, and Quebec. In addition to the Linnean Society of London, five of these still exist, the Société Linnéenne de Bordeaux (founded in 1818), Société Linnéenne de Lyon (1822), the Linnaean Society of New South Wales (1875), the Linnaean Society of New York (1878), and the Swedish Linnaeus Society (Svenska Linnésällskapet, founded in 1917). A search for "Linnaeus" on the Internet produces about 31,000,000 responses.

But what is remembered of PETER ARTEDI? He is known by a few historically minded ichthyologists, who revere him as the "father of ichthyology," but even they know very little about him. We have his *Ichthyologia* published by LINNAEUS in 1738, but it is written in difficult, mid-eighteenth-century Latin, a language very few of us living today can decipher. The brief story of ARTEDI's life, included by LINNAEUS as a preface to the *Ichthyologia*, has been translated into Swedish, but this too provides only very limited access. There are, however, at least three permanent memorials to ARTEDI: two small stone monuments in Sweden, one at his birthplace in Anundsjö and the other at Nordmaling. The third memorial is depicted here:

PETER ARTEDI
SUECUS
ICHTHYOLOGORUM PRINCEPS
NATUS IN
ANGERMANNIA SUECORUM
MDCCV
OBIIT AMSTELODAMI
MDCCXXXV

An eight-foot stone of red-granite set in the Amsterdam Zoological Gardens (*Natura Artis Magistra*) just behind the old *Artis* aquarium, unveiled on 28 June 1905, on the occasion of the bicentenary of ARTEDI's birth. It is inscribed as follows:

PETER ARTEDI

SWEDE

PRINCE OF ICHTHYOLOGISTS

BORN IN
ÅNGERMANLAND, SWEDEN
1705
DIED IN AMSTERDAM
1735

MONUMENT ERECTED
IN DEVOTION
BY THE
ROYAL SWEDISH ACADEMY OF SCIENCES
1905

Chronology

1735 February: LINNAEUS and SOHLBERG depart Uppsala for Germany

27 April: LINNAEUS and SOHLBERG arrive in Hamburg

15 May: ARTEDI visits HANS SLOANE in London

28 May: LINNAEUS and SOHLBERG depart Hamburg for Amsterdam

29 May: ARTEDI visits Stratford on the east side of London

13 June: LINNAEUS and SOHLBERG arrive in Amsterdam

14 June: LINNAEUS visits JOHANNES BURMANN in Amsterdam

15 June: LINNAEUS visits ALBERTUS SEBA in Amsterdam

16 June: LINNAEUS departs Amsterdam for Harderwijk

17 June: LINNAEUS arrives at Harderwijk

18 June: LINNAEUS is made Candidate of Medicine

23 June: LINNAEUS received his doctorate in medicine

24 June: LINNAEUS returns to Amsterdam

5 July: LINNAEUS visits HERMANUS BOERHAAVE in Leiden

8 July: LINNAEUS and ARTEDI meet unexpectedly in Leiden

17 July: LINNAEUS introduces ARTEDI to SEBA in Amsterdam

Early August: LINNAEUS and ARTEDI meet in Amsterdam for the last time

13 August: LINNAEUS and BURMANN visit GEORGE CLIFFORD at Hartekamp

24 September: LINNAEUS departs Amsterdam for Hartekamp

27 September: ARTEDI dines with friends at the house of SEBA on the Haarlemmerdijk

28 September: ARTEDI's body is discovered floating in a canal

29 September: LINNAEUS at Hartekamp, learns of ARTEDI's death, departs for Amsterdam

30 September: LINNAEUS, arriving in Amsterdam by late morning, views ARTEDI's body

30 September: Amsterdam public notary DORPER inventories ARTEDI's possessions

2 October: ARTEDI is buried in ST. ANTHONY's Churchyard

Mid-November: LINNAEUS acquires ARTEDI's manuscripts

9 December: Printing of the first edition of *Systema Naturae* is completed in Leiden

13 December: LINNAEUS receives the first copies of his *Systema Naturae*

19 December: Copies of *Systema Naturae* are sent to HANS SLOANE in London

1736 LINNAEUS publishes *Bibliotheca Botanica* and *Fundamenta Botanica*

2 May: ALBERTUS SEBA dies in Amsterdam

21 July: LINNAEUS departs for London

Late August: LINNAEUS returns to Holland

1737 LINNAEUS publishes *Musa Cliffortiana*, *Critica Botanica*, *Flora Lapponica*, *Genera Plantarum*, *Methodus Sexualis*, and *Hortus Cliffortianus*

1738 LINNAEUS publishes *Classes Plantarum*

April: LINNAEUS publishes ARTEDI's *Ichthyologia*

May: LINNAEUS departs Holland for Sweden by way of Paris

23 September: HERMANUS BOERHAAVE dies in Leiden

1739 June: LINNAEUS marries SARA ELISABET MORAEA

1751 LINNAEUS publishes *Philosophia Botanica*

1753 LINNAEUS publishes *Species Plantarum*

1758 LINNAEUS publishes the tenth edition of his *Systema Naturae*

1774 May: LINNAEUS suffers a stroke that leaves him partially paralyzed for a time

1777 Winter: LINNAEUS has another stroke

1777 30 December: LINNAEUS has a severe seizure

1778 10 January: LINNAEUS dies in Uppsala

Biographical Notes

AELIANUS, CLAUDIUS (c. 175–c. 235), often seen as just AELIAN: Born at Praeneste, a Roman author and teacher of rhetoric who flourished under SEPTIMIUS SEVERUS. He wrote *On the Nature of Animals*, a curious collection, in 17 books, of brief stories of natural history.

ALDROVANDI, ULISSE (1522–1605): Italian nobleman in Bologna who spent his life and fortune assembling the materials for a great natural history, which was eventually published, mostly posthumously, in 13 folio volumes between 1599 and 1688; commemorated by LINNAEUS with the name *Aldrovanda*.

ALSTRÖMER, Baron CLAES (1739–1794): Son of the more famous JONAS ALSTRÖMER (1685–1761) and student of LINNAEUS who traveled through Spain and other European countries; later a government advisor and owner of Alingsås textile manufacturers; honored by LINNAEUS with the name *Alstroemeria*.

ANDERSSON (?–?): Burgomaster (and his brother) of Hamburg during LINNAEUS's visit to that town in May 1735.

ANTONISZ, JAN MOL (?–?): Lawyer in Amsterdam commissioned by the court to represent PETER ARTEDI after the latter's death in 1735.

ARCTAEDIUS, MÅRTEN (1669–?): Son of PETRUS MARTINI ARCTAEDIUS and ANNA OLOFSDOTTER GRUBB, and uncle of PETER ARTEDI.

ARCTAEDIUS, OLAUS (1670–1728): Son of PETRUS MARTINI ARCTAEDIUS and ANNA OLOFSDOTTER GRUBB, and father of PETER ARTEDI.

ARCTAEDIUS, PETRUS MARTINI (c. 1635–shortly after 1716): Father of MÅRTEN and OLAUS ARCTAEDIUS and grandfather of PETER ARTEDI.

ARISTARCHUS of Samos (c. 310–c. 230 B.C.): Greek philosopher, often referred to as the COPERNICUS of antiquity, laid the foundation for a scientific examination of the heavens. According to his contemporary, ARCHIMEDES, ARISTARCHUS was the first to propose not only a heliocentric universe, but one larger than any of the geocentric universes proposed by his predecessors.

ARISTOTLE (384–322 B.C.): Greek philosopher, famous for his *Historia Animalium*, among many other writings.

BÄCK, ABRAHAM (1713–1795): Swedish physician, president of the *Collegium Medicum*, Stockholm, and close friend of LINNAEUS.

BANKS, Sir JOSEPH (1743–1820): President of the Royal Society of London who went on Captain COOK's first circumnavigation of the globe aboard the *Endeavour* (1768–1771), with LINNAEUS's student DANIEL SOLANDER employed as botanist; honored by LINNAEUS with the name *Banksia*.

BAUHIN, CASPAR (1560–1624): Swiss botanist, brother of JOHANN BAUHIN, professor of anatomy and botany in Basel, and author of *Pinax Theatri Botanici* (1620); he and his brother commemorated by LINNAEUS with the name *Bauhinia*, a genus of evergreen shrubs, the bi-lobed leaves of which exemplify the two brothers.

BAUHIN, JOHANN (1541–1613): Swiss botanist, brother of CASPAR BAUHIN, responsible for, among other works, the great *Historia Plantarum*, published in 1652, nearly forty years after his death; he and his brother commemorated by LINNAEUS with the name *Bauhinia*, a genus of evergreen shrubs, the bi-lobed leaves of which exemplify the two brothers.

BELON, PIERRE (1517–1564): French naturalist who published, among other things, a number of books on fishes and other aquatic organisms, the most important of which are *Histoire naturelle des estranges poissons marins*, Paris, 1551; and *De aquatilibus, libri duo*, Paris, 1553; commemorated by LINNAEUS with the name *Bellonia*.

BENZELSTIERNA, MATTHIAS (1713–1791): Student of STOBAEUS and friend of LINNAEUS at Lund.

BERGIUS, PETER JONAS (1730–1790): Student of LINNAEUS and later a botanist, physician, and professor of natural history in Stockholm.

BERLIN, ANDERS (1746–1773): Student of LINNAEUS who traveled to present-day Guinea Bissau and Senegal, where he died without having accomplished his mission.

BEUDEKER, CHRISTOFFEL (1675–1756): Wealthy merchant and landowner in Amsterdam who maintained a cabinet of insects, shells, coins, and especially printed maps.

BLACKWELL, ELIZABETH (1700–1758): Scottish botanist, among the first women to achieve fame as a botanical illustrator, wife of ALEXANDER BLACKWELL.

BLANCARDUS (BLANCKAERT or BLANKAART), STEPHANUS (1650–1704): Anatomist and pharmacist in Amsterdam, who in 1679 published a *Lexicon novum medicum* that went through several other editions appearing as late as 1748.

BOERHAAVE, HERMANUS (1668–1738): Professor of botany, medicine, and chemistry at Leiden, and LINNAEUS's patron during the time he spent in Holland (1735–1738); honored by LINNAEUS with the name *Boerhavia*.

BRODERSONIA, CHRISTINA (1688–1733): Mother of LINNAEUS and daughter of SAMUEL BRODERSONIUS; married NICOLAUS (NILS) INGEMARSSON LINNAEUS (1705).

BRODERSONIUS, SAMUEL PETRI (c. 1658–1707): Father of CHRISTINA BRODERSONIA, LINNAEUS's mother; rector of Stenbrohult, Småland.

BROMELLIUS, OLOF (1629–1705): Swedish botanist; honored by LINNAEUS with the name *Bromelia*.

BURMANN, JOHANNES (1706–1776): Dutch botanist and professor of medicine at Amsterdam; LINNAEUS's friend and colleague during the latter's years in Holland (1735–1738); honored by LINNAEUS with the name *Burmannia*.

BURMANN, NIKOLAAS LAURENS (1733–1793): Son of JOHANNES BURMANN; pupil of LINNAEUS in Uppsala in 1760 and later a Dutch botanist and professor of medicine at Amsterdam.

CATESBY, MARK (1682–1749): English naturalist and artist, best known for his illustrated work *The Natural history of Carolina, Florida, and the Bahamas*, published in London in two volumes, 1731–1743.

CAVALLIUS, OLAUS (1648–1708): Bishop of Växjö.

CELSIUS, ANDERS (1701–1744): Professor of astronomy at Uppsala; invented the Celsius or centigrade thermometer, but used 100 to denote the freezing temperature of water and zero for its boiling point, which numbers were later reversed by LINNAEUS to create the present standard.

CELSIUS the Elder, OLOF (1670–1756): Professor of theology at Uppsala; teacher and patron of LINNAEUS who employed him to help botanize around Uppsala during LINNAEUS's impoverished student days; honored by LINNAEUS with the name *Celsia*.

CESALPINI, ANDREA (1519–1603): Italian botanist, philosopher, and physician to Pope CLEMENT VIII, author of *De Plantis* (1583) and other works.

CHARLES XII (1682–1718): King of Sweden (1697–1718), came to the throne at the age of 15, a precocious boy filled with martial ardor and fanatical courage; during the Great Northern War, which lasted from 1699 to 1721, he defended his country with such fury that he earned the title of the "madman of the North" and went down to final defeat only after an incredible struggle against overwhelming odds. During the rest of the eighteenth century, Sweden rapidly fell to the position of a second-rate power.

CLIFFORD, GEORGE (1685–1760): Wealthy Dutch merchant-banker of English descent, the plants of whose magnificent garden at Hartekamp were described by LINNAEUS in his *Hortus Cliffortianus* (1738); LINNAEUS's most important patron during his time in Holland (1735–1738); honored by LINNAEUS with the name *Cliffortia*.

COLLEN, JEREMIAS VAN (?–?): Alderman in Amsterdam during the time of ARTEDI's death.

COMMELIN, JOHANNES (?–?): Alderman in Amsterdam during the time of ARTEDI's death; no doubt related to the great Dutch COMMELIN family of scholars.

COOK, JAMES (1728–1779): Officer of the English Royal Navy, renowned explorer, navigator, and surveyor, who commanded three major voyages around the world, the last of which resulted in his death on Hawaii, killed by islanders in January 1779; accompanied by JOSEPH BANKS, he took LINNAEUS's student DANIEL SOLANDER with him as botanist on his first circumnavigation of the globe aboard the HMS *Endeavour* (1768–1771).

COURT, PIETER DE LA (?–1772): Alderman during the time of ARTEDI's death who held several public offices in Amsterdam, including administrator of the Dutch East Indies Company (1744), member of the city council (1744–1772), sheriff's officer, and burgomaster (1769); he lived on the Herrengracht, between Huidenstraat and Wolvenstraat.

CREIGHTON, J.A. (?–?): Alderman in Amsterdam during the time of ARTEDI's death.

DESCARTES, RENÉ (1728–1779): French philosopher and mathematician who worked out a philosophic system that set God and the human soul aside as not susceptible to human observation and which was otherwise materialistic.

DILLENIUS, JOHANN JACOB (1684–1747): Physician and professor of botany at Oxford; an early critic of LINNAEUS; honored by LINNAEUS with the name *Dillenia*.

DORPER, SALOMON (?–1784): Notary public at Amsterdam who inventoried ARTEDI's estate on 30 September 1735.

DREYERN (?–?): Merchant in Hamburg, apparently in partnership with HAMBEL; one time owner of the famous Seven-headed Hydra of Hamburg.

EDWARDS, GEORGE (1693–1773): English naturalist and artist, the "father of British ornithology," best known for his *History of Birds*, published in four volumes from 1743 to 1751.

EHRET, GEORG DIONYSIUS (1708–1770): Celebrated German botanical draughtsman, who settled in England—one of the greatest artists of natural history of all time, and said to be the finest flower painter of his age; illustrated, among other things, LINNAEUS's *Hortus Cliffortianus* (dated 1737, but not actually published until 1738).

EIBSEN, F. (?–?): Preacher in the town of Wursten in the Duchy of Bremen who provided ALBERTUS SEBA with information on the Seven-headed Hydra of Hamburg.

ELVIUS, PETER (1710–1749): Student who came to LINNAEUS for private instruction during the latter's early years at Uppsala; later secretary of the Swedish Academy of Sciences.

FABRICIUS, JOHANN ALBERT (1668–1736): German philologist, theologian, and professor of philosophy at Hamburg.

FALCK, ANDERS (1740–1796): Astronomer, brother of LINNAEUS's student JOHAN PETER FALCK.

FALCK, JOHAN PETER (1732–1774): Student of LINNAEUS who traveled to Russia, the Caucasus, Kazan, and West Siberia (1768–1774) as part of the Orenburg Expedition; professor and curator of the botanic garden at St. Petersburg; honored by LINNAEUS with the name *Falkia*.

FORSSKÅL, PETER (1732–1763): Student of LINNAEUS who traveled to Egypt and the region of present-day Israel, Jordan, Saudi Arabia, and Yemen (1761–1763); made professor of botany but died before he could take up the post; honored by LINNAEUS with the name of the common nettle *Forsskohlia*, given in memory of his "bitter death."

FOTHERGILL, JOHN (1712–1780): Quaker physician at Stratford, Essex, England, and famous collector, whose cabinet of zoological and mineralogical specimens, as well as his botanical garden at Upton Park, was well known; honored by LINNAEUS with the name *Fothergilla* for the dwarf alder.

FRANKLIN, BENJAMIN (1706–1790): American printer, scientist, philosopher, and statesman; met with LINNAEUS's student PETER KALM during the latter's visit to Philadelphia in 1748.

GALILEO GALILEI (1564–1642): Great Italian astronomer, mathematician, and physicist, who laid the foundations for modern experimental science; by the construction of astronomical telescopes he greatly enlarged humanity's vision and conception of the universe.

GAUBIUS, HIERONYMUS DAVID (1705–1780): German physician, and professor of chemistry and medicine at Leiden.

GEORGE I (GEORGE LOUIS) (1660–1727): Hanoverian King of Great Britain and Ireland from 1714 to 1727.

GEORGE II (GEORGE AUGUSTUS) (1683–1760): Hanoverian King of England from 1727 to 1760.

GESSNER, CONRAD (1516–1565): Most celebrated naturalist of his day, the father of bibliography, and one of the most learned men of all time; published *Historiae Animalium* (1551–1587), a vast encyclopedic review of zoological knowledge from the time of ARISTOTLE; commemorated by LINNAEUS with the name *Gesneria*.

GORTER, DAVID DE (1717–1783): Dutch botanist and physician; succeeded his father JOHANNES DE GORTER as personal physician of Empress ELISABETH of Russia; published *Flora Belgica* in 1767.

GORTER, JOHANNES DE (1689–1762): Dutch physician and professor of medicine at Harderwijk; served as LINNAEUS's sponsor during the latter's examination for the degree of doctor of medicine in 1735.

GRILL, ANTHONI (1705–1748): Swedish merchant and assayer in Amsterdam during the 1730s.

GRONOVIUS, JOHAN FREDERIK (1686–1762): Dutch botanist, physician, and senator in Leiden; one of LINNAEUS's most important patrons during his years in Holland (1735–1738); a member of the celebrated GRONOVIUS family of classical scholars and author of *Flora Virginica* (1739–1743).

GROOT, JOHAN WILLEM DE (?–?): Dutch printer in Leiden.

GRUBB, ANNA OLOFSDOTTER (c. 1652–1731): Wife of PETRUS MARTINI ARCTAEDIUS, mother of MÅRTEN and OLAUS ARCTAE-DIUS, and grandmother of PETER ARTEDI.

GÜNTHER, JOHANNES (?–?): Apprentice apothecary and assistant at the house of ALBERTUS SEBA, contracted for a two-year period on 1 November 1733.

GUSTAF III (1746–1792): King of Sweden, reigned 1771–1792.

HAAK, THEODOR (?–?): Dutch publisher in Leiden; produced the first edition of LINNAEUS's *Systema Naturae* in 1735.

HALLER, ALBRECHT VON (1708–1777): Swiss botanist and anato-mist, professor of medicine at Göttingen, and prolific correspondent of LINNAEUS, but seemingly in constant combat with the latter; hon-ored by LINNAEUS with the name *Halleria*.

HALLEY, EDMOND (or EDMUND) (1656–1742): English astronomer who established the first observatory in the southern hemisphere on the island of St. Helena; discovered the comet that bears his name; was appointed Royal Astronomer at Greenwich Observatory after the death of JOHN FLAMSTEED in 1720.

HAMBEL (?–?): Merchant in Hamburg, apparently in partnership with DREYERN; one time owner of the famous Seven-headed Hydra of Hamburg.

HASSELQUIST, FREDRIK (1722–1752): Student of LINNAEUS who traveled to Egypt and the region of present-day Israel, Lebanon, and Turkey (1749–1752); teaching fellow in medicine at Uppsala; died in Smyrna at age 30; honored by LINNAEUS with the name *Hasselquistia*.

HEBENSTREIT, JOHANN ERNST (1703–1757): German anatomist and explorer; professor at Leipzig in 1729; traveled in North Africa, 1731–1735.

HEISTER, LAURENTIUS (1683–1758): German anatomist and surgeon, considered the father of German surgery; professor of anatomy and surgery, later of theoretical medicine and botany, at Helmstädt; best known for his *Compendium anatomicum*, published at Altdorf in 1727.

HENCKEL, JOHANN FRIEDRICH (1678–1744): German chemist and mineralogist, councillor of mining and mine physican at Freiberg, and author of *De medicorum chymicorum appropriatione in argenti cum acido salis communis communicatione*, published in Dresden in 1726.

HERMANN, PAUL (1646–1695): German botanist, physician at Batavia, and later professor of botany at Leiden.

HOMRIGH, ROELAND WILLEM VAN (1711–sometime after 1762): Son-in-law of ALBERTUS SEBA, husband of JOHANNA SEBA, who he married on 26 October 1734; instrumental in the publication of the third (1759) and fourth (1765) volumes of SEBA's *Thesaurus*.

HÖÖK, GABRIEL (1698–1769): Lecturer at Växjö and later rector of Wirestad in Småland; one of LINNAEUS's early tutors; married LINNAEUS's sister ANNA MARIA LINNAEUS.

HOUBRAKEN, JACOBUS (1698–1780): Dutch engraver, born at Dordrecht, resident of Amsterdam in 1707; devoting himself almost entirely to portraiture, his best works are probably scenes from the comedy of *De Ontdekte Schijndeugd*, produced in his eightieth year.

INGEMARSSON LINNAEUS, NICOLAUS (NILS) (1674–1748): Father of LINNAEUS, perpetual curate of Råshult (1705) and rector of Stenbrohult, Småland (1708); married CHRISTINA BRODERSONIA in 1705.

JAENISCH (JÄNISCH), GOTTFRIED JACOB (?–1784): German doctor of medicine at Hamburg.

JONSTONUS, JOANNES (1603–1675): Born at Lessno (Lissa) in the palatinate of Posen of a family originally from Scotland, he was an assiduous encyclopedic compiler, publishing numerous works. He is best known for his *Historiae Naturalis*, which appeared in installments at Frankfurt am Main, seven parts in folio, from 1649 to 1662.

JÜTTINCK, HENDRICK WILLEM (?–?): Owner of the lodging house at 16 Warmoesstraat, near the Nieuwebrugsteeg, in the dock area on the riverfront of Amsterdam, where PETER ARTEDI resided in 1735.

KÄHLER, MÅRTEN (1728–1773): Student of LINNAEUS who traveled in Italy (1752); later served as physician for the admiralty at Karlskrona.

KALM, PETER (1715–1779): Finnish student of LINNAEUS who traveled in northwest Russia (1744–1745) and to the British colonies of North America and to southern Canada (1748–1751); later professor of economics and natural history at Åbo; honored by LINNAEUS with the name *Kalmia*.

KEERSEBERGH, PHILIP (?–?): Apprentice apothecary and assistant at the house of ALBERTUS SEBA from 1 January 1726 to SEBA'S death on 2 May 1736.

KOHL, JOHANN PETER (1698–1778): German professor of ecclesiastical history in St. Petersburg; later author and journalist in Hamburg.

KÖNIG, JOHAN GERARD (1728–1785): Student of LINNAEUS who traveled in the region of present-day Thailand, Sri Lanka, and Tranquebar (1767–1785); appointed Danish trade-post physician at Tranquebar, he remained there until his death.

KÖNIGSMARCK, HANS KRISTOFER, COUNT VON (1600–1663): Swedish field marshall; one time owner of the famous Seven-headed Hydra of Hamburg, later inherited by COUNT VON LEEUWENHAUPT.

KOULAS, DAVID SAMUEL (1699–1743): Friend of LINNAEUS while resident at the house of STOBAEUS in Lund; later instructor in Malmö.

KREEK, JAAP DE: Fictitious tavern owner on the nearby corner of the Warmoesstraat and Nieuwebrugsteeg, just across from the Sign of the Lompen.

LAWSON, ISAAC (1704–1747): Wealthy Scottish botanist and physician; assisted LINNAEUS in the publication of the first edition of the *Systema Naturae* in 1735.

LEEUWENHAUPT, COUNT VON (?–?): One time owner of the Seven-headed Hydra of Hamburg, inherited from COUNT VON KÖNIGSMARCK.

LEIBNITZ, BARON GOTTFRIED WILHELM VON (1646–1716): One of the most profound philosopher-scientists of modern times, but probably best known as ISAAC NEWTON's antagonist in an ill-fated priority battle over the invention of the differential calculus. A philosopher of the Enlightenment, he put great stress on the importance of pure reason, and thought that by it man could transcend the material universe.

LETSTRÖM, PETER (1707–1748): Student who came to LINNAEUS for private instruction during the latter's early years at Uppsala; later assessor of the Royal College of Medicine in Stockholm.

LIEBERKÜHN, JOHANNES NATHANIEL (1711–1756): German physician, anatomist, and physicist, most widely known for development of the solar microscope, studies of the intestine, and invention of a reflector for improving microscopic viewing of opaque specimens. He was also a member of the mathematics department at the Berlin Academy of Sciences and created a lens that enhanced the use of early portable microscopes for botanical fieldwork.

LILJA, LARS (?–?): Owner of a tavern, the King of Sweden, in the harbor district of Shadwell, frequented by ARTEDI during his visit to London in 1734–1735.

LINNAEA, ANNA MARIA (1710–1769): The oldest of LINNAEUS's three sisters; married GABRIEL HÖÖK, a clergyman and one of LINNAEUS's early tutors, with whom she had ten children.

LINNAEA, CHRISTINA BRODERSONIA (1688–1733): LINNAEUS's mother, wife of NILS LINNAEUS.

LINNAEA, ELISABET CHRISTINA (LISA STINA) (1743–1782): LINNAEUS's eldest daughter; married CARL FREDRIK BERGENCRANTZ (1726–1792).

LINNAEA, LOVISA (1749–1839): LINNAEUS's third daughter (his second, SARA MAGDALENA, born 1744, died in infancy) who never married and outlived the family.

LINNAEA, SARA CHRISTINA (SARA STINA) (1751–1835): LINNAEUS's fourth daughter.

LINNAEA, SOPHIA (1757–1830): LINNAEUS's fifth daughter.

LINNAEUS, CARL the Younger (1741–1783): LINNAEUS's first child and only surviving son (a second son, JOHANNES, born in 1754, died in 1757); demonstrator at the Uppsala botanic garden at age eighteen, and later (1763) joint Professor of Botany with his father, at whose death (1778) he was elected also to the chair of medicine; he never married and died without issue.

LINNAEUS, JOHANNES (1754–1757): Second son of LINNAEUS, died before the age of three.

LINNAEUS, NICOLAUS (NILS) INGEMARSSON (1674–1748): Father of LINNAEUS, perpetual curate of Råshult (1705) and rector of Stenbrohult, Småland (1708); married CHRISTINA BRODERSONIA in 1705.

LÖFLING, PEHR (1729–1756): Student of LINNAEUS who traveled in Spain and Spanish South America (1751–1756); died of fever in present-day Venezuela; honored by LINNAEUS with the name *Loeflingia*.

LOON, VAN (?–?): Alderman in Amsterdam during the time of ARTEDI's death in 1735.

LOOPES , ANNA (1674–1738): Wife of ALBERTUS SEBA, who he married on 3 June 1698.

LOOPES, ENGEL (?–?): From the Egelantiersgracht in Amsterdam, father of ANNA LOOPES and father-in-law of ALBERTUS SEBA.

LOVISA ULRIKA (1720–1782): Queen of Sweden and sister of FREDERICK the Great of Prussia, whose curiosity cabinet and that of her husband, ADOLF FREDRIK, was arranged by LINNAEUS.

MÅNSSON, ARFWIDH or ARVID (c. 1590–c. 1649): Swedish teacher of natural history from Rydaholm, Småland; author of *En myckit nyttigh Örta-Bok*, a herbal first published in 1642 at Stockholm.

MARSIGLI, LUIGI FERDINANDO, COUNT DE (1658–1730): Italian geographer and naturalist whose principal works include *Histoire Physique de la Mer*, translated by LECLERC (Amsterdam, 1725); and *Danubius Pannonico-mysicus* in seven volumes (The Hague, 1726).

MARTIN, ANTON ROLANDSSON (1729–1785): Student of LINNAEUS who traveled in Norway and along the Arctic coast (1758–1760); later instructor at Åbo.

MARTIN, PETER (1686–1727): Son-in-law of RUDBECK the Younger who in early 1724 took over RUDBECK's teaching duties at Uppsala University; later Professor of Medicine in Uppsala and member of the Royal Medical Board; married VENDELA CHARLOTTA RUDBECK in 1714.

MEAD, RICHARD (1673–1754): Influential English physician who advanced the practice of inoculations; appointed to King GEORGE II in 1727.

MERIAN (MERIANA), MARIA SIBYLLA (1647–1717): German artist and naturalist who, at age 52, undertook a three-month expedition to Surinam in 1699, with her twenty-one-year-old daughter DOROTHEA, financed in part by the city fathers of Amsterdam; her most important work is *Metamorphosis Insectorum Surinamensium*, published in 1705.

MILLER, PHILIP (1691–1771): English horticulturist of Scottish extraction, gardener of the Chelsea Physic Garden; he corresponded with many contemporary botanists; his large and valuable herbarium was later sold to Sir JOSEPH BANKS.

MOLENBEEK, ANNA (?–?): Most probably a maidservant in the employ of HENDRICK JÜTTINCK, who registered ARTEDI as a pauper unable to pay for his own funeral.

MONTIN, LARS (1723–1785): Student of LINNAEUS who traveled in Lapland (1745–1751); later a regional public doctor in Halland.

MORAEA, SARA ELISABET (LISA) (1716–1806): LINNAEUS's wife, married in June 1739.

MORAEAUS, JOHAN (1672–1742): LINNAEUS's father-in-law; public doctor of the copper-mining town of Falun in Dalecarlia.

MORTIMER, CROMWELL (c. 1693–1752): English doctor of medicine and secretary of the Royal Society of London.

NATORP, JOHN FREDERICK (?–?): Naturalist from Hamburg who provided ALBERTUS SEBA with a drawing of the Seven-headed Hydra from which SEBA's engraving was made.

NEWTON, ISAAC (1643–1727): English physicist and mathematician who produced the most important and influential works on physics of all times, including formulation of the three laws of motion, now known as NEWTON's Laws; he invented the calculus years before LEIBNIZ, but failed to publish his work until after LEIBNIZ had published his; president of the Royal Society of London preceding HANS SLOANE.

NIEBUHR, CARSTEN (1733–1815): Danish voyager of discovery (with PETER FORSSKÅL), only survivor of the Arabian Expedition; member of the Swedish Academy of Science.

ORANGE, Prince of (WILLIAM V) (1748–1806): Stadholder of the Dutch Netherlands from 1751–1795, famous for his menagerie and large collection of natural curiosities.

ORPHEUS: In Greek mythology, the son of CALLIOPE and either OEAGRUS or APOLLO. He was the greatest musician and poet of Greek myth, whose songs could charm wild beasts and coax even rocks and trees into movement. He was one of the Argonauts, and when the *Argo* had to pass the island of the Sirens, it was ORPHEUS's music that prevented the crew from being lured to destruction.

OSBECK, PEHR (1723–1805): Student of LINNAEUS who traveled to Guangzhou (1750–1752) as ship's chaplain for the Swedish East India Company; later country parson at Hasslöv, Halland; commemorated by LINNAEUS with the name *Osbeckia*.

PALMBERG, JOHANNES (c. 1640–1691): Botanist, and lecturer at Stängnäs; later rector of Turinge; author of *Serta Florea Suecana eller Svenske örtekrantz* published in 1684.

PETER the Great (1672–1725): Czar of Russia from 1682, emperor of Russia from 1721; opened Russia to the West by inviting the best European engineers, shipbuilders, architects, craftsmen, and merchants to come to Russia; hundreds of Russians were sent to Europe to get the best education and learn different arts and crafts.

PLATO (427–347 B.C.): Greek philosopher and a pupil of SOCRATES who formed a school in the garden of Academus in 386 B.C.; the best known of all the Greeks, most famous for his *Republic*.

PLUMIER, CHARLES (1646–1704): French botanist, friend of TOURNEFORT, and priest of the Order of the Minims, who made three voyages to Martinique and neighboring islands; among a number of botanical works, he is best known for his *Description des plantes de l'Amérique*, which appeared in 1693, and *Plantarum Americanarum*, published posthumously under the editorship of JOHANNES BURMANN from 1755–1760; commemorated by LINNAEUS with the name *Plumeria*.

PORTLAND, Duchess of (MARGARET CAVENDISH-BENTINCK) (1715–1785): English aristocrat and one of the foremost private collectors of the eighteenth century, her main interest was in shells, some of which she acquired from COOK's expeditions; when she died, her huge collection was auctioned, attracting buyers from all over Europe.

PREUTZ, ELIAS (1696–1739): Medical assistant at Uppsala University; later provincial physician in Skara; replaced for incompetence as lecturer at Uppsala by LINNAEUS.

QUINKHARD, JAN MAURITS (1688–1772): Dutch painter and art dealer who painted a portrait of ALBERTUS SEBA.

RAY, JOHN (1627–1705): English theologian and one of the great naturalists of the seventeenth century; Fellow of Trinity College, Cambridge; perhaps best known for his *Catalogus Plantarum* of 1660 and *The Wisdom of God Manifested in the Works of the Creation* of 1691; associated with FRANCIS WILLUGHBY, whose *Ornithologiae* (1676) and *Historia piscium* (1686) were completed and edited by RAY after the death of their author in 1672.

RENARD, JEANNE (1714–1746): Daughter of LOUIS RENARD; committed suicide by drowning herself in an Amsterdam canal shortly after her father's death in 1746.

RENARD, LOUIS (1678/79–1746): French Huguenot book-dealer, publisher, foreign agent, and seller of medicinals in Amsterdam.

ROBERG, LARS (1664–1721): Professor of medicine at Uppsala, responsible for theoretical and practical medicine, surgery, physiology, and chemistry; renowned for his miserliness.

ROLANDER, DANIEL (1725–1793): Student of LINNAEUS and specialist in entomology who traveled to Surinam (1755–1756); on his return, instead of presenting his collections to LINNAEUS, he sold them to two Copenhagen professors; later became insane and lived on public charity until his death.

RONDELET, GUILLAUME (1507–1566): Chancellor of the University of Montpellier and influential professor of natural history and medicine; composed two works on fishes and other aquatic animals: *Libri de Piscibus Marinis*, published in 1554, and *Universae Aquatilium Historiae*, dated 1555; commemorated by LINNAEUS with the name *Rondeletia*.

ROSÉN, NILS VON ROSENSTEIN (1706–1773): Professor of anatomy and medicine at Uppsala who cooperated with LINNAEUS in a campaign for breastfeeding babies.

ROTHMAN, JOHAN STENSSON (1684–1763): LINNAEUS's teacher and benefactor at Växjö who introduced LINNAEUS to the works of TOURNEFORT and other prominent naturalists.

ROYEN, ADRIAAN VAN (1705–1779): Dutch professor of botany and director of the botanical garden of Leiden.

RUDBECK the Elder, OLOF (1630–1702): Swedish professor of botany and anatomy at Uppsala whose nearly finished manuscript of an illustrated edition of CASPAR BAUHIN's *Pinax* (1620), along with several thousand finished woodcuts, was lost in the great Uppsala fire of 1702; commemorated, along with his son of the same name, by LINNAEUS with the name *Rudbeckia*.

RUDBECK the Younger, OLOF (1660–1740): Son of OLOF RUDBECK the Elder; professor of botany and medicine at Uppsala, succeeding his father; LINNAEUS's teacher and primary benefactor at Uppsala at whose house he lived as tutor to his sons; commemorated, along with his father of the same name, by LINNAEUS with the name *Rudbeckia*.

RUDBECK, JOHAN OLOF (1711–1790): Son of OLOF RUDBECK the Younger; tutored by LINNAEUS.

RUDBECK, VENDELA CHARLOTTA (1692–1729): daughter of RUDBECK the Younger and wife of PETER MARTIN.

RUMPHIUS (RUMPF), GEORGIUS EVERHARDUS (1628–1702): Dutch naturalist and merchant in the service of the Dutch East India Company and governor of the Dutch colony at Ambon; he published two works on the flora of the island of Ambon.

RUYSCH, FREDERIK (1638–1731): Dutch physician and naturalist; professor of botany at Amsterdam, later in anatomy; human and comparative anatomy were his primary interest, but he spared nothing to add additional objects of nature to his collection; he was especially well known for his collection of injected human bodies, which he was able to maintain in a fresh state for long periods of time; his museum in Amsterdam displayed entire bodies of infants and adults in a state of mummification, all arranged to express dramatic gestures.

RUYSCH, HENDRIK (1663–1727): Son of FREDERIK RUYSCH; like his father, he followed a medical career, inheriting the post of city obstetrician of Amsterdam from FREDERIK in 1712. HENDRIK is said to have shared the secret composition of his father's embalming fluid, the use of which enabled FREDERIK to preserve entire corpses "which appear still to be alive but which have been dead for about two years."

SALTER, JAMES (?–?): Proprietor of "DON SALTERO'S" coffee-house in Chelsea, England, originally established in 1695; SALTER was nicknamed DON SALTERO by Vice-Admiral MUNDEN who had spent time in Spain and acquired a fondness for Spanish titles. The coffee shop is mentioned in FRANCES (FANNY) BURNEY'S 1778 novel *Evelina*. SALTER's bizarre collection of curios epitomized the non-scientific approach to natural history prevalent at the time. He promoted his shop as a place of marvels and wonder. An advertisement placed in *Mist's Weekly Journal* in 1728 spoke of "Monsters of all sorts here are seen, Strange things in Nature, as they grew so, Some relics of the Sheba Queen, And fragments of the famed BOB CRUSOE. Knick-Knacks, too, dangle round the wall, Some in glass cases, some on the shelf, But what's the rarest sight of all? Your humble Servant shows Himself."

SALVIANI, HIPPOLYTE (1514–1572): Italian physician who published a magnificently illustrated book on fishes, the *Aquatilium Animalium Historiae*, in folio, from 1554–1558.

SCHEUCHZER, JOHANN JACOB (1672–1733): Swiss naturalist, physician, historian, and mathematician, said to be the founder of paleontology; not to be confused with his brother, JOHANN SCHEUCHZER (1684–1738), Swiss botanist and professor of physics at Zürich.

SCHNELL (SNELL), CARL CHRISTOPHER (C.1688–1771): Physician at Lund who in KILIAN STOBAEUS'S absence treated

LINNAEUS for an insect bite that had become infected, thereby perhaps saving his life.

SEBA, ALBERTUS (1665–1736): Rich pharmacist residing in Amsterdam who assembled at great cost a large cabinet of natural history, a part of which was purchased by PETER the Great and transported to St. Petersburg, and the rest dispersed upon SEBA's death. He had his collection described and magnificently engraved in four folio volumes, published at Amsterdam in 1734, 1735, 1759, and 1765, the last two volumes appearing posthumously. The text of the third volume contains articles on fishes prepared by ARTEDI.

SEBA, JOHANNA (1710–1758): Youngest of the four daughters of ALBERTUS SEBA and ANNA LOOPES; married ROELAND WILLEM VAN HOMRIGH in 1734.

SERENIUS, JACOB (1700–after 1771): Bishop of the Swedish parish in London from 1723 to 1734, who provided ARTEDI with a letter of introduction to HANS SLOANE.

SHAW, GEORGE (1751–1813): Curator of the zoological collections of the British Museum, author of *The Naturalists Miscellany*, published from 1789–1813; a *Zoology of New Holland*, published in 1794; and in particular, a compilation titled *General Zoology or Systematic Natural History*, thirteen volumes published from 1800–1826.

SHAW, PETER (1694–1763): English medical doctor, author of *A New Practice of Physic, wherein the various diseases incident to the human body are orderly described, their causes assign'd, their diagnostics and prognostics enumerated, and the regimen proper in each deliver'd . . . , the whole formed on the model of Dr. Sydenham, and completing the design of his Processus Integri*, second edition in two volumes, London, 1728.

SHERARD, JACOB (?–?): Unknown member of the large SHERARD family of scholars.

SIDENIA, HELENA (1682–1759): Second wife of OLAUS ARCTAEDIUS and mother of PETER ARTEDI.

SIDENIUS, PETRUS (1592–1666): Court chaplain in Stockholm; father of HELENA SIDENIA and maternal grandfather of PETER ARTEDI.

SIEGESBECK, JOHAN GEORG (1686–1755): Medical doctor and botanical demonstrator at St. Petersburg; LINNAEUS's bitter antagonist who challenged his theory of plant sexuality, partly on moral grounds; remembered by LINNAEUS with the name *Sigesbeckia*, a small-flowered weedy plant.

SLOANE, HANS (1660–1753): English physician, naturalist and fanatical collector; secretary of the Royal Society of London in 1693, president from 1727 until his death; his vast collections of objects of natural history were donated to the English nation and formed the foundation of the British Museum; among his publication, he is best known for *Voyage to the islands of Madeira, Barbados, Nièves, St. Christopher's, and Jamaica*, London, 1707–1725, two volumes in folio, with two hundred and seventy-four plates.

SMITH, WILLIAM (?–?): Printer in Amsterdam who, in collaboration with JANSSONIUS VAN WAESBERGE and WETTSTEIN, produced the first volume of ALBERTUS SEBA's *Locupletissimus rerum Naturalium Thesauri* in 1734.

SOBIESKI, JOHN (JOHN III) (1629–1696): King of Poland from 1674 to 1696; avid collector of art and objects of natural history; champion of Christian Europe against the Ottomans.

SOHLBERG, CLAES (1711–1773): LINNAEUS's friend, fellow student, and traveling companion on the journeys to Dalarna and Holland, whose father was inspector of mines at Falun, Dalecarlia, and at whose house LINNAEUS spent the Christmas holiday of 1734.

SOLANDER, DANIEL CARLSSON (1736–1782): Student of LINNAEUS who traveled to Lapland (1753) and later, as botanist, accompanied JOSEPH BANKS on COOK's first circumnavigation of the globe (1768–1771); keeper of natural history at the British Museum, London, and honorary doctor of medicine and of law at Oxford.

SPARRMANN, ANDERS (1748–1820): Student of LINNAEUS who traveled around the Cape of Good Hope and joined COOK's second circumnavigation of the globe (1772–1775); later professor of natural history and pharmacology in Stockholm; honored by LINNAEUS with the name *Sparrmannia*.

SPREKELSEN, JOHANN HEINRICH VAN (1691–1764): German naturalist and collector in Hamburg.

STOBAEUS, KILIAN (1690–1742): Physician and professor of history at Lund University; LINNAEUS's teacher and patron during his years in Lund (1727–1728).

TÄRNSTRÖM, CHRISTOPHER (1703–1746): Student of LINNAEUS who traveled to Java and Cambodia (1745–1746) as ship's chaplain for the Swedish East India Company; died off Cambodia on the outbound voyage; honored by LINNAEUS with the name *Ternstroemia*.

TELANDER, JOHAN (1694–1763): LINNAEUS's first tutor and later a parson; remembered by LINNAEUS as morose and ill tempered.

TERSMEEDEN, CARL GUSTAV (1743–1828): Friend of LINNAEUS who, with CLAES SOHLBERG, brought the news of ARTEDI's death to LINNAEUS at Hartekamp on 29 September 1735; witnessed, with SOHLBERG and HENDRICK JÜTTINCK, the inventory of goods left behind by ARTEDI; later a Swedish admiral.

THEOPHRASTUS (c. 371–c. 270 B.C.): Greek philosopher, a disciple of LEUCIPPUS, PLATO, and ARISTOTLE, succeeding the latter in his teaching post in 324 B.C.; he created one of the first botanical gardens. His two main works of natural history are *Enquiry into Plants*, in nine books, and *De Causis Plantarum*, in six books, a kind of plant physiology. He is said to have lived nearly a hundred years, and that all of Athens turned out for his funeral.

THUNBERG, CARL PETER (1743–1828): Student of LINNAEUS who traveled to southern Africa, Ceylon, Java, and Japan (1770–1779) as a surgeon for the Dutch East India Company; became professor of

medicine and botany at Uppsala in 1783 on the death of CARL LIN-
NAEUS the Younger.

TILIANDER, SVEN (1637–1710): Domestic chaplain to Count HORN
at Bremen; later rector of Pietteryd and maternal uncle of LINNAE-
US's father NICOLAUS (NILS) INGEMARSSON LINNAEUS, in whose
house NILS spent a part of his boyhood.

TILLIANDER (later TILLANDZ), ELIAS (1640–1693): Swedish botanist and professor of medicine at Åbo; author of *Catalogus Plantarum
quae prope Aboam tam in excultis* published in 1683; honored by LIN-
NAEUS with the name *Tillandsia*.

TORÉN, OLOF (1718–1753): Student of LINNAEUS who traveled to
Guangzhou (1750–1752) as ship's chaplain for the Swedish East India
Company; an account of his travels was published by LINNAEUS in
1759; honored by LINNAEUS with the name *Torenia*.

TOURNEFORT, JOSEPH PITTON DE (1656–1708): French botanist
and voyager of discovery whose plant classification was the standard
until the major revisions of LINNAEUS; the first botanist to properly
define genera, many of LINNAEUS's generic names of plants
were taken from his works; commemorated by LINNAEUS with the
name *Tournefortia*.

TRAESE, MADAME (?–?): Proprietor of a famous eighteenth-century
brothel in Amsterdam; it was so well known that even Prince EUGENE
of Savoy visited it in 1722 during his official stay in Amsterdam.

TYSON, EDWARD (1650–1708): English physician, anatomist, classical scholar, and bibliophile in London; abandoning human for
comparative anatomy, he is said to be the first Englishman to investigate animal structure on an extensive scale.

VAILLANT, SÉBASTIEN (1669–1722): French physician and botanist
whose ideas about sexuality in plants were the basis for LINNAEUS's
sexual system of plant classification.

VALENTIJN, FRANÇOIS (1666–1727): Protestant minister at Ambon
and author of a great Dutch work, in five volumes in folio, printed

at Dordrecht and Rotterdam, 1724–1726, titled *Oud en Nieuw Oost-Indiën*.

VALENTINI, MICHAEL BERNHARD (1657–1729): Professor at Giessen; his most important work, *Amphitheatrum Zootomicum*, was published at Frankfurt am Main in 1720.

VASA, GUSTAV ERIKSSON (GUSTAV I) (1496–1560): Regent of Sweden in 1521, after leading the rebellion against the sitting monarch of the Kalmar Union, and King of Sweden in 1523; introduced Protestantism to Sweden.

VOIGTLENDER, GUSTAF FREDRIK (1711–1754): Student of LINNAEUS at Uppsala, later regimental doctor.

VOLTAIRE (1694–1778): French philosopher and author, whose original name was AROUET; one of the towering geniuses in literary and intellectual history, personifying the Enlightenment.

VOSMAER, AERNOUT (1720–1799): A fanatical collector and director of the menageries and "Natuur- en Kunstcabinetten des Stadhouders" of Holland; under his direction the collections were greatly expanded, and many descriptions of the animals under his care were published, most of them founded on specimens that had lived in the menageries.

WAESBERGE, JANSSONIUS VAN (fl. 1709–1749): Publisher in Amsterdam, well known especially for his charts and maps; the son-in-law of JAN JANSSON, succeeding to the publication of cartographic material, much of which had originated with MERCATOR and HONDIUS; with JACQUES WETTSTEIN and WILLIAM SMITH, publisher of the first volume of ALBERTUS SEBA's *Locupletissimus rerum Naturalium Thesauri* in 1734.

WALPOLE, Sir ROBERT (1676–1745): English statesman, appointed first lord of the treasury and chancellor of the exchequer in 1721, essentially controlling Parliament; usually described as the first prime minister of Great Britain.

WETTSTEIN, JACQUES (1706–1775): Bookseller and printer in Amsterdam and Leiden who, in collaboration with JANSSONIUS VAN WAESBERGE and WILLIAM SMITH, produced the first volume of ALBERTUS SEBA's *Locupletissimus rerum Naturalium Thesauri* in 1734.

WHELER, GRANVILLE (1701–1770): English natural philosopher and resident of London who experimented with electricity.

WILLUGHBY, FRANCIS (1635–1672): Wealthy English naturalist whose father of the same name left him a large inheritance; in collaboration with JOHN RAY he undertook to do a complete natural history, he doing the animals and RAY the plants, but these plans were cut short by an early death at age 37; his *Ornithologiae* (1676) and *Historia piscium* (1686) were later completed and edited by RAY; Fellow of Trinity College, Cambridge.

WISHOFF, CONRAD (?–?): Dutch publisher in Leiden from 1710 to 1750. WISHOFF published LINNAEUS's *Genera plantarum* and *Classes plantarum* as well as ARTEDI's *Ichthyologia*.

Bibliography

ARTEDI, P. 1738. *Ichthyologia sive opera omnia piscibus scilicet: Bibliotheca ichthyologica. Philosophia ichthyologica. Genera piscium. Synonymia Specierum. Descriptiones specierum. Omnia in hoc genere perfectiora, quam antea ulla. Posthuma vindicavit, recognovit, coaptavit & edidit Carolus Linnaeus, Med. Doct. & Ac. Imper.* N.C. Wishoff, Leiden, 12 + 68 + 92 + 88 + 104 + 118 pp. + index.

BLUNT, WILFRID. 1971. Linnaeus and botany. *History Today,* 21(2): 107–115.

———. 2001. *Linnaeus, the Compleat Naturalist.* With an introduction by William T. Stearns. Princeton University Press, Princeton and Oxford, 264 pp.

BOERMAN, ALBERT JOHAN. 1953. Carolus Linnaeus, a psychological study. *Taxon,* 2(7): 145–156.

———. 1957. Linnaeus becomes *Candidatus Medicinae* at Harderwijk. A neglected Linnaean document. *Svenska Linné-sällskapets Årsskrift,* Uppsala, 40: 33–47.

BOERMAN, ALBERT JOHAN. 1979. Linnaeus and the scientific relations between Holland and Sweden. *Svenska Linné-sällskapets Årsskrift,* Yearbook of the Swedish Linnaeus Society, Commemorative Volume for 1978, Uppsala, pp. 43–56.

BOORSTIN, DANIEL JOSEPH. 1983. *The Discoverers: A History of Man's Search to Know His World and Himself.* Random House, New York, xvi + 745 pp.

BRIGHTWELL, CECILIA LUCY. 1858. *A Life of Linnaeus.* John van Voorst, London, viii + 191 pp.

BROBERG, GUNNAR. 1992. *Carl Linnaeus.* Swedish Portraits, a series of biographies of eminent Swedes, The Swedish Institute, Stockholm, 32 pp.

CADDY, FLORENCE. 1887. *Through the Fields with Linnaeus: A Chapter in Swedish History.* Little, Brown, and Co., Boston, Vol. 1, 347 pp., Vol. 2, 376 pp.

CAIN, ARTHUR JAMES. 1992. The *Methodus* of Linnaeus. *Archives of Natural History*, 19(2): 231–250.

ENGEL, HELMUT. 1936. Linnaeus' voyage from Hamburg to Amsterdam: An explanation of some obscure points in his almanac. *Svenska Linné-sällskapets Årsskrift*, Uppsala, 19: 50–58.

———. 1937. The life of Albert Seba. *Svenska Linné-sällskapets Årsskrift*, Uppsala, 20: 75–100.

———. 1951. Some Artedi documents in the Amsterdam Archives. *Svenska Linné-sällskapets Årsskrift*, Uppsala, 34: 51–66.

FARBER, PAUL LAWRENCE. 2000. *Finding Order in Nature: The Naturalist Tradition from Linnaeus to E.O. Wilson.* Johns Hopkins University Press, Baltimore and London, xii + 136 pp.

FRÄNGSMYR, TORE (editor). 1983. *Linnaeus, the Man and His Work.* With contributions by Sten Lindroth, Gunnar Eriksson, and Gunnar Broberg. University of California Press, Berkeley, Los Angeles, and London, xii + 203 pp.

GAGE, ANDREW THOMAS, and WILLIAM THOMAS STEARN. 1988. *A Bicentenary History of The Linnean Society of London.* Academic Press, London, x + 242 pp.

GOURLIE, NORAH. 1953. *The Prince of Botanists, Carl Linnaeus.* Witherby Ltd., London, xiv + 292 pp.

GREENE, EDWARD LEE. 1912. *Carolus Linnaeus.* With an introduction by Barton Warren Evermann. Christopher Sower Co., Philadelphia, 91 pp.

HAGBERG, KNUT. 1952. *Carl Linnaeus.* Translated from the Swedish by Alan Blair. Jonathan Cape, London, 264 pp.

HOLMBERG, BO R., and ERIC NYLANDER. 2004. *Linnés vän Peter Artedi.* Naturhistoriska Riksmuseets, Stockholm, 24 pp.

JACKSON, B. DAYDON. 1926. The visit of Carl Linnaeus to England in 1736. *Svenska Linné-sällskapets Årsskrift*, Uppsala, 9: 1–11.

KOERNER, LISBET. 1999. *Linnaeus: Nature and Nation.* Harvard University Press, Cambridge and London, x + 298 pp.

LANDELL, NILS-ERIK. 2008. *Doctor Carl Linnaeus, Physician.*
Translated from the Swedish by Silvester Mazzarella, edited by
Lars Hamsen. Mundus Linnaei Series No. 3, IK Foundation &
Company, London and Whitby, ix + 10–316 pp.

LINDROTH, STEN. 1979. Linnaeus in his European Context.
Svenska Linné-sällskapets Årsskrift, Yearbook of the Swedish
Linnaeus Society, Commemorative Volume for 1978, Uppsala,
pp. 9–17.

LINNAEUS, CARL. 1736. *Caroli Linnaei, sueci, Methodus.* Angelum
Sylvium, Leiden, 1 p.

———. 1738. Vita Petri Artedi descripta a Carolo Linnaeo. pp.
[iii–xiii], In: *Petri Artedi sueci, medici, Ichthyologia, sive Opera omnia
piscibus scilicet: Bibliotheca ichthyologica, Philosophia ichthyologica,
Genera piscium, Synonymia Specierum, Descriptiones specierum.
Omnia in hoc genere perfectiora, quam antea ulla. Posthuma vindicavit,
recognovit, coaptavit & edidit Carolus Linnaeus.* Conradum
Wishoff, Leiden.

———. 1964. *Systema Naturae, 1735.* Facsimile of the First Edition,
with an Introduction and a first English translation of the
"Observationes" by Dr. M.S.J. Engel-Ledeboer and Dr. H. Engel.
Nieuwkoop, B. de Graaf, 30 + [17] pp.

LÖNNBERG, EINAR. 1905. *Peter Artedi, a Bicentenary Memoir Written
on Behalf of the Swedish Royal Academy of Science.* Translated by W.E.
Harlock. Almquist & Wiksells, Uppsala and Stockholm, 44 pp.

MALMESTÖRM, ELIS, and ARVID HJALMAR UGGLA. 1957. *Vita
Caroli Linnaei: Carl von Linnés Självbiografier.* Almquist & Wiksell,
Stockholm, 235 pp.

MERRIMAN, DANIEL. 1938. Peter Artedi–systematist and
ichthyologist. *Copeia,* 1938(1): 33–39.

———. 1941. A rare manuscript adding to our knowledge of the work
of Peter Artedi. *Copeia,* 1941(2): 64–69.

NYBELIN, ORVAR. 1934. Tvenne opublicerade Artedi-manuskript.
Svenska Linné-sällskapets Årsskrift, Uppsala, 17: 35–90.

————. 1955. Strödda bidrag till Artedis biografi. *Svenska Linné-sällskapets Årsskrift*, Uppsala, 38: 51–66.

————. 1967. Kring Petrus Artedis vistelse i England. *Svenska Linné-sällskapets Årsskrift*, Uppsala, 49: 9–25.

ODELSTIERNA, INGRID. 1967. Carl Linnaeus: Petrus Artedis liv. Translated and annotated by Ingrid Odelstierna. *Svenska Linné-sällskapets Årsskrift*, Uppsala, 49: 1–8.

PETRY, MICHAEL JOHN. 2001. *Carl von Linné: Nemesis Divina*. Edited and translated, with an introduction and explanatory notes, by M.J. Petry. International Archives of the History of Ideas, No. 177. Kluwer Academic Publishers, Dordrecht, Boston, and London, xviii + 483 pp.

PULTENET, RICHARD (editor). 1805. *A General View of the Writings of Linnaeus, by Richard Pultenet, M.D.F.R.S. The Second Edition; With Corrections, Considerable Additions, and Memoirs of the Author, by William George Maton, to Which is Annexed The Diary of Linnaeus, Written by Himself, and now Translated into English, from the Swedish Manuscript in the Possession of the Editor*. Printed for J. Mawman, London, xv + 596 pp.

ROGER, JACQUES. 1997. *Buffon, A Life in Natural History*. Translated by Sarah Lucille Bonnefoi, edited by L. Pearce Williams. Cornell University Press, Ithaca and London, xvii + 492.

SCHMIDT, KARL P. 1951. The amphibians and pisces in the first edition of the *Systema Naturae. Copeia*, 1951(1): 2–7.

————. 1952. The "Methodus" of Linnaeus, 1736. *Journal of the Society for the Bibliography of Natural History*, 2(9): 369–411.

SMITH, JAMES EDWARD. 1821. *A Selection of the Correspondence of Linnaeus, and Other Naturalists, from the Original Manuscripts*. Longman, Hurst, Rees, Orme, and Brown, London, Vol. 1, xiv + 605 pp.; Vol. 2, iv + 580 pp. + index.

SPRINGER, LEONARD F. 1936. Hartekamp på Linnés tid och dess senare öden. *Svenska Linné-sällskapets Årsskrift*, Uppsala, 19: 59–66.

STEARN, WILLIAM T. 1958. Botanical explorations to the time of Linnaeus. *Proceedings of the Linnean Society of London*, 169(3): 173–196.

———. 1981. *The Natural History Museum at South Kensington: A History of the British Museum (Natural History) 1753–1980.* Heinemann, London, England, xxiii + 414 pp.

STRANDELL, BIRGER. 1973. An introduction to Linnaeus. Pp. 3–45, In: Gilbert S. Daniels (editor), *A Linnaean Keepsake*, Issued to Commemorate the Opening of The Strandell Collection of Linnaeana at The Hunt Botanical Library, Carnegie-Mellon University. Published by The Hunt Botanical Library of the Hunt Institute for Botanical Documentation, Carnegie-Mellon University, Pittsburgh, Pennsylvania.

UGGLA, ARVID HJALMAR. 1957. *Linnaeus.* Translated from the Swedish by Alan Blair. Swedish Institute, Stockholm, 18 pp, 16 pls.

WALDE, OTTO. 1951. Nya bidrag till Artedis biografi. *Svenska Linné-sällskapets Årsskrift*, Uppsala, 34: 41–50.

WHEELER, ALWYNE C. 1961. The life and work of Peter Artedi. pp. vii–xxiii, In: Alwyne C. Wheeler (editor), *Petri Artedi Ichthyologia, Historiae Naturalis Classica*, J. Cramer, Weinheim.

———. 1979. The sources of Linnaeus's knowledge of fishes. *Svenska Linné-sällskapets Årsskrift*, Yearbook of the Swedish Linnaeus Society, Commemorative Volume for 1978, Uppsala, pp. 156–211.

———. 1987. Peter Artedi, founder of modern ichthyology. *Proceedings of the Fifth Congress of European Ichthyologists*, Stockholm, 1985: 3–10.

———. 1991. The Linnaean fish collection in the Zoological Museum of the University of Uppsala. *Zoological Journal of the Linnean Society*, 103(2): 145–195.

Acknowledgments

In preparing this work, I have relied heavily on EINAR LÖNNBERG'S remarkable memoir on the life of PETER ARTEDI (1905), which, in turn, is based almost exclusively on *Vita Petri Artedi* published by LINNAEUS in 1738 as an introduction to ARTEDI's *Ichthyologia*. I have also made wide use of LINNAEUS's autobiographies, one of the most extensive of which appears in English in RICHARD PULTENET's *A General View of the Writings of Linnaeus* (1805). Other significant sources include WILFRID BLUNT's *Linnaeus, the Compleat Naturalist* (2001); TORE FRÄNGSMYR's *Linnaeus, the Man and His Work* (1983); NORAH GOURLIE's *The Prince of Botanists* (1953); LISBET KOERNER's *Linnaeus: Nature and Nation* (1999); and two important articles by HELMUT ENGEL, "The life of Albert Seba" (1937) and "Some Artedi documents in the Amsterdam Archives" (1951), both published in issues of *Svenska Linné-sällskapets Årsskrift*, Uppsala.

Others who have helped along the way include SVEN O. KULLANDER, FANG KULLANDER, and BO FERNHOLM of the Swedish Museum of Natural History, Stockholm; WILHELM ARNÖR, Decerno AB, Stockholm; HANS VISSER, CORINNE STAAL, and ERIK SCHULTZ of the Amsterdam Municipal Archives; YOUSEF IWAN, proprietor, Cafe-restaurant Het Karbeel, Warmoesstraat 16, Amsterdam; PAUL G. HOFTIJZER, Department of Book and Digital Media Studies, Leiden University; WILLEM BACKHUYS and MICHAEL RUIJSENAARS, Backhuys Publishers, Leiden; GINA DOUGLAS, Librarian and Archivist of the Linnean Society of London; CATHY BROAD of the Linnean Society and The Natural History Museum, London; E. CHARLES NELSON of the Society for the History of Natural History, London; ELAINE PORDES, archivist at the Department of Manuscripts, British Library, London; SAM FLEISHMAN, Literary Artists Representatives, New York; CHRISTIE HENRY, Senior Editor at the University of Chicago Press; and CHARLOTTE TANCIN, librarian at the Hunt Institute for Botanical Documentation, Carnegie Mellon University, Pittsburg. I am especially grateful to MARK VAN BRONKHORST of MVB Fonts, Albany, California, for the cover design; and to ABBY J. SIMPSON of Seattle,

Washington, who provided an early critique of the entire manuscript and greatly improved the final draft. Others who read the manuscript, either in whole or part, and provided advice and encouragement include WILLIAM D. ANDERSON JR., MICHAEL J. COOKSEY, SARAH GAGE, MARTIN GEERTS, MILTON S. LOVE, DAVID L. G. NOAKES, JOANNE M. PAVLAK, DIANA M. RUBIANO, and PETER WARD. Finally, at Scott & Nix, grateful thanks are extended to GEORGE SCOTT and CHARLES NIX for the design and production of this volume.